Arranged

Also from Lexi Blake

Arranged

A Masters and Mercenaries Novella

By Lexi Blake

1001 Dark Nights

EVIL EYE
CONCEPTS

Arranged
A Masters and Mercenaries Novella
By Lexi Blake

1001 Dark Nights

Copyright 2017 DLZ Entertainment, LLC
ISBN: 978-1-945920-25-7

Foreword: Copyright 2014 M. J. Rose

Published by Evil Eye Concepts, Incorporated

Acknowledgments from the Author

As always thanks to Liz and MJ and their crew—Kim and Pam, Fedora and Kasi on the editing side, to that weirdo they have formatting (I can say that. I gave birth to him) and the amazing Jillian Stein working on social media and making pretty things to show off! Thanks to my publicist Danielle Sanchez and the entire crew at Inkslinger.

We all come across hard times in life and in our work. When those two worlds collide into a raging heap of toxic waste, you really need your friends at your side. This book is dedicated to two amazing women—Mari Carr and Lila DuBois. You helped me through a very hard time and I'll never forget it. I love working with the two of you around because you speak my language and make me comfortable. And this book would likely be very different without Lila helping me to see how Kash and Day could work, how even dominance can be light and feminine and lovely.

One Thousand and One Dark Nights

Once upon a time, in the future…

*I was a student fascinated with stories and learning.
I studied philosophy, poetry, history, the occult, and
the art and science of love and magic. I had a vast
library at my father's home and collected thousands
of volumes of fantastic tales.*

*I learned all about ancient races and bygone
times. About myths and legends and dreams of all
people through the millennium. And the more I read
the stronger my imagination grew until I discovered
that I was able to travel into the stories… to actually
become part of them.*

*I wish I could say that I listened to my teacher
and respected my gift, as I ought to have. If I had, I
would not be telling you this tale now.
But I was foolhardy and confused, showing off
with bravery.*

*One afternoon, curious about the myth of the
Arabian Nights, I traveled back to ancient Persia to
see for myself if it was true that every day Shahryar
(Persian: شهريار, "king") married a new virgin, and then
sent yesterday's wife to be beheaded. It was written
and I had read, that by the time he met Scheherazade,
the vizier's daughter, he'd killed one thousand
women.*

Something went wrong with my efforts. I arrived in the midst of the story and somehow exchanged places with Scheherazade — a phenomena that had never occurred before and that still to this day, I cannot explain.

Now I am trapped in that ancient past. I have taken on Scheherazade's life and the only way I can protect myself and stay alive is to do what she did to protect herself and stay alive.

Every night the King calls for me and listens as I spin tales. And when the evening ends and dawn breaks, I stop at a point that leaves him breathless and yearning for more. And so the King spares my life for one more day, so that he might hear the rest of my dark tale.

As soon as I finish a story... I begin a new one... like the one that you, dear reader, have before you now.

Prologue

Fifteen Years Before
Oxford, England

Kashmir Kamdar lay back on the blanket, his face to the sun. He loved England, genuinely adored the years he'd spent here, but sometimes he missed the sun of Loa Mali. It could be so dark here, but on a day like this, he found his way to one of the parks and let the sun soak into his skin and he felt the connection to his island home.

"You don't care at all about quantum mechanics today, do you?"

He didn't open his eyes. He didn't have to see Dayita's frown. Her perfect lips would be turned down, but there would also be a light in those hauntingly gray eyes. "You could read the chapter to me."

"While you snore? I think not."

He felt her settle down beside him, their arms barely touching. Yes, that was better. Dayita Samar was the only other Loa Mali resident here at Oxford, and in the last six months he'd pretty much decided that she was the only Loa Mali resident he needed.

He even adored her name. Day. She scared off all the other guys by putting that insanely thick mound of hair up in a mousy bun, hiding her glorious eyes behind bulky glasses, and wearing somewhat shapeless sweaters. He suspected she simply hadn't figured out how to dress for the cold weather. He wanted to see her on their island home, her body wrapped in a sari that would allow him hints of her copper and gold skin. She scared the men off with her incredible intellect as well. They were all intimidated by how freaking smart she was.

It hadn't intimidated him. After all, he'd lived in his big brother's shadow for all his life. He was absolutely used to being the second smartest person in a room.

"I suppose it won't hurt to take a little nap." She sighed beside him. "Or to watch the clouds. They're different here. I'm thinking about taking a meteorology class in my spare time. I'm fascinated by how different the weather is here in England."

He turned on his side and smiled down at her, his head propped in his hand. "You should feel the way the winds can whip around the Himalayas. There's nothing like a storm at base camp one."

Her eyes came open. "You're telling me they let you climb Everest? I would think the guards would have a problem with that. Did you force poor Rai to be your Sherpa?"

Naturally she knew what he was talking about and that he would need someone to guide him. And she was right about the guards. "I went to Nepal in Shray's place. He got a horrible cold at the last minute, but Father didn't want to cancel the trip. They let me go up to the first base camp. It was more than enough. A storm hit and I froze my poor backside off. I got back to the beach as quickly as possible."

She laughed, the sound musical to his ears. "Did you cuddle with the guard?"

"I have a 'no cuddling' policy with my royal guard. And you know they only really stay close when I'm working for my father. There aren't many people here in Oxford who want to hurt the spare heir of a tiny island country. Shray, on the other hand, oh, let's just say I've learned to be happy that I'm a second son."

"It's one of the things I like about you, Your Highness." She rolled over too, and they were side by side. "I think it would be hard to have your whole life laid out for you. I like that you're not jealous of your brother."

Yes, this was the Day he'd come to... Had he come to love Day? He certainly felt more for her than he'd ever felt for a girl before. He hadn't slept with a single model, or anyone else, since he'd met her, and he hadn't even tried to kiss her yet.

"Most people think I should be saddened by the idea of being the spare. By being so close to the crown and yet so far away. They think I should be jealous of Shray, but I feel sorry for him. Don't get me wrong. I adore my brother, but I don't want to be him. You're right. His life is laid out for him. He'll marry some woman my father approves of, have children as soon as possible, and settle down to be the perfect king one day. Did you know they forced him to major in economics and political science?"

He shuddered at the thought. And Shray hadn't been allowed to go so far from home. He'd studied in India so he could be close to the palace. His leash had been so very short.

Day's nose wrinkled. "How boring. Except the math part. That's probably fun. Maybe I'll study it in my free time."

He had to smile. "You don't have any free time. I'm forcing you to study something else. It's called human dynamics. We're going to a pub tonight and we'll drink and eat and watch the crowds."

Now her eyes went wide. "I need to study. I have a test in differential equations next week."

"Which you can pass in your sleep." Day had forgotten more mathematics than most people ever learned. Still, he knew she would prepare. "You can study later, Day. Tonight you're going to play. You never play."

She sat up and started to gather her books. "I don't and I should remember that, Your Highness."

Okay. That was bad. Even he knew that particular tone in a woman's voice, though he rarely heard it in Day's. It meant he'd screwed up. Normally that tone of voice represented an off ramp, and after a few weeks with a woman, he tended to look for those.

He didn't want one with her. He liked her. They were friends and he was starting to think they should be something more. He wasn't a child. He was twenty years old and maybe Shray wasn't the only one who was thinking about settling down. Not right away. Not marriage anyway, but it would be nice to settle in with her and see where they could go. The truth was he was tired of models and actresses who had no idea who Stephen Hawking was. The playboy was tired and wanted his brainy girl.

"What did I do wrong?"

She stopped, hugging her books to her chest. "Nothing. I'm being exactly what I promised myself I wouldn't be. I'm being a foolish girl. I have a unique chance to make something of myself and here I am mooning over a boy I can't have. I'm sorry, Your Highness. I need to go."

He reached out, gripping her wrist gently. "Stop calling me that. Please call me Kash. I'm not my brother. I'm not destined for the throne. I'm nothing more than a young man trying to ask a lovely woman out for a date and screwing it up terribly."

Those gray eyes went wide. "A date?"

There was something about the breathy way she said the word that let him know all would be well. He got to his knees in front of her, facing her so she could see how serious he was. "A date. It's when a boy and a girl go out into the world and have fun."

Her eyes never left his, never shifted coyly away. It was one of the things he loved about her. Day took charge. "I'm not one of your fun-time girls, Kashmir. You should understand that about me. If you think I'm going to giggle and hook up and walk away happy I screwed around with a prince, you don't know me at all."

He liked the strength in her voice. "That's what I've been trying to do all these months. Get to know you. We've become friends. I would like to see if we could be more. Dayita, I know you think you're nothing but a brain on two legs, but I see you as something more."

"More?" She stared at him as though trying to find the definition in her head.

Yes, this was one of the things he needed her to understand. "You're brilliant, but you're also a woman. You treat all the men around you as if you couldn't care less."

"I don't think the men around me like me."

"I like you," he said quickly, not willing to let a moment of misunderstanding pass. "I like who you are."

Her cheeks had flushed, a deep color coming to them. "They don't think I'm especially feminine."

Because she knew what she wanted? He liked that most about her. "How do they know what femininity is? You're a woman because your body is different, but I...I like your soul, too. You don't have to be different with me. You can be exactly who you are and I'll still like you."

"If this is some kind of game to you..." she began and he could see the shimmer of tears in her eyes.

The last thing he wanted to do was ever make her cry. She was so strong. He wanted to add to that strength, never take from it. "It's not a game. I like you, Day. Even better, I like me when I'm around you. Does that make sense? I like how I feel when you're with me."

"How do I make you feel?"

How to explain it? It was something he thought about a lot lately. He'd started to study it like a scientist would, considering all the angles, measuring his feelings versus others and coming up with the theory that Day was the right woman for him. "I feel peaceful around you. I feel secure."

He knew it was a risk. Some women would see that as unmanly. He should have talked about protecting her. He wanted to protect her from everything, but he'd never in his life felt like a woman wanted to protect him, too.

She bit her bottom lip and seemed to think things over before she reached up and pulled the tie out of her hair, shaking it out. "Let me kiss you."

He stopped, his whole body going on high alert. His dick twitched in his slacks. When he'd proposed this little picnic, he'd known he was going to start to ease her into a more traditional male/female relationship, but he hadn't expected this. He'd thought he would get her to go to a pub with him and they would have fun, and after three or four outings she might not even recognize as dates, he would kiss her.

He should do it now. He should lean over and fist his hand in her hair and show her how masculine he could be.

"Yes." He stayed still because she hadn't asked him to kiss her. She'd been clear and plain in her intent. She wanted to kiss him. She'd asked his permission as though he was something precious.

Women threw themselves at him. They plopped themselves down in his lap and offered him all manner of sexual favors. Not once had anyone asked if they could kiss him. Certainly not in that strong tone that let him know he really should say yes because he would miss out on something if he didn't.

Her lips curled in a smile he'd never once seen from her. That smile was wicked and it got his cock hard as a freaking rock. He hadn't touched her yet and he was erect and ready.

She reached her hand up, fingertips brushing his skin. "Don't move. Let me touch you. Let me learn you."

For Day, learning was serious. She studied him, her fingers moving along his jawline. She was studying him, assessing and categorizing him. It wasn't a bad thing. No. Day wouldn't find him wanting. Day viewed the world itself as something marvelous, something to explore.

How would she explore him? The question made his body tighten, his whole being focus on her. The rest of the world seemed to fall away as Day leaned in and finally, finally brushed her lips against his.

He felt a spark deep inside. Her hands moved up, sliding into his hair and twisting ever so slightly. His scalp tingled and his breath caught. She kissed him softly, the ease of her lips contrasting with the sharp tingle to his scalp. Her chest came up, rubbing against his, and he felt something he hadn't before. He felt…wanted. Not for his royal position. Not for his money.

For himself.

She went up, as tall as she could get on her knees. He was sitting back and he found the way she towered over him incredibly sexy. He didn't have to do a damn thing. Day was in control. She would take what she wanted and what she wanted was him.

"Open your mouth for me. Let me in."

He found himself giving in, the whole moment spiraling out of control. It wasn't what he'd meant to do, but that was all right. He didn't have to decide. All he had to do was follow her path and she would lead him somewhere incredible.

He was so hard he could barely breathe as her tongue slid along his. It didn't matter that they were in a park. It wasn't that crowded at this time of day. The River Cherwell was off to his right and there was a lovely copse of trees to his left they could go into when she wanted to fuck. Yeah, he would move the blanket, open his slacks, lay back and let her ride the hell out of him.

He'd known it would be good.

The *thud thud* of a helicopter broke through the intimacy of the moment. Damn it. They needed to go away. He leaned in, but she was already pulling back. Her face turned up to the sky.

"I think they're landing," she shouted over the hard scream of the blades rotating.

She leaned in as though to try to cover him.

He wasn't having that. Not for a second. He moved out from under her, placing his body over hers. He felt her stiffen but he wasn't giving in.

"Your Majesty!" A familiar figure moved toward him. His guard. Rai. He'd come with him all the way from Loa Mali. He'd left his family and spent the last four years of his life here, only short visits home connecting him with the ones he loved. Rai had been his steadfast companion, giving him space when he needed it, taking care of him when he got too wild.

Why was Rai calling him "your majesty"? He stood, reaching down to help Day up. "What's wrong?"

Rai had a grim look on his face. "I have to get you to Heathrow, Your Majesty. There's a plane waiting for you. Something's happened at home. We need to go as soon as possible."

Kash shook his head. He wasn't leaving in the middle of a semester. "I'll call Dad. And what's wrong with you? It's 'your highne…'"

He stopped, the world shifting and twisting and turning until he couldn't quite stand. Day was there, holding him up.

There was only one reason to ever call him "your majesty." No one should have called him that. Not ever in his life. It was what his people called the king and queen. Only ever the king and queen.

"What happened to my father?" His gut twisted and he choked back a cry. "My brother?"

Rai shook his head. "There was a car accident, Your Majesty. The king and your brother were caught in a storm. Your brother was driving and he lost control and went over a cliff. I'm so sorry." He went down on one knee. "The king is dead. Long live the king."

King Kashmir.

Day's arms went around him, but now they were surrounded

by guards. Rai had brought an army with him.

Because he was no longer the spare. Because he was the last of the Kamdar line and he was king.

"We have to go." Rai was back on his feet, nodding toward the helicopter.

Kash felt himself being pulled away from Day, but there was nothing he could do. He had to go home. He glanced back, saw her standing there with tears in her eyes.

And he knew the whole world had changed.

Chapter One

Present Day
Miami, Florida

Kash woke when the pillow beneath his head shifted. Confusion set in even as his head started to pound. His mouth was dry as the desert. Why was the bed moving?

He wasn't going to wake up this morning. There was no reason to. He was going to lie here and pretend he had absolutely nothing to do.

In some ways it was true. He was fairly inconsequential recently.

He groaned as he realized the pillow he'd been lying on wasn't a pillow at all. It had been a woman's hip, soft and warm.

Where the hell was he?

"That's right, Your Majesty. Time to wakey, wakey," a male voice said. "I'd offer you eggs and bakey, but I saw what you drank last night. We might want to hold off on the food for a while. Wish I could let you sleep this off, but I got orders."

The voice was familiar, but he struggled to attach a face. Whoever had invaded his bedroom was speaking English with a Western accent. Kash didn't want to open his eyes. The world was far too bright. "Well, I'm the king so I can override any orders you've been given. Where is my guard? And who the hell are you?"

"Yeah, I take my orders from Big Tag. I think he's far scarier than you are. Especially right now." More light invaded his previously darkened room. "That's right, darling. You should get dressed. The king is thankful for your company last night. And your sister's. And whoever the other lady was."

"Oh, good lord. Does he owe you cash?" An upper-crust British accent split the air and Kash did recognize that one. Simon Weston. And his partner, Jesse Murdoch, was the laconic Western guy.

"They're not hookers." Why the hell was McKay-Taggart here?

"Yes, we are," a feminine voice said. "And we agreed on a thousand for each of us. Are you telling me we're about to get stiffed?"

"I'll make sure you get everything he promised you and a bit more if you'll please avoid the paparazzi outside," Weston was saying. "If not, you'll find I'm good at suing people. Your choice, ladies. Easy cash or a nice lawsuit. Jesse, would you please escort his majesty's friends to the taxi that's waiting for them?"

"Sure thing, partner. You going to deal with our charge?" Murdoch asked.

"Hopefully our charge isn't about to vomit all over the hotel suite. Let management know that we'll be leaving soon and will require a security escort off the grounds. Michael will be here with the limo and Boomer is watching to ensure none of those reporters get to this floor. I'll have the king down in thirty minutes."

"We'll be ready. Ladies, let's get you home. You should probably put on some clothes...oh, huh. I didn't know those counted as clothes. All right then."

The door closed and Kash forced himself to sit up. The room immediately started spinning, but he wasn't going to give in. "Where is my guard? I don't remember much about last night, but I do know I didn't call McKay-Taggart. I certainly didn't need you to rescue me from three lovely ladies."

Weston looked perfectly neat and clean in his three-piece suit with shiny loafers. He crossed the suite to where someone had brought in coffee service. He poured a cup and started back across the room. "One of them isn't a hooker. One of them is a reporter and she's about to discover that the film she took last night of your antics is going to go missing. Jesse's quite excellent with sleight of hand."

He frowned. "A film?"

"Some would call it pornography." Weston placed the cup on the nightstand. "I'll choose to call it a reality show that will never be aired. As for your guard, apparently he quit last night. He was fed up because he'd figured out who the lovely lady was, but you refused to listen. He called home and explained the situation and your mother hired us. You're lucky you were here in Miami. If you'd been in Europe, you would be dealing with a cranky Aussie. I assure you I'm going to handle you with more care than he would. Well, unless you give me trouble."

Kash reached for the cup. Some of it was coming back to him. He'd fought with Rai. The man had been his personal guard for years, but lately they'd been squabbling like an old married couple. Rai knew him, knew how to deal with him even when he was a complete ass. Lately Rai kept getting on him, pointing out all the ways Kash was failing.

Shit. Rai had found out about Lia. Shit. Shit. Shit. Someone had told Rai about the fact that Lia had once been in his bed. Years before she'd married Rai. It had meant nothing to either one of them. It had been one night of pleasure and he hadn't seen her again. Fuck, he'd meant to go to the grave with that secret.

"Damn it. I certainly didn't mean to fire anyone. Is he still here in Miami?"

He needed to talk to Rai. He had to put things right. There was also the added problem that if he didn't have an approved guard, he would be forced to go home. Kash had come to Miami to attend a meeting with a company that claimed it could help protect the pipeline that brought Loa Mali's oil to the refineries. His country spent millions to ensure the drilling they did left their natural resources and the beauty of their island untouched.

Until such time as Kash found a way to get rid of fossil fuels altogether. That was the ultimate goal, to find a way to free the world from its dependence on oil. Well, and then to license the technology and make an enormous amount of money, but first and foremost it was about the science.

He'd been close. So close when an asshole rabid former CIA agent had blown up his fucking lab and killed several of his best engineers. Good men and women who were trying to help the world and now they were gone.

Their research had only survived because of Simon Weston's boss. Ian Taggart and his wife, Charlotte, had saved Kash, too. So he owed them.

And damn, but he owed Rai.

"He's already gone home." Weston sank into a chair beside the big bed. "Your mother has hired him to work a position that allows him to stay in Loa Mali most of the time. Apparently he's recently married and wants more time with his wife."

Guilt swamped him. Since that CIA bastard had ruined years of Kash's work, he'd dragged Rai around the globe, partying and pretending to enjoy life. The last few years had been one long sinkhole he couldn't seem to come out of.

He was even tired of sex. Not that he was going to let anyone know that. He had a reputation to uphold. A bad, horrible, playboy reputation.

"That's good for Rai. I need a younger guard anyway. I need one who can keep up with me. Rai has become an old man. All he cares about is his job and his wife."

"Yes, how boring of him."

Kash nodded. "I'm glad you see that. I offered him a world of travel and to be surrounded by the most beautiful of all women. He gives me lectures on how I should settle down. He tells me my liver will die soon. My liver is as strong as I am. My liver is a bull."

"Well, I do suspect you're full of bullshit, as my cousins would say. You should think about getting dressed. Our plane leaves in two hours. I need to get you out of here. The paparazzi will be swarming the place by now."

The coffee was starting to work. He was vaguely beginning to remember that Rai had called him an idiot. That hadn't been polite of him. He could remember Rai's dark eyes rolling and him saying something about how he'd given up, how he'd become everything his father would have detested.

Rai had been so sanctimonious. Then his own guilt had caused him to hit the bottle hard. It was why he'd brought those women to his room even though he'd figured out one of them wasn't a well-paid call girl.

Still, he was fairly certain he'd performed admirably, and what was one more sex tape? Why did everyone overreact?

"Don't worry about the paparazzi. They're perfectly harmless. How many do you expect? Five? Prince Harry's in New York. Most of the royal watchers will be after him. He's only shown his willy off a few times. Mine is everywhere. The Internet is awash in my beauty. The upside of that is the paps merely want a picture of me smiling and then they'll leave me alone." He stood up, feeling infinitely better.

Rai had poked his personal buttons, but Kash had behaved abominably. He needed to get Rai on the phone and apologize. The truth was he *had* neglected his research for the last few years. It was a setback and nothing more.

And the last several months had been particularly bad, and he blamed the Taggarts. He'd hosted the wedding of the youngest Taggart and it had left him feeling restless. Being around all those happy families had done something terrible to him. It had made him wonder if he wasn't missing something. Those smiling men with their women and children had caused him to wonder if his life wasn't a bit on the shallow side.

And for the first time in forever, he'd thought of her. He'd stood as Theo Taggart had promised to love Erin Argent for the rest of his life and he'd had a vision of Day with her gray eyes and silky hair. Day, with those ridiculous glasses.

Innocent Day.

They were worlds apart now. She was probably married and teaching somewhere in the States or England. She would have a professor husband who would argue fine points of theory with her and she would be raising a couple of genius-level children. He wondered if she saw him in the papers and laughed about the time the playboy prince had kissed her.

He hoped she was happy.

And for a moment, he'd mourned. Not for his father and brother. He did that every day. He'd mourned the Kash he'd been. He'd ached at the thought of what that Kashmir would think about who he was today.

"Good lord, man, put on some clothes." Weston stood and walked back to the coffee service. "Everyone else might have seen that, but I've been careful not to."

He wasn't sure why Weston was such a prude. The man was known to be a member of Sanctum. It was a club in Dallas that catered to people in the BDSM lifestyle.

"My mother has overreacted. I'm sure she was terrified when she learned I was over here in America without a proper guard, but she certainly shouldn't have called McKay-Taggart to escort me home. I assure you I can find my way. You don't have to make the twenty-hour flight." Who had he brought with him? Yes, that lovely girl from the east side of the island with the pretty breasts was the flight attendant. He could spend some time with her.

"There are currently around two hundred members of the press outside waiting to get a statement from you."

Kash stopped. "Two hundred?"

"Give or take a few. That's why we're going to require a police escort." Weston continued on as though nothing was wrong. "I've got my man with a limo in the parking garage. We'll meet Jesse down there and Boomer will join us in the lift. The hotel has agreed to shut down one of the lifts so it only stops on this floor and the parking garage. Boomer will ensure no one gets through. Miami PD has offered an escort to the airport. You should hurry and shower. We don't have much time."

His head was reeling in a way that had absolutely nothing to do with the unholy amount of vodka he'd downed the night before. "Why is the fact that I had sex with three women news? Believe me, it happens all the time. Second, why would I need a bloody police escort? And what is a Boomer?"

"A Boomer is one of two new former Special Forces bodyguards your mother has hired until Jesse and I train a new group to protect the royal family since it's expanding. I hope you have a large refrigerator. Boomer eats constantly, and you should watch out for any erratic behavior. He's a nice lad, but he's been hit on the head more than anyone could imagine. However, he's a bit of a savant when it comes to marksmanship. No one cares that you had sex with three women last night because no one knows. I took care of that and your mother is not going to be happy about all the bribes I had to expense to accomplish that. You need a bloody police escort to get through the throngs of reporters, as I mentioned earlier. Now could you please put that thing away? My wife is meeting us at the airport. I would like to be able to tell her the amount of nudity I witnessed was minimal."

He was getting irritated. He tossed on last evening's slacks. If the Brit wanted to power play him, he could get with the game. It wasn't like he would allow them to come in and drag his ass home like he was some kind of wayward child. He was a king. "Don't bother to bring your wife. I'm sure she's lovely, but my mother has overstepped herself. I will choose my guard and I will select who will train them."

Weston checked his watch. "How soon can you be ready?"

"Have you heard a word I've said? I thank you for helping me out last night and keeping that tape from hitting the web, but I can manage from here."

Weston picked up the newspaper that had been delivered along with the coffee service. He tossed it Kash's way. "If you feel that way, I can certainly let Michael and Jesse know they should stick to her majesty's side and allow you to be brutally murdered if it comes to that."

"Mother already has guards." He clutched the newspaper. She'd had the same set of guards for years. She liked to call them her girls. Four women who'd served in the military and had been trained by...well, by McKay-Taggart. Had something happened? "Why is Mother so afraid she needs more guards?"

"Not for your mother," Weston replied casually. "It's for your future bride. As for firing me and Jesse, you can't. We've been hired by your parliament to provide security and assistance for the royal wedding and to train the new queen's guard."

Yes, he'd had far too much to drink. He was still sleeping and having the oddest dream.

Weston shook his head. "It's all right there in the paper, if you don't believe me. Now hurry and take that shower. You've got to get home because the formal engagement ceremony is in two days."

Kash opened the paper and stared down at the headline.

Playboy King to Claim His Bride

"I'm not getting married."

Weston stepped up and patted his arm. "You are or you'll give up your throne. I'll explain it all on the plane. The other reason your mother hired me is I have a degree in law. I've read the clause in your constitution that your mother intends to use to force you to marry. I assure you, it will hold up. You can attempt to change the constitution but that requires a two-year review process, another year of public forums, and a vote. You'll be replaced by then. Like I said, I can explain it all on the incredibly long plane trip. Are you all right, Your Majesty? You went a bit green."

Kash ran for the bathroom.

He'd been right. He shouldn't have bothered to wake up.

* * * *

Dayita Samar stepped into the queen's private reception room with a smile. Not for the stunning décor or the view of the ocean in the distance, though both were worthy of great praise. No, Day's smile was for the woman herself. Queen Yasmine was one of the kindest women she'd ever had the pleasure of meeting. The queen mother was a stabilizing influence on the country, someone to look up to and admire for her willingness to serve her people.

How she'd managed to produce a son who was a walking venereal disease was beyond Day's comprehension.

Day curtsied even as the queen waved off such formalities.

"Darling Day, come here. It's been so long," the queen said, enveloping her in a hug.

She was far too thin. It had been a while and the queen seemed frailer than before.

"Your Majesty, it's always a pleasure to see you." Day had learned how to maneuver her way around a bureaucracy, but she genuinely enjoyed dealing with the queen. After the morning she'd had, it was a nice way to spend her afternoon. "You said it was urgent. How can I help you?"

"Oh, my dear, you won't simply be helping me. You'll be helping your country. You might be helping the world." The queen took a step back and there was no way to miss the sheen of tears in her eyes, though she took a deep breath and seemed to banish them. She turned and walked to the sitting area, a cluster of lush chairs on a carpet that was likely worth more than Day's yearly salary at the ministry.

The queen took a seat, gesturing for Day to take one of her

own.

"I'm certainly intrigued, Your Majesty." Day studied the queen. There was a weariness to her that couldn't be missed, even though she smiled like nothing was wrong. "How can I help?"

"You can marry my son."

Day smiled and couldn't help the laughter that bubbled out. The queen was also quite funny. The idea of Kashmir marrying anyone was ludicrous. He was far too busy screwing supermodels and actresses and other men's wives. After a long moment, she sat back with a sigh. "Thank you, Your Majesty. I needed a laugh today. I've spent the morning fighting with parliament over funding for my elementary science education program."

The blustery old men who ran parliament didn't see the need. She'd argued that early science and math intervention worked to get more girls involved in those areas of study. By the time they hit junior high it was too late, and certain societal norms took over, making the classes less interesting to female students. Apparently that was perfectly fine with parliament. One of the men had even told her she would be far happier if she quit her job, got married, and had a husband to occupy her time.

Oh, how she would love to take a whip to that bastard, and not in a pleasurable way.

The queen frowned in Day's direction, getting her attention quickly.

Day sat up. "You're serious? About me marrying the king? I haven't spoken to the king in years. I hardly think he wants to marry me."

The queen's hands tightened around the arms of her chair. "I'm dead serious. The time has come and passed and I can't wait another second more. Have you ever heard of the Law of Rational Succession? It's a tiny clause set into our constitution over two hundred years ago."

She'd read the constitution, of course. History, and in particular Loa Malian history, was a subject she enjoyed. Since becoming the head of the country's education department, she spent her time reviewing public school books. She didn't remember the law, however. "I've never heard of it."

Her majesty seemed to relax a bit, as though she'd half

expected Day to run for the hills. "I'm not surprised. Few people outside of constitutional lawyers have, but I've been assured that it will hold and that it's perfectly legal. The Law of Rational Succession states that the king can be forced to marry or give up his throne if he has not selected a bride by his twentieth birthday."

"Twenty?" Kash was thirty-five.

"Yes, well, it was written long ago when men and women were expected to marry and reproduce at a young age," the queen explained. "I've given him fifteen years but there's no end in sight. According to the law, the king or queen's parents have the right to select a proper spouse, and the wedding must take place within two weeks of the invocation or the king's crown is forfeit. It was placed into law in an attempt to avoid the kind of trouble that comes from the line of succession being broken. There is also a clause about being able to remove a monarch who will not abide by the constitution or one who is too sick to care for the people."

"Has it ever been used?"

The queen shook her head. "It has never been invoked before. Now, I am going to assume that my son will work to block me, but I've got a legal team on that as well. Changing the constitution will require roughly three years. I can end the monarchy in two weeks. The only place for the crown to go is to my nephew, Chapal, and he will refuse it. He has already signed the documents of abdication in case Kashmir proves stubborn."

End the monarchy? Day tried to process the idea. The Kamdars had held the crown for centuries. The family had been the one to put into place the constitution that protected the citizens— even from a bad king. Kash's grandfather had been the one who shared the revenue from the country's oil with every Loa Malian, making them the wealthiest citizenship in the world.

Loa Mali had a parliament, but the crown worked hand in hand with them and the king could have the final say if he chose to use his power.

Not that King Kash paid much attention anymore. He was far too busy running around the world having his picture taken at parties.

"You would have us move to a purely representative government? I don't know if that is a smart move, Your Majesty.

Some people in this country are still extremely set in their ways. I spent all morning arguing with a group of elected officials who believe a woman's place is in the home and that educating our girls in anything beyond how to keep a house is a waste of time."

The queen's lips curled up in an encouraging smile. "Excellent. As queen, you will be able to direct education from a much more powerful position. They won't be able to refuse you. Smile when you force them to eat crow, darling. That is the one thing we shall have to work on. You frown far too much. I know it's not proper to ask a woman to smile these days, but a queen is different. You must never allow them to see anything but strength. A good smile while you're gutting some idiot's argument is a perfect show of strength. Come along. Give me one. I know you can do it."

What surreal dream was she having? She was going to wake up any minute. She had to. "Your Majesty, I don't understand."

"It's easy. Look." The queen's mouth curled up in a restrained smile. "You see, the key is to not look too joyous. Save that for moments when you need the public to see you as a woman and not a queen. Those times come too. The key is knowing when and how to use the power to its best effect."

"What?"

The queen waved away the question. "I know you young people love your resting bitchy faces, but you have to save that for particular people. Like those men today. You may use this bitchy face on them to show your queenly power, though I assure you smiling will set them off their games more. And don't let the cameras catch you frowning or they do those miming things on the Internet now. There was a terrible one of me and some Harry Potter character. If you smile, they can't do this to you."

Day had seen it. Some Potter fan had likened the queen to Professor McGonagall. It had been Day's screensaver for over a month.

"I think you're talking about memes. No one makes memes of the head of education." Of course, no one really listened to her either.

"But they will make the memings when you are queen," Queen Yasmine announced solemnly. "Now, we must talk about your dress. I think traditional is best for the actual ceremony, but you should wear couture to the reception. The whole world will be watching. We need to present a true vision of our country as a cosmopolitan nation. I've already called the heads of three fashion houses to submit designs. And, darling girl, I love you, but we must pluck those eyebrows. They're growing together. They're not supposed to do that."

She wasn't... She felt her forehead and grimaced. Technically hair was supposed to grow. Plucking it was the unnatural force here. It was also not the point. "Kash hasn't spoken to me in fifteen years. Why would he want to marry me now?"

The queen sighed. "Have you listened to a word I've said? Kash doesn't want to get married at all. I'm rather certain he doesn't want to come home. That's why I hired guards to drag him here. I was even smart enough to hire the particularly handsome one with the British accent and the law degree. Even now he's explaining to Kash that there's no way out of the trap I've set and that he should accept this beautiful gift of love and stability I'm offering him."

"Is it a gift or a trap?" The queen had used both words, but it was definitely starting to feel like a trap to Day.

The queen's smile turned beatific. "It's both, of course. That's the beauty of it all. You're going to be perfect for him. You're the girl to keep him in line. My boy is lovely and so smart, though he often forgets to use his brain. I wish his penis wasn't so large. I think that was where we went wrong. It has to have come from my side of the family, because my husband certainly wasn't that large. And I was happy with that. It meant he didn't feel the need to use it on every woman who walked by. And you must get Kashmir to stop having it photographed. It's unseemly."

Day felt herself blush. Damn it. She didn't blush. Ever. She'd seen almost everything there was to be seen and she was cool with it all. Sex was part of a good and natural life. Accepting her own sexuality had been important. But something about the elderly queen talking about Kash's penis had Day's skin flushing. "Your Majesty, I'm not marrying Kashmir. He's been a halfway decent king, especially in the early years, but he would make a terrible husband."

"But he won't once you show him the way."

"The way?"

"Dayita, there's a reason I chose you." The queen was quiet for a moment and then she looked back up, not even attempting to quell the tears in her eyes now. "You can save him. You can give him the stability he needs. You can show him he doesn't have to destroy himself."

"I don't know why you think I can do that."

The queen seemed to come to some inner decision because she sniffled and then sat back, her head coming up regally. "You are smart enough to lead this country. You are perfect to be the face of the monarchy. If I allow Kash to continue, we will be obsolete and our country will go the way of so many other small nations. You are right. At this point we still have a faction that would love to see us go back into the Dark Ages. I worry that there is a group of men waiting to take over. They would privatize something that has always been public. That oil was found on public land and therefore belongs to all of us. They would change this and that would send many of our people into poverty. Women and girls, most of all. Are you willing to risk that?"

Something was wrong with the queen. Day had never seen her like this before. Her majesty was so gentle and gracious. "Your Majesty, I understand that you're upset with Kashmir, but I'm not going to marry him. You need to talk to him about this. You need to make him see reason. He should marry, but he needs to find the right woman."

"You are the right woman, but he is far too foolish to see it. He's spent fifteen years avoiding you."

"He doesn't remember my name." He'd refused to see her the one time she'd shown up to the palace in person. He'd never written her back. She'd sent him letters for more than a year until she finally realized he was ignoring her.

"Then introduce yourself, darling, because I won't be swayed," the queen announced. "I will see the two of you married and settled and working for a brighter future or I will destroy it all and let the cards fall as they may."

"Why are you doing this?"

"Because it's my last chance to make things right for him. He wasn't raised to be the king. The pressure has been too much. He chafes at the bit because he was allowed too much freedom in his younger years. I must leave him with a woman who can handle him, who can direct him in how he should go. Someone who can be a partner to him, even lead him when he needs to be led. Someone strong, and if I allow him to he will choose poorly. If I had more time… I do not so I will place this bet on the table. I will put everything I have into it and see if you will call me. I'm not bluffing, Dayita. I will do this."

Day felt her breath flee as she realized the truth behind the queen's words. "Does Kash know you're dying?"

"No."

"You have to tell him."

"I will, when the time is right." She waved a hand and the door to the hallway opened. A servant rushed in, carrying a tray. It was as though she'd been hovering outside, waiting for the moment when the queen would call upon her, anxious to do her part.

Was Day's country calling her now? It was insane to think that in this day and age she would be asked to marry in order to help her country, but some of what the queen was saying made sense.

"I'm a commoner." She tried to come up with any way out of this trap.

The queen took the pills her servant had brought her. She reached for them and clasped the older woman's hand when they touched. This wasn't a mere servant. Day had seen Mrs. Pashmi Indrus every time she'd met with the queen. She hovered in the background, but it was obvious she was close to her majesty. She handed the queen a glass of water.

"So is the English girl and she's done quite well," the queen replied. "She is the new royalty and you are very much like her."

"I'm not a virgin."

That made the queen laugh. "Darling, no one is anymore. And to marry a virgin off to my son would be like handing one over to a dragon and expecting her to know how to slay it."

"I'm afraid I would be more likely to kill your son than to find happiness with him."

"You cared for him once." She swallowed the pills and that proved to Day more than anything how serious the queen was. Her majesty would never allow herself to do something so personal around anyone but her small family. By showing Day her weakness, she was bringing her in. "I know the two of you were close in England. You can find this again."

Day shook her head, even though she knew damn well she was already sliding down the queen's slippery slope. "We're two entirely different people now."

"No, you're not. You're merely older and time has worn off some of your joy," the queen said quietly. "It will do this to you, time will. Only if you let it. It's easy to let time and pain change you into someone less than you were. Less able to love. Less able to forgive. Less able to look at this world of ours and see that it is so beautiful. Time teaches us to see the ugly parts so we can protect ourselves. But, darling, when we spend all of our energy protecting ourselves we miss out on all the reasons we're alive in the first place."

Day felt a tear slip down her cheek and missed her mother so much in that moment. Her father had moved on, starting another family and leaving her behind, but she could hear her own mother in the queen's words. Perhaps they were the words of every mother to her child, the prayer that her child would find love, joy, happiness. And a place in the world. A reason to be.

"I cared for him a long time ago," Day admitted. "But even then I didn't think it could work."

"Then what fun it will be when it does," the queen replied. "Am I taking you away from someone you truly care about? My intelligence says you haven't had a serious man in your life for years."

Not since she'd made the decision to move home. She'd dated a few men in England and then had a more serious relationship when she'd taken the head of education job back here. It hadn't worked out and now she threw herself into work. She was nearly thirty-six. There was plenty of time to find a mate.

But would she find a calling as well? Already there was a part of her that wondered what she could do with that crown on her head. She could ensure that a whole generation of children got what they needed. She could be an ambassador for science around the world. The Professor Queen.

She didn't have to love Kash. She merely had to be a good

partner to him. Perhaps some people found their true love in the form of another human being, but Day could find it in helping her people.

"No, Your Majesty. I'm not in love. I don't think I've ever been in love." Except she'd thought she'd loved Kash. Those months with him had haunted her for years. She could still remember how it felt to brush her lips against his.

If the queen knew how she spent some of her nights, would she want her as a daughter-in-law?

"There are personal things we should talk about." Day couldn't not be honest.

"Is this about that club you go to? And the one in Paris? What was it called?"

Mrs. Indrus piped up. "The Velvet Collar."

"Yes, that is the one." The queen's eyes lit with mirth. "Pashmi and I looked at their website. Very interesting place."

The queen's servant giggled a bit behind her hand and suddenly looked years younger.

And Day found herself blushing again. "It's for relaxation. I rarely indulge myself physically."

"Well, that's good because I'm sure that my son does. He needs a good spanking, if I do say so myself. You both like those clubs. That's one thing you have in common. Excellent. It's a start." The queen clapped her hands together. "Now let's talk about your wedding. Pashmi, could you get us some tea and then perhaps you will join us? You have such a good eye when it comes to colors. We shall fill the palace with flowers."

Pashmi strode away to do the queen's will and Day realized she was trapped.

Utterly and completely trapped in a cage she couldn't force her way out of because there was a piece of her that still wanted to know if it could work.

That was the most dangerous trap of all.

Chapter Two

Kash strode into the palace, well aware every single person he met had taken one look at him and fled the other way. The guards at the gates hadn't questioned him, simply waved him by as they attempted to not look him in the eyes. The maids and servants he'd passed hadn't offered a single greeting.

The only person standing between him and his mother now would be the lord chamberlain. He had heard one of the maids calling for him. It wouldn't do any good. Hanin Kota had taken over the running of the palace a few years before the king and Shray had been killed. He was a somewhat cold man who lived for formality. His family had worked for the Kamdars for decades. Kash had always thought it would be fun to fire him, but he'd deferred to his mother's wishes.

If Hanin gave him trouble, Kash would boot him out. There was a freedom in what his mother had done.

He was angry. As angry as he could ever remember being.

"You might chill out before you scare the shit out of the entire palace, Kash." Jesse Murdoch easily kept up with him.

He ignored his so-called guard. Murdoch wasn't alone. The Boomer was with him. Yes, Kash would fire him, too. All of them.

The one thing in his life that should have been his choice was being taken from him. Everywhere he turned he had responsibility weighing on him. Lately he'd tried to handle it by giving more and more to parliament. They seemed happy. Now he was supposed to give up his much-needed time away and take some unknown wife and stay at home and deliver a brood of mewling children to his mother?

Chapal could have the crown. He'd decided that after the Brit had explained the situation he was in. His mother had used some antiquated rule of law to force his hand? Oh, she would find out he couldn't be forced into this.

"This is a real palace. It's cool." The mass of muscular flesh the others called Boomer was smiling at everything like this was all one long vacation. "Hello, ma'am. Real nice place you got here."

"She's a servant," Kash shot back. "The palace doesn't belong to her."

The young woman, who had to be all of twenty, turned back to her dusting, but not before he'd seen the way her skin had flushed with shame.

When had he taken to hurting young women with careless words? He wasn't this man. He was a charmer. He never shamed anyone for their position in society. Bloody hell. He was going mad.

"Please accept my apologies," he said quickly before turning back toward his destination. The queen mother's wing was off to the left.

"Don't you mind him," Boomer was saying to the maid. "He's a massive asshole."

"He's the king," the woman whispered.

"King Asswipe," Boomer replied. "I was told he was cool and everything, but he's real mean. He even sent away the lady with the mints on the airplane. Do you happen to know where the kitchen is? I'm a little hungry."

Good god, the man had eaten everything on the plane and he was complaining again? "Boomer" apparently meant never-ending gut in American English. "Ana, would you please escort Mr. Boomer to the kitchen and inform the chef that he's in need of sustenance? He's only eaten two full meals in the past few hours."

"Thank god. I'm starving." Boomer let himself be led off.

Which left him with only one intrusive guard. He'd managed to ditch Weston and the Texan, Michael Malone. They'd declared they needed to do a quick tour of the grounds so they could get something called a "lay of the land." Now all he had to do was get rid of Murdoch and his life would be perfect. "Why don't you go with him?"

Murdoch simply smiled. "Because I would rather be with you."

"I'm going to yell at my mother," Kash explained. "I would prefer to do it alone."

Murdoch shrugged. "I can stand out here. Please don't try to run off."

"I'm not being run out of my own palace." Kash turned for the door. His mother would be in her parlor at this time of day. He'd snuck in the back way in the hopes of catching his mother off guard. Surely she knew his plane had landed, but he'd moved quickly. She would be expecting him in another thirty minutes or so. He wanted her off guard so he could tell her exactly what she could do with her bloody wedding plans.

His anger had been building over the course of the long flight. How dare she throw this at him? With everything else he had to deal with, the last thing he needed was his mother losing her mind.

Yes, perhaps that was the way to go. His brain was working overtime and on almost no sleep. He'd tossed and turned all the way over. Not even drinking had helped ease him into peace. The whole time he'd fumed and raged, and he was ready to play as dirty as she was.

Dementia. It wasn't so surprising at her age. So what if she was only seventy and had all her faculties? The fact that she'd decided to take him on was proof enough that she'd lost her mind.

He'd have her in a nice home shortly, and then when she cried and begged him to allow her to come home, he would. But only after she'd taken back that stupid invocation. She would go to parliament and explain that she would never question her son again.

And anyone who ever did would find out that he was the damn king.

He was about to open the doors when the lord chamberlain showed up, stepping right into the way. "I think you should wait, Your Majesty. The queen mother is busy at this time. I'll set an appointment for you if you like."

Hanin stood there, a smug smile on his face and his suit in perfect condition.

"I would like to fire you and punch you in the face on the way out. If you don't move out of the way and allow me access to my mother, I will."

"You always were a bit of an animal, weren't you, Kashmir?" But he stepped aside.

"Don't ever forget it. And that's 'Your Majesty.'" At least it was until he shoved the crown somewhere the sun didn't shine.

He opened the outer doors, ready to have it out with his mother.

"Be quick, Pashmi. They say he's on his way. I can't have my son seeing this."

Seeing what? Oh, he would see everything. He would control everything since it seemed he was never allowed to be out of control. They came at him from all sides. When he wasn't dealing with parliament, he was fighting with OPEC or some other oil cartel. When he finally found something he felt good about, some asshole ex-CIA guy blew it all up, and now he was expected to take this from his own mother? No way.

He shoved through the inner doors and stopped.

Hanin moved past him. "Your Majesty, I'm so sorry. I tried to stop him but he threatened me with physical violence."

"It's all right," his mother was saying. "He would have found out anyway."

His mother's long-time maid was helping her to sit up and a woman in medical scrubs was wrapping up an IV that had obviously been used on his mother.

His mother, who had taken to not eating supper. Or breakfast.

His mother, whose clothes hung off her lately and she'd waved off his worry by telling him she was trying a new diet.

His mother, whom he'd neglected so much he hadn't seen that she was ill.

Hanin turned on him. "Can I expect that his majesty will be civil to the queen mother? I told her you wouldn't take this well. She insisted. As you can see, she's not strong enough for a fight, much less a wedding. You should convince her not to do this."

All thoughts of yelling fled as his whole soul seemed to sink. How had he not seen this? How had months gone by and he hadn't recognized that his mother might be dying? "Please allow me to talk to my mother. I'll take care of her."

Hanin strode out the door, closing it behind him.

"What is it? Is it cancer?" The thought made his heart seize. He moved to her side, dropping to one knee. Grandmother had died of cancer. He'd watched her waste away even as she'd smiled and tried to pretend everything was all right.

The lines around her eyes tightened. "I didn't mean for you to know."

She would probably tell him there was nothing to worry about. Pashmi wouldn't care that he was the king. Pashmi had changed his damn diapers at one point. She was practically a second mother, so he turned to the one person in the room he could intimidate.

He stood and faced the nurse. "What does my mother have? What is this treatment you're giving her?"

"A blood transfusion, Your Majesty. She was down two pints, a side effect of the chemotherapy for her cancer. She'll feel better now. She'll have much more energy." The nurse looked back at his mother. "She's very sick, Your Majesty. It's stage four ovarian cancer. She had a full hysterectomy but the cancer had spread to her colon and the doctors no longer think the chemo is working."

He felt as though the wind had been knocked out of him. Those words kicked him in the gut and left him gasping for breath.

This was why she'd done what she'd done.

"You're going to die and you don't want to leave me alone."

"Could we have the room, please?" His mother straightened up, her shoulders going back in a regal fashion.

Pashmi led the nurse outside.

He felt sick. How had he missed this?

"It's not your fault, Kashmir."

"I would disagree. How long has this been going on?" How long had he been out there partying while his mother was dying? How many women had he gone through while she'd fought for her life, gone through round after round of hell?

"Please, Kash," his mother implored. "Please sit with me. It's not as bad as the doctors say."

He found the edge of the couch, balancing on it. He wouldn't sit back in case he needed to carry her out. "I'll have the doctors tell me themselves."

"Of course. Don't be angry with them. I asked them to keep things quiet. I didn't want to make a fuss."

No fuss over the fact that she was dying. "Tell me how long you've known."

"I was diagnosed six months ago. I told you I was having surgery."

"You told me it was routine. You then told me they found nothing serious. I didn't go to the doctors because you told me it was all fine." And because he hadn't wanted to believe. He'd been in a bad place, dealing with the fact that he'd come so close and couldn't replicate the experiments that had gone well before. He'd come up against failure after failure so he'd done what he did now. He'd found a party and become the life of it. For a month.

He'd offered to come home for the surgery but he'd been somewhat relieved when she'd told him not to, when she'd waved off his worry and laughed that she would rather be alone. She'd told him if he came home, the press would come with him.

He should have come home. He should have been sitting at her bedside when she woke up. She'd had no one. Her husband and eldest son were dead. Shray would never have allowed their mother to go through this alone. Shray would have seen.

Why had God taken Shray and left behind the lesser brother?

"Kashmir, listen to me. I know you're angry."

He was angry, but it was muted now. The rage he'd felt was buried under an avalanche of pure guilt. And pain. "You have no idea."

She sat back, looking older than he remembered. "Yes, I do, and I don't blame you. I hoped I could get better, but it looks as though I will not."

"I'll call in all the doctors." He would take her anywhere he needed to take her. He would find the best specialist and bring him or her in. "There are new therapies coming out every day."

"I don't want them. I'm tired, son. I've fought my battle and it's time to be with your father and your brother."

All he heard was it was time to leave him alone.

"Please forgive me. I didn't want to disrupt your life," she said quietly.

Nope. He couldn't sit at all. "Not disrupt my life? You don't allow me to take care of you because you don't wish to disrupt my life, but you come up with this insane plan to force me to marry?"

Despite her obvious weariness, there was a light in her eyes. "It's not insane. It's quite good, my plan. And you will marry, won't you, Kashmir?"

So neatly was her trap sprung. Still, he couldn't say the word. He couldn't give this up. She would be gone and he would be trapped in some loveless, sexless, hopeless marriage.

"I want to see you happy." The words sounded more like a plea coming out of his mother's mouth.

"Then don't ask me to marry." He stood in front of the floor-to-ceiling windows that looked out over the city. In the distance, he could see the Arabian Sea. When he'd been a child, he and Shray had played on those beaches, building sand castles to rival their home.

He was going to be alone. No one would remember who he'd been. He would be who he was now for the rest of his life. He would be the player king, the party boy.

"What do you think of this one, Your Majesty?" a feminine voice said. "I like it but I worry it's a bit revealing."

He turned as a woman in a brilliant yellow dress walked in from the side room.

For the second time in minutes, he felt the world flip and realign.

"Day?"

She turned and her spine straightened. Her body, so relaxed before, seemed to grow a few inches, and her gaze took him in.

She looked like a queen with her steely eyes.

"Hello, Kashmir," she said, her voice deeper than he'd remembered. That voice of hers washed over him. "I wasn't expecting to see you today."

Dayita Samar. How many years had flown by? She didn't look older, merely more mature. As though the beautiful girl he'd cared for had turned into a gorgeous woman who knew exactly who she was.

Day. The first woman he'd ever thought about settling down with.

God, was she really the only woman he'd ever thought about settling down with? He'd had a few girlfriends over the years, women he'd spent time with, escorted to the world's glittering events, but none of them had ever been like Day. None of those women had talked science and politics and put him on his ass when he needed it.

"Hello, Day." He couldn't help but stare at her. It was like a ghost had walked back into his life at the precise moment he needed to be reminded of his past.

"Well, are you going through with it or should I take off this dress and get back to work?" There was no mistaking the challenge in her eyes.

Oh, she should take off the dress. He remembered vividly how he'd wished he could get her out of those ridiculously prim clothes she'd worn at Oxford. Gone were the heavy sweaters and thick, too-long skirts. The gossamer yellow fabric skimmed her every curve and she was luscious.

More than that. She looked like home, a home he'd long thought lost to him.

His mother looked up at him expectantly. "Well, I thought if I was going to force you into a quickie marriage, I should at least give you a bride, too. Should I tell you why I selected Dayita? She's lovely and of the right age and you have much in common. She has a master's degree in physics from Oxford, so she's intelligent. We don't want an uneducated queen."

"I thought you planned to go for your doctorate." He couldn't seem to take his eyes off her. While he was looking at Day, he didn't have to acknowledge that his mother was dying.

"Circumstances changed," she replied, gathering the flowing skirt around her. "My father required help at home so I returned to Loa Mali and I eventually took over the education department, with her majesty's blessing."

His mother smiled Day's way. "She's been brilliant, but the parliament is giving her trouble about funding for elementary education. It seems they would prefer to spend it on other things."

Day had been here on Loa Mali all this time? She headed his education department? And what the hell was his parliament doing? "There is nothing more important than our children receiving the best possible education we can afford."

"Our girls and our boys," Day said with a quiet will.

Those old men were giving her hell about educating girls?

Another thing he'd allowed to slip by. "You'll have your funding."

"Will I have my wedding?" His mother started to stand, her hands shaking. "Or should I prepare the lawyers?"

She was really going to do it. His mother was lovely, but when she decided, her mind was made up. She would force them into a constitutional crisis and he had no idea what the fallout would be. Day had reminded him what was at stake. Education and equality for an entire generation of Loa Mali's daughters.

"You'll have your wedding." He rushed to steady his mother, her hand so small and frail in his.

Small of body, great of will. That was his mother.

"Excellent." She straightened up. "Let's talk to the seamstress, darling girl. I think the dress is perfect, but they must bring the hem up slightly. We can't have you tripping at your wedding. And Kashmir, I have a tailor coming for you as well. The appointment is at four. Please don't be late. We shall dine tonight as a family. Seven p.m. sharp."

He watched as Day led his mother back toward the room they appeared to have set up as a dress shop. Of course. Day would need new clothes.

Kash walked out, ignoring Murdoch, who followed behind him. He strode through the palace until he got to his room. He ordered everyone out, locked the doors, and when he was absolutely certain he was alone, he sat at his desk. He stared at the picture of his family, his father and mother, smiling and proud. Shray at twenty-two, the almost king. Himself, grinning though the photographer had asked them all for restraint.

Kash stared at the photo and wished he could cry.

* * * *

The papers didn't do the man justice. He was far more beautiful in person. Even more handsome than she'd remembered him.

Day sighed as she walked out onto the balcony. Their small family supper had turned into a twenty-four-person state dinner after the parliament heads learned that Kash was back home and a bride had been selected.

Her first lesson in politics—family couldn't come first when one was the king.

She'd sat at the opposite end of the table from Kash, but she'd managed to watch him. He'd been charming and witty and he'd deflected many of the rather rude questions about how his marriage would change the way things were run.

On her end of the table she'd been asked numerous questions about what she would wear and who would arrange her hair for the ceremony, and did she worry about how the public would take a commoner queen?

She rather thought they would prefer a Loa Malian on the throne. Unfortunately, all the females who could claim some royalty were related to Kash, the downside to one family holding a crown for so long. If Kash wanted royalty he would have to marry a foreigner.

That was the moment the minister of infrastructure went back to asking about her hair. Apparently he had a niece who was a hairdresser.

She took a deep breath and stared out over the city. At this time of night, it was quiet in this sector, though she could see the lights twinkling downtown and closer to the beach. All the tourists and young people would be dancing the night away or sipping a cocktail after a long day of surfing and fishing.

God, she loved this place.

Was she doing the right thing? Perhaps she was for her country. For herself and Kash, she wasn't so sure.

She'd watched him from across the long, formal table and she hadn't seen any hint of the boy he used to be. Somehow, in the back of her mind she'd thought they would meet again and he would be the same.

So foolish of her.

"Did you enjoy the dessert? They had been planning on serving crème brûlée, but I remembered you like gelato. Strawberry."

She turned and Kash was standing in the doorway, the tie to his tuxedo undone and the first few buttons of his shirt open, showing off golden skin.

Oh, how the girls must swoon over that man.

Unfortunately for him, she was a woman and not a girl. She curtseyed, recalling her etiquette classes and going down deep, to show her respect for the crown. "I thank you, Your Majesty."

"Come now, Day. I asked you not to call me that long ago, and now it appears there's even less reason. We were friends then. We're going to be husband and wife in a week. Shocking how quickly that woman can move when she wants to."

He looked so composed, but she couldn't forget that he'd only found out his mother was dying this afternoon. That was when she'd seen the real man. She'd interrupted them with her silly dress and she'd seen the shock and pain on Kash's face before he'd smoothed it out and gone back to being the polite royal he'd become.

"Are you all right?" She asked the question for two reasons. First, she wanted to know the answer and second, to see if they really were still friends.

His lips curved up slightly. "I'm faring quite well. We Kamdars are made of sterner stuff than this. Did you enjoy the dinner?"

So, not so friendly he would talk about private things with her. It was good to know where they stood. They needed to have a long conversation about how this was going to work. They might be marrying to protect the Kamdar line and to give his mother some peace, but they needed a plan of action about how best to achieve their goals.

Partners. That was how she'd decided to look at this. They were partners. And if she ended up governing the kingdom while he was out fucking around with supermodels, she wouldn't get her heart broken.

Just humiliated.

Yes, they needed a talk and perhaps a contract.

"I enjoyed the meal very much. The company left something to be desired, but I suspect I'll get used to dining with windbag politicians." She turned back to the balcony, leaning against it. The view from here was spectacular. Beyond that, it was soothing in a way.

"Yes, Mother told me they're giving you trouble." He joined her, leaning beside her, their bodies so close but not touching. "I'll talk to them, ensure you have your funding."

"Don't. It can wait a few weeks. I need to go back to them and introduce myself as their new queen." She wasn't about to let them think she sent her husband in. If he behaved as he so often did, he wouldn't be around much and it would be up to her to keep everyone in line.

"Is that why you agreed to this arrangement? Because you wanted power?"

"I agreed because I care about this country. I've spent the last ten years of my life working here and trying to ensure that our children get what they need to make it out in the world. I agreed because your mother is excellent at putting one in a corner. I agreed because someone has to and I wasn't sure who you would bring home if given the chance." She shuddered at the idea of some brainless model attempting to be a role model for Loa Malian girls.

"Ah, you don't think I have good taste in women."

"I think you have an unquenchable appetite for them, Your Majesty, and that is something we should talk about."

"Ah, the wifely lectures begin," he said with a sigh. "Please proceed. I'm anxious to get this over with so I can be properly chastened."

"I only ask that you attempt some discretion, Kashmir. I don't expect you to be faithful in any way, but I do expect you to not humiliate me."

He turned, frowning a bit as though she'd surprised him. "You don't expect me to be faithful?"

It was time for some honesty. "I don't think you can be. How long have you kept a single woman? A month? Three?"

"Six," he replied. "I was with Tasha Reynolds for six months before we went our separate ways."

"And were you faithful to her?" She already knew the answer to that question.

"We had an agreement." He frowned as though the conversation wasn't going at all as he'd expected. "She was on set much of the time. She knew I had a highly stressful job, so she was understanding. I gave her the same options."

"Excellent, then let's be fair with each other. As long as we're both discreet, this marriage of ours doesn't have to mean the end of our lives."

"You have a man?"

"No, but I do have a life and I can't imagine never sleeping with someone again."

He stopped, his body going still for a moment. "What is that supposed to mean? I'll be your husband. You'll sleep with me. I know biology wasn't your field of study, but do I have to explain how babies are made? That's what my mother is doing. She's buying your womb."

So he wasn't as sanguine about the marriage as he'd seemed earlier. That was another thing she needed to know. "There are many ways to make a baby, several of which don't involve sex."

He frowned. "You can't be serious. We're going to be married. We're going to have sex."

"When I decide I'm ready, we'll talk about it." This brought her to the place she needed to be. "I think we need to negotiate our own private marriage contract. I would feel much better if we understood the parameters. It would help us both to know how to act and what our roles are."

"Your role is as my wife, and part of that is sleeping with me," Kash insisted.

"Not until you've had an STD test and I'm certain I want to sleep with you. I've already confirmed that it's traditional for the king and queen to keep separate rooms."

"There's nothing traditional about this."

She had to laugh. "I think it's quite traditional."

"Not for my family. My father was deeply in love with my mother. He met her at a ball in Bombay. Her father was the king of a small South Pacific island. I was told they danced all night and he went to her father the next day and demanded her hand in marriage or there would be war. As neither country had much of a standing army, they chose wedding."

She'd never heard the story. "That's sweet, but it's not how most royals wed."

"My grandfather selected his own bride as well. I'm the first in a hundred years to be arranged by someone else. I suppose my mother thinks I'm incapable of selecting a proper bride."

She had to offer him an out if he wanted one. They would both be miserable if he truly thought he could do better. "You should talk to her if you have someone you care for. I don't think she wants you to be unhappy. If there's a woman you love, you should present her to your mother."

Kash huffed, a disdainful sound. "After she's presented you to the parliament? I think not. Anyone I could bring in would be less than perfect. You really are, you know. I spent the last several hours studying up on you. Top of your class at Oxford. Accepted into MIT's doctoral program, but you turned it all down because your mother was sick. You had the whole world laid out for you, but you came home and took a job so far beneath you it's ridiculous. This one is beneath you, too, you know. You should be in a lab somewhere mapping the universe, not trying on designer dresses."

"I assure you I can make a difference." There were times when she wished she'd been able to follow through on the plan she'd made so long ago, but things changed. Dreams changed. "I have a purpose here. There are many brilliant minds working on the universe. The former head of education barely passed her O levels, much less university. I've thought this through. I can have a voice in this position, a unique one."

"Yes, you'll be my better half. My smarter half. Everyone will know the only way a woman like you marries a man like me is because it was arranged."

He was being frustrating, threatening to bring out the piece of herself she'd decided to suppress. No matter what the queen said, she wasn't sure Kash would be able to handle her when she got into that state of mind. She forced her voice to be gentle. The last thing she needed was to hear from another man how unwomanly she was. "What are you worried about, Kash? I told you if you have another woman, I'll step down."

He pushed away from the wall. "And I told you there is no single woman. Do you know where they found me? The bodyguards my mother hired to drag me home, that is."

"Miami, I heard." She was curious where he was going with this. Something seemed to be raging in the king this evening. Something that needed soothing, but she wasn't sure that was her place.

"They found me in bed with not one woman, but three." He said it like she was supposed to gasp and quiver with shock and distaste.

Did he think she didn't read the papers? Didn't see the way the press covered his antics? "Hence my offer to negotiate a path that will please us both."

His eyes narrowed, anger flaring as though he wasn't getting the reaction he wanted. "You think I was pleased?"

"If you weren't then you were doing it wrong. And with three women. You would think one of them would know how to do it right." She wasn't about to feed into his beast tonight.

He chuckled but there was no humor in the sound. "I wasn't talking about the sex. Or maybe I was. Maybe I was talking about how hollow it is now, how nothing fills me. There is no other woman, but there won't be any love for you either. Don't think you can win me back by following through on this ridiculous plan of my mother's."

It was her turn to laugh. "I haven't thought of you that way in years."

He was quiet for a moment. "You never think of that kiss?"

She wasn't going to lie. Despite what he'd said, she'd had time to think. This wasn't a ridiculous plan. This was the queen's way of knowing someone would be watching out for her country after she died. Day did want this to work. Not the relationship. Not in any romantic way. Rather, she wanted the job. She was ready to do her duty, and only Kash could keep her from it. That meant if they couldn't be friends, at the very least they had to respect each other. "I think about it from time to time, but we were two different people then. Those children are gone. I get wistful when the memory washes over me, but I don't mourn for some lost love between us."

She sometimes wished things had turned out differently. She certainly wished Kash hadn't lost such a huge chunk of his family. But she knew the Kash whom she'd kissed that day by the river wasn't the Kash standing with her tonight. He'd changed in that moment. He'd become a king, and it was obvious the weight didn't sit well.

"Well, it's for the best that you didn't. Did you even think of me after I left or did you move on to the next bloke? I heard later on that you dated Neville Hightower after I left. Quite a step down, I should say." He turned to go. "I'll bid you goodnight. I'm sure there's something Mother has planned for us tomorrow."

"Stop right there." She wasn't putting up with that. She needed to make that clear. "You will not talk to me like that again."

He turned, his lips quirking in an arrogant smirk. "I'll talk to you any way I like. Haven't you heard that I'm the king?"

Now she was finding a little rage of her own. "I don't care who you are. You will not speak to me like that. If you have a question, I'll answer it. If you need comfort, I'll talk to you. Do you think I don't see through this? This behavior is one of two things. Either you are truly the arrogant ass you're presenting to me or the day has been too much and I'm a convenient punching bag."

His face lost that smooth smile. "I didn't mean to hurt you. It has been a long day."

There was the moment she'd been waiting for. When he realized what he was doing, he backed off. For that, she could reward him. She moved closer, putting her hand on his shoulder and leaning in. "Kashmir, you found out your mother is dying. Of course it's been a long day."

His head shook. "I can't. I can't even process it right now. Answer my question. It's easier to focus on this, on us. Please."

The *please* did it. Something about a polite man always softened her up. His question. Had she thought about him after that day by the river? "I wrote you letters for a year or so. I came home for the coronation and tried to see you, but they wouldn't let me through. Too many people and I wasn't important enough, I suppose. I don't blame you, Kash. I was some girl you knew at university. You had other things to deal with back then."

She didn't blame him. Not anymore. In those first years, she'd been angry with him, mad at herself for letting him in. Now she saw them for what they'd been. Two children trying to navigate a world that constantly attempted to drown them. They were all swimming as hard as they could and there was no blame to be placed.

He stiffened, coming to his full height. "You did what?"

She stepped back. "I wrote you."

"You wrote me a letter?"

"No, I wrote you probably fifty or sixty. I was lonely after you left. I knew after you didn't reply to the first five or so that you weren't going to, but I still liked talking to you. It was probably a silly thing to do. I should have gotten a journal or something, but I didn't."

He put his hands on her shoulders, looking her straight in the eyes. "Dayita, I never got a single letter from you."

He hadn't sent one either. It was so long ago. "I sent them to the palace post office. I suspect they deal with hundreds of letters."

"I should have gotten them. I asked my secretary to send me anything from my friends at Oxford. I got nothing. I was desperate back then. I wanted something, anything to make me feel normal, but all my friends deserted me. I wanted to see you. How can you say you came to the coronation? I offered to send a plane for you. You refused. You said you had too much to do. Why are you lying to me?"

Oh, someone had lied and she could guess whom. Her heart twisted at the thought of Kash being all alone and longing for his friends only to have none reply. "Kash, I never got any correspondence from you. No offer at all. Why would I have turned you down? I came to try to see you. I have pictures of me and my father at the coronation celebrations outside the palace. I assure you I wouldn't have made a twelve-hour flight in economy if you would have sent a plane. I know Matthew and Roger tried to contact you, too. Your friends didn't abandon you. They couldn't get to you."

"Why?" Kash let go and seemed to stumble a bit before regaining his balance. "Why would she do that to me? My mother is the only one who could have done this. No one else in this palace would have kept something like this from me."

The last thing he needed was to get angry with his mother. "I'm sure she had her reasons. You needed to be focused on your new duties. You couldn't spend all your time mooning over a beautiful girl."

His hands, fisted before, relaxed, and he gave her the first genuine smile she'd seen from him all evening. "Mooning? You think I would moon over you?"

Yes, she was remembering how to handle him. Perhaps there was a bit left of the happy boy she'd fallen in love with all those years ago. "I'm sure you did, Your Majesty. I can picture you right here, staring out and wishing for your lost love. Maybe you even bought a guitar and learned how to play. You wrote sad songs about how much you missed me."

He laughed, a magical sound. When Kash laughed, his body shook with it. It reminded her of how passionate he'd been about everything. Kash had an enthusiasm for life that brightened a room when he walked in, that made her look at the world around her differently. He'd been the one to bring her out of her shell.

Had she gone back into it for years because he'd gone away?

He smiled down at her, his hands coming up to frame her face. "I did miss you, Dayita. Those first years, I missed you like crazy." He sobered a bit. "But I've changed. You're right. I'm not the man I was back then."

Her heart twisted in disappointment. She'd almost been sure he would kiss her, but he moved back. She tried not to show how much that hurt. A few hours back in his life and she was the one with longing in her heart. It was dangerous, but luckily she was a disciplined woman. She wasn't a girl anymore. She knew better. And deep down, she'd always known that they'd had their chance and it wouldn't come again. "I'm not the same either. I'm older, more restrained. I'm comfortable with myself now so I can go into this arrangement with my eyes wide open."

"Can we not make any more major decisions tonight?" Kash asked.

He looked so tired and she wondered if he had slept at all. She was worried that if she left him alone, he might confront his mother, and they all needed cooler heads to prevail. The past was the past and they had to deal with the future. If she was going to be his wife, she needed to be his friend again, and friends took care of each other. "Come to my room and I'll get you a drink."

He cocked a single brow.

Yes, she still remembered how to speak Kashmir. "No, I'm not inviting you into my bed. Have a drink with me and I'll tell you all about our friends, if you want to know. I'm still close with Roger and Matty."

He frowned. "And Neville?"

Such a jealous man. "Neville got a bit handsy, and once I broke his fingers he seemed to lose interest in me."

"Ah, that's what I like to hear." Kash reached a hand out. "Are we really going to do this, Day?"

"Only if you want to, Your Majesty." It had to be his choice in the end, even if most of his options had been taken from him.

He seemed to come to some decision and he pulled her hand to his lips. "All right then, my bride-to-be. I hope Mother stocked your room with whiskey. I could use some. Don't mind the bodyguards. They follow me. I think they think I'm going to run."

She'd seen his new American guards. She'd been assigned a couple herself. Michael Malone was a lovely man, and the oddly named Boomer was like a beautiful, massive golden retriever.

She nodded to Mr. Murdoch as they walked back into the palace. He'd been hovering close all night and seemed like a perfectly kind man.

Kash began talking about the old days.

It was time to figure out what kind of man her future husband was. And if he could handle what she needed.

Chapter Three

Kash came awake and sat up in bed. Something was wrong. Different. Definitely different. He was also dressed. He was wearing a pair of pajama pants because he'd sat up for the longest time with Day, talking about old times. They'd started out drinking Scotch, but when she'd switched to tea, he'd gone along with her. They'd called down to the kitchens and had tea and sandwiches and tiny cakes sent up.

He'd been sad to leave her.

"I feel odd."

"That's what it feels like when you don't wake up with a hangover, Your Majesty," Simon Weston said as he strode into the bedchamber. "I know it's terribly odd to realize you remember the evening before, but that's how it goes. I need to talk to you about security for tonight's official engagement announcement and celebration. I'm afraid things are going to move quickly over the course of the next two weeks."

Yes, he did remember. He was getting married to Day. His mother had set it all up, but then it had been his mother who had kept Day from him in the first place. "I need to talk to my mother."

"She'll be here in a few moments." Weston nodded toward the door and the flood of servants began. "She's coming in with the lord chamberlain. I've had breakfast brought in."

Yes, Kash could see that. His normal breakfast was usually coffee and a protein bar, but this was a full breakfast. Full English. He hadn't had a full English since his college days. Mostly because it was absolutely terrible for him. He smiled, the memories wafting over him as he smelled the sausages and fried eggs, baked beans and bacon. There was toast and hash browns and tomatoes. "Did you order this? I don't think my mother's ever had a fry-up."

Weston shook his head. "This is for you. I've gotten to be too American to possibly handle that breakfast. I've got an omelet and some fruit. Your fiancée ordered for you. She's attempting to take over some of the queen's duties."

His stomach grumbled and he couldn't help but smile. Day remembered. They'd often had breakfast together and he would always order a full English breakfast. She would wrinkle her nose as she ate some tiny thing and drank an enormous cup of coffee. He'd never had a woman other than his mother order breakfast for him.

There were only four plates. He hoped Hanin was sitting off to the side somewhere and he could ignore him, but somehow he doubted the world would be so kind to him. That meant there wasn't a place for Day.

"Should we invite my...?" He'd almost called her his wife. It was weird. He would have a wife in two weeks' time. "Should we invite the future queen? She might have something to say about her schedule."

Weston took a cup of coffee from the young woman serving breakfast. "Ms. Samar is also indisposed. She's having a spa day. I hope you don't mind, but my Chelsea and Jesse's wife, Phoebe, offered to join her. Apparently Ms. Samar doesn't have many close girlfriends, and spa days are much more fun when shared. I also think we should talk about a few specific threats that could be rather stressful for your bride-to-be. I thought I would talk about those before your mother gets here."

"Threats?" He smiled at the maid, who handed him a perfectly brewed cup of coffee. Usually he gulped it down, desperately needing the caffeine. It was nice to savor it, to truly taste the unique flavor. He'd missed this coffee. Loa Mali coffee was unlike anything else he'd ever tried. "Are you talking about the antimonarchists? They love to threaten me. They never do anything at all about it."

All talk. Blah. Blah. Kill the king. Blah. Blah something boring and political. Death to the Kamdars. Blah. So typical and yet they never even tried to murder him.

"I think there's something different now," Weston said.

"Why now?"

"Because up until now you've shown no signs of any chance that you would marry soon. Without marriage there was always the possibility that the monarchy would end with you."

"I'm not the last Kamdar. My cousin could take the throne if something happened to me."

"Chapal?"

"Yes, he is obnoxious but quite intelligent." After all, he was a Kamdar.

"He's also gay."

Kash waved that thought off. "Yes, though he is a terrible dresser. No style at all. What his husband sees in him I will never know."

"By constitutional law, he can take the throne, but unless he is willing to procreate, the line would end with him."

Ah, he hadn't thought of that. He'd always thought that Chapal would carry on and be the absolute worst-dressed homosexual king in the world. His husband, Ben, would have to do all the hard work of making things livable in the palace. Chapal was too attached to his bloody computer.

But after Kash, Chapal was the last Kamdar. "I'll start the wheels to change that. The world is not where it was two hundred years ago. If Chapal adopts, his child should not be punished. We're not in the Dark Ages, though the antimonarchists would have you believe it. So you think they're serious this time because I'm getting married?"

"You've gotten threats?" His mother walked into the room, her voice strong but her body seemingly so frail.

Kash stood and walked to her, offering her his hand to steady her. He ignored Hanin, who walked in behind her. Hanin would be gone soon enough. He would allow the man to stay around because his mother favored him, but the minute she was gone so was Hanin.

His stomach turned. Had he really just thought about his mother being dead?

"Are you all right?" His mother stared up at him.

"I'm fine. I'm adjusting." And not well. He was floundering.

"Come along. We have much to talk about and your breakfast is ready."

She waved him off but found her chair. "I'll have some tea, please."

"Your son's fiancée ordered you tea and toast," Weston said.

"I told the cook the queen wasn't interested in food." Hanin sat down to his own breakfast, setting aside his ever-present planner.

"And my daughter-in-law-to-be wished to give me the choice." His mother picked up a knife and began to butter her toast. "I think this should be quite nice. My stomach can't handle much right now, but this looks good."

Day was getting his mother to eat even when she wasn't here. Still, he was angry with her. Oddly, not as angry as he'd been the night before. He'd wanted to rage at her, but hours in Day's company had defused the anger and what that hadn't calmed, seeing his mother's frail figure had. He settled himself into his chair, his appetite coming back. "Mr. Weston was talking about the antimonarchists."

Hanin's mouth curled in obvious distaste. "Animals, all of them."

"I'm sure they would say they're fighting for democracy," Weston replied.

"They're threatening my son?" His mother carefully scooped out the jam Dayita had sent with the toast. "They do this all the time. I'm sure they're particularly nasty now that the wedding has been called and they know the monarchy shall persevere."

"They're threatening to stop the wedding." Weston sat back. "I've sent each of you my plans for security. It will be very tight, and everyone will be vetted by my firm. I suggest allowing in one sanctioned photographer and one reporter. The queen-to-be would like to auction off the photos, with all proceeds going to a charitable fund for education."

The future queen was practically a saint. "Whatever she would like. I don't think I want to do a ton of press though. How are we framing this? Does the world know this is an arranged marriage?"

"Of course not," his mother replied. "As far as anyone knows, you and Dayita met in England and drifted apart but now you've gotten close again. Everyone knows you're a bit on the reckless side. They will assume Day is pregnant and that is the reason for the hasty wedding. If you could make that happen on the honeymoon, it would be wonderful."

Ah, there was his irritation. Not even the lovely eggs could get rid of it. "My procreation will be my choice, Mother. You've interfered enough."

Hanin sat straight up. "You can't talk to the queen mother that way."

"Bah," his mother replied. "I'm happy he's talking to me at all. If I have one thing to be grateful to the cancer for, it's the guilt that's kept my son from running away to be with loose women. He always runs for the loose ones."

"Or the spies," Weston added helpfully. "When I first met him he was entertaining several hookers and a couple of undercover spies."

Ah, the beautiful Kayla. Yes, he'd called her his Asian lily, and she'd been an American double agent. She'd quite scared him at times. Brutal girl, but lovely. "Could we forego hashing through ancient history? Well, not entirely. I would like to know why you chose Day as my bride when you did everything you could to keep us apart fifteen years ago."

His mother flushed but remained steady as a rock. "Because I figured out I was wrong all those years ago. You have to understand that everything was crazy after your father and Shray died. You came home and all you would talk about was some young lady I'd never met before. I needed you focused on taking the crown. We were desperate at the time. I was desperate at the time."

She'd been alone, her whole world washed out from under her. Perhaps a few years before he wouldn't have been able to see things in such a fashion, but he could now. Still. "I only wanted to see her. I wanted something that was mine."

"And I needed you to see the crown as yours. I needed you focused on the country." His mother reached out, sliding her hand over his. "I was wrong, but at the time I thought I was right. I thought the feelings you had for Dayita were nothing more than a childish crush on a girl who likely reminded you of home. You didn't fight hard. You sent her a single invitation and then we heard nothing more. She sent years of letters. I thought it was one sided."

Had that really been it? At the time he'd felt so crushed. She hadn't answered a single request and he'd given up, moved on. Day had written him letter after letter. She'd flown a thousand miles to see him.

He'd been the faithless one.

"You read the letters? Are they still around?"

Hanin put his fork down. "I kept them for history's sake. Your mother asked me to keep them from you, but I always worried she would change her mind. So I kept them instead of trashing them. Three years ago she asked about the young woman, asked me if I knew her. I said no, but I did know a way her majesty could get to know her. And I gave her the letters."

"And I fell in love with Day," his mother said quietly. "I found out she was here in Loa Mali and I did everything I could to bring her into my sphere so I could watch over her. When the time came, I made my move to bring her back to you. I don't know if I was wrong to do what I did in the beginning. I don't know if she would have been a steadying hand or a distraction, but I do know you need her now."

"You had no right to keep those letters from me." But he kept his tone calm. He hated the fact that he couldn't let his rage fly. And he truly loathed the reason why he couldn't. How could he be angry with his dying mother? There was someone he could deal with. "Hanin, you became my employee the day my father and brother died. I consider following my mother's orders in this case tantamount to treason. Would you like me to have your head cut off?"

The man had gone a nice shade of gray.

His mother gasped. "Kashmir!"

Weston merely chuckled. "You have the right, Your Majesty. Still, I think a public execution might overshadow the wedding."

Hanin stood. "I did my job. I serve this country and the palace. Do you have any idea how hard you make my job? She was right to do what she did. Getting you to focus is like being forced to work with an untrained monkey."

"Hanin!" At least his mother was shocked by all of them. "Please don't refer to his majesty in such a fashion or he'll be right to fire you."

"He's planning on firing me anyway." Hanin stepped back. "The minute you're gone, I'll be gone, too, and he'll probably get rid of his bride as well. A man like him doesn't change. I feel sorry for your poor bride. She'll either find herself divorced in a year or the object of everyone's pity because there's no chance that you don't go back to your partying ways within weeks of your mother's death. Perhaps before. After all, it's not like you ever cared what she and the world thought of you anyway. Her majesty is trying to save the country, but you won't care. You'll ruin us all in the end. I always saw that."

"Hanin, please," his mother began.

"Oh, no, Hanin, you continue on." It was good to see his lord chamberlain for who he really was. "Let me know exactly how you feel."

Tears had started in his mother's eyes. "I can't plan this without him."

Damn it. She shouldn't be planning anything at all. She should be resting, trying to maintain her strength.

Fucking fuck and fuck fuck.

Kash stood and attempted to moderate his tone and his expression. All the sweet words in the world wouldn't mean a thing if he looked like he felt—like he wanted to murder someone. He had to be the king, and the king remained calm and made reasonable decisions. "Hanin, please accept my apologies. It is true that I believe my bride and I will be happier with a new lord chamberlain after we're wed and I am in the palace most of the time. I would like to do things in a modern way, and you have always emphasized the traditional. Perhaps that is why we seem like we're at cross purposes. I do, however, promise to make your retirement a lucrative one. And I certainly won't ever speak of beheading you again. That wasn't well done of me."

Hanin turned and walked back to the table. "I will stay for your mother's sake."

His mother reached over and patted his hand as though he was a child and had done something well for the first time.

"Shall we talk about the guest list? I've got it down to seven hundred." Hanin opened his notebook.

"I'll need all those names. Every single person will have to be vetted," Weston replied. "We've got almost no time so I need a finalized list by this afternoon."

"Seven hundred." It horrified Kash. The one good thing he could think of about his two-week engagement was going to be the smallness of the wedding. No one could put together a true royal wedding in two weeks. "No. We have so little time and there are no plans. We should keep it small. No more than twenty."

His mother's face lit up, and for a brief moment he saw the woman who had raised him, youthful and full of joy and strength. "No plans? I've been planning for years. Everything is already in place. It will be the grandest wedding, Kashmir. I've already found someone who will release a hundred doves as you and Day are pronounced husband and wife. And, of course, we must be seen observing all the rituals."

He shook his head. "Absolutely not."

Weston was watching his mother. "Rituals?"

"Yes, Loa Mali has many beautiful rituals for the bride and groom." His mother put her hand over her heart. "The Palm Ritual is lovely. I have many pictures from your father's and mine."

"Mother, it's the twenty-first century. I'm not hiding in a group of palm trees getting my arse cut up so I can steal a woman who has already agreed to marry me. Nor will I allow my best friends to tie me up and beat my feet with fish."

What Loa Mali had was a group of crazy antiquated and downright ridiculous rituals meant to ward off evil spirits and generally make everyone getting married think twice about doing it in the first place.

He saw the glint in his mother's eyes and knew he was in trouble.

* * * *

Day sat back with a smile, the steam from the spa deliciously warm. "It's supposed to ward off bad spirits and build the groom's strength for the wedding night."

Phoebe Murdoch's lips curled up as she laughed. "Fish? They're going to beat Kash's feet with fish and that will give him virility?"

It was silly, but she suspected the queen mother was going all out with this wedding. "I suspect the practice was created by fish merchants. One of our main industries is fishing, but we have a problem with bycatch. These are the unwanted fish that are caught by our commercial fishermen. Several of our local fish are quite horrible to eat, but legend has it those fish are imbued with the potency of our ancient sea god, so they're prized for wedding and fertility rituals. Not only will Kashmir have his friends beat him with the fish, he'll have to eat a good portion of one raw in order to ensure our wedding night is productive. And since we haven't yet agreed to have relations on our wedding night, I fear it will be for nothing."

"You're not sleeping with Kash?" Chelsea Weston sat on the bench to Day's left. "I would love to have seen the look on his face when you told him. That man thinks he's God's gift to women. Not that I don't like Kash. He's fun to be around, but he does think a whole lot of that face of his."

Did he? Day wondered about that. "I think a lot of it is armor. I knew Kash before he became the king. In some ways he did everything he did to differentiate himself from his older brother. He became the playboy because Shray was so serious. But you have to understand that playboy prince was studying theoretical physics at Oxford when I met him, and he didn't get in because of his name. Kash is incredibly smart."

"Oh, I know that," Phoebe replied. "When Jesse first met him, he was close to a working prototype of a car that ran on water."

Day had been grateful for the company when she'd been told Chelsea and Phoebe would accompany her. Normally this day would be spent with Day's sisters and her female in-laws-to-be. She had some cousins, but they had mostly moved to Europe or the States. She'd been unable to see herself spending this time with the little mice who worked with her at the department. They were sweet women, but her two assistants were mostly biding their time until they could find husbands. She liked these two women. They were smart and strong of opinion.

It was interesting that she also thought they would be quite submissive when it came to sex. But then she had started to wonder the same thing about Kashmir.

"I'd heard a rumor that the explosion in the Arabian Sea wasn't an accident." She hadn't talked to him about it the night before. They'd sat together and drank and talked about their old friends. She hadn't wanted to bring up anything that might make him sad or angry. He'd been in a good place, and she'd been the one to take him there. She wasn't one to undo her own work.

How would he feel if he knew she was looking at him as if he was a potential sub to top?

Chelsea shook her head. "Not an accident at all. It was all the work of a group of major douchebags known as The Collective."

Phoebe stared at her friend. "You are the worst CIA employee in the world. You know that's probably classified."

Chelsea shrugged. "It's also good gossip, and I don't work for them anymore. Right now, I'm a happy housewife. Well, a housewife who works ten hours a day writing code for the new business. And let me tell you, dealing with Adam is not a picnic. He thinks he's way smarter than he is. Satan's right about him."

Chelsea talked a lot about Satan. Day was fairly certain it was an oddly affectionate nickname for someone, and not that Chelsea had a weird religious bent. Still, she wanted to shift the flow of conversation back to the important stuff. "Why would this Collective come after Kashmir?"

Phoebe and Chelsea seemed to have an entire conversation through frowns and the narrowing of eyes.

Finally, Phoebe gave in. "Fine. It is good gossip and I don't work for the Agency anymore either. Also, you're about to become like the head of the country and stuff, so I think you could probably find this out on your own. The Collective was a group of the world's biggest companies and they basically Star Chambered the rest of the world. They helped each other out, you know. Some business needed to sell their firearms, so The Collective helped out by starting a civil war somewhere. They manipulated stock prices, practiced all the worst things humanity can do. Kash's experiments would have cost the oil industry everything, so they sent an agent to blow the lab up."

"They were also supposed to kill Kash," Chelsea explained. "But my Simon jumped off a cliff and saved him."

"I think Big Tag would say that's a gross oversimplification of that story," Phoebe continued. "But Jesse does say it was pretty cool. It was actually Kayla who got the king out."

Chelsea shook her head. "Don't."

Phoebe had flushed. "Yeah, uhm, but mostly Si. It was a team effort."

Day could guess what they were covering up. She hadn't been blind for fifteen years. His womanizer reputation had been the reason she'd held back during college. Until that moment when he'd allowed her to take control, when she'd realized she might truly have something to give him that no one else could. Of course, at the time she hadn't understood that there was a word for what she needed.

Dominance.

"I know what he used that boat for. He kept his harem out there. So did he seduce her after she saved him? Did he offer to pay her off with his body?" That sounded like Kashmir, the manwhore.

Chelsea winced. "She might have been a spy at the time, and he thought she was a supermodel."

Day let her head fall back as she laughed. It was a good play by the Agency or whoever had hired this Kayla person. Going at Kash through his cock was the only way to go. "I pray his cousin found out about that. Chapal runs the country's technology and security. I believe most of his migraines come from Kashmir's many women. I'm afraid your husbands taking over security even for a brief period of time will be difficult for them. Kash acts out when he's angry. I expect him to misbehave a lot before this wedding actually occurs."

"And after?" Phoebe was studying her.

It was easy to forget these two lovely women were both former CIA. Of course, that was likely exactly why they'd been so good at their jobs. "After, we will find our way. I suspect we will be friends and try to get along as much as possible. He'll have his life and I'll have mine."

"That sounds terrible," Chelsea shot back.

But Day had come to some terms with it. She hadn't expected to marry at all. Now she had the prospect of children. Oh, they might be implanted with the medical equivalent of a turkey baster, but they would have two loving parents. "I never thought I would marry when I made the decision to stay here on Loa Mali and work."

"You're beautiful," Phoebe remarked. "You're intelligent and kind. Why would you think you wouldn't marry?"

"There aren't a lot of prospects on this small island, and despite all of our wealth and our freedoms, we're still quite old fashioned in some ways. The king has done a good job by steering parliament away from laws that would curb a woman's freedom, but there are still many who believe a wife's place is at home. I'm not that woman. It would have been difficult to find a man here who wouldn't want me at home. Home is a place I go to after work. It's not that I look down on women who do stay home. My mother did and I loved her very much. I simply am not built that way. I wouldn't find the same satisfaction that she did. As I believe she would have hated working the way I do. We need choices. We need to be free to be who we are."

"A queen isn't free," Chelsea said.

She'd thought about this, too. "But a queen makes a contract with her people. She knows what she will do and what is not acceptable. I quite like a contract. My marriage to Kash will be contracted. We will have our roles, agreed upon between both of us."

"There is nothing wrong with a good contract, but don't write out spontaneity." Phoebe adjusted her towel. "You cared about Kash once. Why not see if you can again? Some men like Kash settle down after marriage and make lovely husbands."

"She should know. Her brother was the only person I've met who was worse than Kash. Well, I mean he didn't have a harem boat or anything, but Ten tore through some women, if you know what I mean," Chelsea confided. "And now he's faithful to his wife. Whose name is Faith. Yeah, that's terrible. Sorry about that."

"Faith is wonderful," Phoebe replied. "And Chelsea's right about my brother. He was a horrible manwhore. Kashmir is actually a nice man. I've always thought the right woman could settle him down. All the women I've ever seen around him are too superficial. They're flighty things. I think he picks them because he never has to get serious with any of them. At least that's what my husband thinks."

"Si thinks he's..." Chelsea bit her bottom lip and sighed. "Sorry. New friends."

"Thinks he's what?" Day was intrigued. She'd heard a bit of gossip concerning these friends of Kash's. She wasn't sure how to ask without embarrassing anyone, but perhaps direct was the best bet. "Does your husband, who I would guess is the top, think Kashmir would be happier as a bottom?"

Phoebe's jaw dropped.

Chelsea merely laughed. "Yes. Yes, that's exactly what he thinks. A lot of us do, but we wouldn't say it. He's a little sensitive. He's been to Sanctum, but he just played around. I've heard he's gone to several clubs around Europe and plays, but at least outside the actual bedroom he tops."

That was what she'd been a bit afraid of. Yet last night when she'd taken control of the situation, when she'd seen to his comfort and given him direction, he'd responded beautifully. He'd been happier at the end of that night, though she would have bet he hadn't realized what she was doing.

Phoebe curled her legs underneath her. "So, how long have you been in the lifestyle, Mistress?"

Well, that hadn't taken her long. "Ten years. I met a man in graduate school. He was lovely and he had certain needs that I found I enjoyed indulging. We broke up because I came home to Loa Mali. Not much of the lifestyle here. I go on retreats two or three times a year. I have Mistress rights at some clubs in Europe. I find it relaxing, but I worry my husband-to-be will prove very traditional in this sense."

"How will you know until you try?" Chelsea asked. "I doubt anyone has ever offered to top him before. Not in a serious way. You don't have to pull out a whip."

"You want me to be the sneaky top." What she'd been so far.

"I think some subs need to be eased into what they need," Phoebe explained. "I know I did. I thought it was distasteful until someone convinced me to try. And I probably still wouldn't have found myself if I hadn't been with a man I truly connected with. I can certainly see how Kash might need it. Submission for some of us is relaxing. It's a way to find a place where we don't have to think. For all his playboyness, he still has an enormous amount of pressure on him."

"He did back then, too. I can see now it was why we worked. I was different than the other girls. I thought he liked to talk to me because we came from the same place, that he merely missed home. Now I look back and realize he liked it when I would take charge. I didn't force him to make all the decisions. It's hard to make all the choices. And I wouldn't want a sub who needed me to direct him in his daily life. But sexually, I prefer to be in control. Again, it's the way I'm built, but it can be hard to be different."

It could be impossible. Lately, the trips to her clubs had been unsatisfying. She needed a permanent partner, someone she could connect with for more than a weekend or a few weeks. Someone who needed her.

She was coming up on a time in her life when she would have to decide if she would suppress that need for the rest of it. Perhaps that was why she'd given in to the queen mother so easily. Being the queen meant having a nation that needed her, a whole island of people she could fight for.

Or perhaps she'd done it because for years she'd dreamed of Kash kneeling for her, asking her for discipline, his face peaceful when she gave it to him.

That one kiss had changed her life in ways he couldn't have dreamed of.

Should she give her marriage an actual shot?

"He might surprise you," Phoebe said. "Ease him into it. Like I said, it really worked for me. He's already comfortable in the lifestyle. It doesn't scare him or make him squeamish. I know the few times he's visited Sanctum, he tends to like to watch some of the heavier scenes. But when it comes time to play at anything beyond spanking or light scenes, he won't participate even when there are other Doms to supervise and teach him."

"Because he's not truly interested in being the one holding the crop," Chelsea said with a smile. "He likes to watch and fantasize about those heavy scenes, but I would bet real money he's not the Dom in his head."

Day breathed in the steam of the room, letting it relax her. "I could run a test, I suppose. If I know my future mother-in-law, she's going to want all the bells and whistles a Loa Malian wedding can have. One of those is the Palm Ceremony."

"Do you get hit in the face with palm fronds?" Phoebe asked. "That's still better than fish."

She had to chuckle at the thought. It was obvious Phoebe had never been hit with one. They could be sharp. "No, it's a ritual to honor the first king of Loa Mali. Supposedly, he found his bride wandering on a beach. He would hide and watch her from a copse of palm trees. He asked her father for her hand in marriage, but he refused because she was from another island. The king decided to steal his bride. He rode onto the beach and scooped her up on his stallion and whisked her to the palace, where he made love to her for the first time. Her father, seeing how happy he'd made the daughter, acquiesced and the couple was married one week later. So you see, the whole fish ceremony is silly because most married couples get it on after the Palm Ceremony. We might be one of the only cultures in the world that actively tell engaged couples to take a test drive."

"I like it." Chelsea stood. "I've got a massage in five. I think we should help the Mistress plan."

Phoebe winked her way. "You know I'm always up for a good plan."

It was probably a horrible idea, but sometimes a woman had to take a chance. Perhaps when her king stole her away, he would find he was the one who was claimed.

Yes, she liked the sound of that.

Chapter Four

"You're sure you want to do this?" Chapal moved a palm frond, sneaking a peek at the beach where Dayita would soon be walking.

Kash sighed and tried not to step on anything the horse decided to leave behind. "It's considered good luck."

His cousin looked somewhat ridiculous wearing traditional clothes. His chest was on display and he wore a pair of lightweight pants that reached just below his knee. On his head rested a headdress made of shells and palm leaves.

On Chapal's skinny, never-hit-a-gym-in-his-life, how-was-a-brown-man-so-damn-pale body, it looked a bit silly.

Kash rather thought it made *him* look dashing and romantic. Otherwise, he looked like an idiot douchebag about to reenact a bit of history almost no one gave a damn about.

Except for all those crazy people on the beach waiting to watch the ceremony. They lined the beach and the road that would take them back to the palace. Weston had the route guarded by a number of the new guard he had hired in the last week. He'd doubled the amount of palace guards and was working with the small police force and military to get them trained.

Even his old bodyguard Rai had agreed to come back for the royal wedding. He stood outside the staging area, his back to Kash and his eyes moving across the crowd.

"Do you really want good luck?" Chapal asked. "You want this marriage to work? I ask because I like Day. I've known her for the last few years and she's a lovely woman. I would hate to see her get hurt."

Days had passed and this was all he'd heard. It had been a solid week since he'd agreed to the arrangement and every moment he spent with Day made him think it wouldn't be so bad. Every moment he spent away from her made him wonder if he was a monster.

"Why would she be hurt? Have you ever once known me to hurt a woman?"

Chapal turned, crossing his arms over his chest and then uncrossing them because he was wearing a horrible necklace made of the aforementioned itchy palm fronds. "You would never physically hurt a woman. I know that. I'm talking about her tender heart."

He had to smile at that one. "Tender heart? Have you seen what she does to members of parliament who don't get on board with her education plans? She can eviscerate a man with that sharp tongue of hers."

Day had been keeping her appointments as the head of education despite the fact that the last week had been a whirlwind. He'd gone with her to an advisory meeting with the parliament's committee on schools. He'd stayed in the background as she'd requested, watching from the back of the balcony seats. They'd given her a rough interrogation about her budget and why they should increase it. At two points in time he'd nearly stood up and gone after a few of the bastards for the way they'd spoken to her. Day had been cool and calm, explaining everything patiently and then threatening to go straight to the press with a story about how the Loa Mali parliament had spent three hundred thousand dollars on a party to celebrate their own anniversary, a party the public wasn't invited to, but they refused to spend a paltry seventy-five thousand to update computer software for their children. They'd sputtered and cursed and Day had gotten her way.

And Kash had gotten a hard-on. A really massive, wouldn't-go-away-for-a-long-time hard-on.

That had felt good. It had been a long time since he'd wanted more than sex, since he'd wanted one particular woman, and for more than to prove he could have her.

Maybe he was a bit of a monster, but he never lied to the

women he took to his bed.

And he wasn't going to lie to Day.

"She doesn't date often," Chapal continued. Why his cousin believed he had to also be his conscience, Kash had no idea. "The whole time I've known her she's dated two men. One was a setup and she never saw him again. She spends all of her time on work. When she goes on vacation, she goes alone."

That didn't seem right. "Where does she go? And what happened with the other man?"

"She dated the minister of transportation for about six months. They seemed well suited, but then she broke things off with him and he was married to another woman within six weeks. She won't talk about what happened. I think he asked her to marry him, but only if she gave up her job and came home. I think she comes up against this quite a bit. As for her vacations, she goes to Europe. Ben and I asked if she would like company once, but she said she was fine alone."

He didn't like the thought of her roaming around Europe by herself. Not because she couldn't take care of herself, but rather because he didn't like the thought of her being lonely. He could see her wandering about museums and soaking up all the history, perhaps meeting with friends she'd made, but she would be essentially alone. There would be no one holding her hand or ensuring she had everything she needed. No one would bring her coffee in the morning or cuddle with her at night.

"I want to make this marriage work." He was saying the words aloud for the first time and they felt right. "I do not intend to do anything that would break my bride's heart. If I do this, I'm going to do my best to be a good and faithful husband."

Chapal's jaw dropped and he stared for the longest moment.

"You don't have to look at me like I've grown two extra heads," Kash complained. "I can say the word faithful. Listen to this one. Monogamy. See. It rolls off the tongue. Don't you back up, you ridiculous ass. Lightning is not going to strike."

"You have to admit you've never used those words unless they were accompanied by a vomiting sound." Chapal stepped closer. "I think you could hurt her if you aren't careful."

No one cared if she hurt him, of course. "Leave that to Day

and me. We've been talking things through. We're going about this in an intellectual way, determining the best way to handle things. We've decided to make a contract between us and if and when we choose to have sex, we will be faithful to each other. If things seem to be difficult, we'll be honest and revisit the contract to allow more freedom."

He hadn't liked that thought. She was surprisingly open to…well, to being open if things didn't work. She said she would rather they had a healthy, happy friendship and partnership than put the country and whatever children they might have through a divorce. No married king and queen of Loa Mali had divorced before. He didn't intend to be the first, but he didn't like the thought of some passionless friendship between them.

"She's a sensible woman and it appears she's being realistic about this marriage, so I'm going to completely back off." Chapal held his hands up as if they were proof he would interfere no more.

He should leave it there. He wasn't some lovestruck idiot who needed to talk about his feelings. He didn't have feelings. He had responsibilities that he tried his hardest to forget about. Of course, they were the same responsibilities that Day had been bearing some of the burden of. He didn't need to talk this out before the evening came around.

It was simple. The tradition was that the groom and bride-to-be spent the evening together, getting to know one another. The groom attempted to seduce the bride.

That was one tradition he intended to keep up.

"Prince Chapal, it's time to do your part. Ms. Samar is about to start her stroll along the beach." Weston stepped out of the copse of trees, his three-piece suit completely pristine somehow, despite their walk in the forest.

Chapal shook his head. "I truly never thought I would have to do this. I'm so glad Ben and I eloped."

His cousin sighed and proceeded to step out into the clearing. He would be the king's "eyes," the servant who first saw the long-ago queen and told his sovereign about the beauty on the beach.

Kash heard a loud shout go up, the royal watchers all cheering as the ceremony began.

"I want you to move quickly when you get to the road

approaching the palace," Weston said matter of factly. "The police are having some issues. I advised them that I believed the crowd would be quite a bit bigger than their estimates. They chose to disagree with me and now we're understaffed there. Smile and wave and move through quickly. It's the only place I worry about. I've got Michael and Boomer here, and Jesse and I will monitor the road."

"All right." He wanted to see her. He wanted to be done with all this pageantry. Which was odd, because usually the pageantry was what he craved.

"We've also had an issue with a woman claiming she needs to see you."

He sighed. Yes, he'd gotten several phone calls from Tasha Reynolds. "She's the only woman I dated for more than a few days in the last several years. She's an actress and she's very aggressive." He'd found her aggression, her take-charge personality, attractive in the beginning. He'd enjoyed having a strong woman who was capable of making decisions. Until she'd proven that all her decisions were based on what was best for Tasha and only Tasha. She'd been mean to her staff and rather cruel to him as well. He'd walked away after a terrible fight and refused to take her calls even after she'd threatened to go to the press. "Ignore her. It's best not to feed into her neuroses."

It was after Tasha that he'd taken to finding his gentle "flowers." Even the thought of how he'd called them that made him think of what Day would say. Likely she would roll her eyes and walk away, shaking her head and calling him a douchebag. She called him on his douchebaggery at every turn and yes, he liked that, too.

Day was take-charge, but without the hard aggression. Day made decisions based on what was best for the people who depended on her.

Day was the kind of woman he could depend on.

He wanted to see her. Why did Chapal get to see her first? Chapal couldn't even appreciate her curves. Chapal didn't want to let his hands skim her hips while he kissed her gently. He would have to be gentle with her. Like his cousin had said, she probably didn't have a lot of experience. He would have to treat her with the respect she deserved, but in a way that let her know he could take care of her. Herd her gently toward their bed. Once she was there, he would keep convincing her to stay there.

He found himself looking forward to the chase. He never chased any woman. They came after him. He winked their way and they fell into his arms.

And he wasn't so unaware that this behavior was far more about the type of woman he spent time with and how interested each of them was in his money and his fame. It was rarely about him.

Somehow he thought Day was different. Perhaps he was being foolish, but he couldn't help himself. Dayita was going to be his bride. His. No one else's. Dayita was going to be at his side when he needed her. She was the type of woman who would take an interest in his job, beyond smiling for the press and spending money on shoes.

He tried to peek through the palms but all he could see was Chapal's backside.

"I like your bride," Weston said. "So does my wife. She thinks Dayita is perfect for you."

He wasn't sure about perfect. He didn't believe in perfection. Even in his happiest moments there was always a sense that something was missing, but that wouldn't be her fault. It was because he was a fraud. Because he wasn't Shray. "I think we've got a good beginning. Now I have to convince her to actually give this thing a try."

"I thought she was doing that."

He sent the Brit a grin. "I'm talking about sex. I don't want a sexless marriage."

"Somehow I think you'll find a way, Your Majesty. But you should talk about it with her," Weston said.

He pulled back a frond and there she was. Dayita was dressed in all white, no shoes on her feet, and her glorious hair wild and free. He felt the tug of arousal in his groin. Yes, there was the unruly beast he'd known when he was younger. His cock didn't need any foreplay when it came to this one. All he needed to do was look at her. "I would rather show her how I feel."

A shadow fell over him and Rai was suddenly standing in the

small clearing Kash would soon ride out of. "I hope you've taken all the tests, Your Majesty. Otherwise our fair queen-to-be might not last long."

"Excuse me?" Weston's whole body had tensed.

Kash put a hand up. He knew damn well what Rai was talking about and why they'd had the fight that had ended their friendship. "Don't, Mr. Weston. Rai has a long lead when it comes to me. He's more friend than bodyguard." He turned to the man who'd been at his side most of his life. Right up until the moment he'd realized Kash had slept with his wife. Oh, they hadn't been married at the time, hadn't even been dating, but Rai had taken deep offense. "And yes, I've had blood work done, but you know I'm careful."

"Careful? You're the single most reckless ass I've ever met." Rai turned his back. "It's almost time to move, you piece-of-shit player."

"You can't allow him to talk to you like that," Weston said.

Kash waved him off. "He's only doing it because we're alone and he knows you and I are friends." There was something he needed to know, something that had his gut in knots when he thought about it. "I need to know that you're not taking this out on Lia."

Rai turned, his face red. "Don't you mention her name, and no. She's innocent. You're the vile animal who seduced her. I would never harm my wife. She's been through enough."

She'd been excellent at fellatio. Not that being good at fellatio was a bad thing. It was a serious plus in Kash's mind, but apparently Rai needed a bloody virgin as his bride. Years before, Lia had come to Kash. He'd been having one of his blow-out parties. She'd wanted to spend time on the boat, and Kash had suspected she wanted a way out of her parents' house. He'd spent a single evening with the girl years before.

Six months before, she'd shown up on Rai's arm and they were engaged.

He'd barely recognized the girl when they'd been introduced. She'd been terribly embarrassed and had made him promise to never tell. God, if he'd ruined Rai's marriage, he would never forgive himself. "I'm glad you're happy with Lia. She loves you very much. She was young and a little wild, a bit like we used to be."

"Used to be? Perhaps I've matured, but I've seen none of that from you."

No, his actions of late weren't those of a mature man, but he was trying. "I'm so sorry for that night, Rai. I know I can't make it up to you, but I miss you, my friend. And I thank you for helping out today. Are you enjoying the new job?"

Rai simply turned away and moved back to his post.

"We can't use him again. I'll make sure he's never on your service." Weston had his phone out. "I have no confidence that man will take a bullet for you."

Once he would have. Once Rai had been his closest friend. It was probably fitting that a woman came between them. What he hadn't expected was how much he would miss his friend, how much he wanted to talk to Rai about Day. Still, Weston had a point. "You can move him around, but don't fire him and you can't move him to a lower position. No cut in salary. He has a wife and mother to take care of."

Weston nodded, but it was easy to see he was still suspicious. "You should get ready. It's almost time."

A great cheer went up and Chapal made his way back to the staging area. He was shaking his head. "I can't believe how many people are out there. I hope you don't fall off that horse. Good god, man, don't step back."

Because the horse seemed to have an active bowel. This could all go horribly south.

And then it did. He heard the crack of gunfire and the screams of people and Kash took off, running with one thought. He had to get to her. He had to get to Day.

A hard arm went around him and he was being pulled back. Kash fought like hell, right up to the moment another arm went around his neck and the world went black.

* * * *

Kash paced the floor in front of her, still garbed in his traditional clothes. He would have made a stunning Horse King if the ceremony hadn't gone so poorly.

"I'll have him killed. I'll use the horse that shits constantly. I'll find three more exactly like him. Terribly gassy horses. I'll tie that motherfucker to each of them and quarter him and then I'll allow the horses to shit on his corpse. His suit won't look so perfect then, will it?"

Day couldn't help but smile because Kashmir looked adorable when he was angry. Also very masculine and threatening, but adorable. She particularly liked the reason for his anger.

"They thought someone was trying to set off a bomb," she pointed out. "They didn't know it was merely fireworks. You know your guard was only doing his job."

"Rai would never have choked me until I passed out." Kash was off, his words spitting out in a rapid-fire volley of rage.

Day simply poured him a glass of Scotch. The poor man had had a long day. Kash had heard the chaos and tried to reach her. When Simon Weston had rightly attempted to get the king out of the line of fire, Kash apparently fought like hell to get to her. He was angry he hadn't been the one to protect her.

The instincts to love and protect and cherish were still there. He wasn't even fighting them. He cared about her, and that was a good thing, since the afternoon had brought on a revelation of her own.

She'd realized when she'd heard that sharp, shocking sound that she'd never gotten over him. Not really. She'd heard that explosion and her first thought had been to get to Kash. The idea that he could be hurt or even dead had chilled her to the bone. She'd known in that moment that she would hate herself forever if she didn't try with him. She'd started running toward where she'd known Kash was waiting.

The intensely large Mr. Boomer had simply scooped her up and run. She'd known she didn't have a chance against him and she hadn't thought to offer him a pizza to let her go. She'd found herself shoved in what was basically a tank masquerading as an SUV, and she'd been at the palace before she could breathe. Kash had come in a second SUV along with Chapal, who'd been forced to explain why her bridegroom was unconscious.

It was now hours later and they'd made an appearance on the balcony of the palace so everyone could see they were alive and unharmed. Her first balcony. She'd stood at Kash's side and waved, her free arm around him. She'd been the one to convince him to calm down and show his people that all was well. She'd also been the one to convince him not to kill the Brit who'd merely been doing his duty.

Now she had to calm him down again, and she thought she knew how she would like to try.

There was nothing holding her back. She wanted him. She needed to see if she could make this work between them. If what Chelsea and Phoebe had said could actually be true.

"Have a drink and let's talk about this."

His eyes narrowed, but he took the drink. "I don't want to talk. I want to punch Weston in the face. Rai would never have overreacted in such a manner."

"Rai was running toward me full tilt when Mr. Boomer tossed me over his shoulder. He reacted to that terrible sound in exactly the same manner as the other bodyguards," she explained. "I think we should have a talk with him about why he didn't stay with you."

Kash took a long sip. "To tell you the truth, I'm glad he went after you. He's unhappy with me right now. At least he thinks enough of his job to try to save you. I wish the ceremony hadn't been ruined. You know now a lot of people will say we're cursed as a couple."

"Only the superstitious ones." She knew there were already rumors spreading, but they didn't matter and he needed to see that they didn't. "We show them how uncursed we are by presenting ourselves as a happy couple."

He was suddenly still, his eyes on her. "Are we a happy couple?"

"I don't think we've had time enough to be sure of that yet, but I know we were once." She'd thought it through in a way she never had before. She had a much different view of those months with Kash in England. "You were courting me back then, weren't you? You wanted me to be your girlfriend."

He sat down in the plush chair that dominated the sitting area portion of his bedroom. Normally they stayed in the living room, but he'd wanted more privacy. This was the only place in his suite that wasn't covered by CCTV, the only place where they could truly be alone. Everything about the space was masculine and decadent, including the man himself. With his hair disheveled and his chest on display, it wasn't hard at all to see him as a primal male.

One she'd dearly enjoy taming.

"I don't think you realized it at the time."

She was willing to admit her faults. "I didn't. I had my nose in a book most of the time back then and I had little experience with men. No, I had no idea you were interested in me beyond copying my notes from class when you slept in."

"It would surprise you to know that I often thought about sleeping in with you." His voice had gone low and gentle. "I was crazy about you back then, Day. I find myself in the same position today, but I don't want to scare you. I know you think we should take this slow and I will honor your wishes, but I want this marriage to work. You see me as a playboy, but I don't want to be some forty-plus player who trades on his money to keep young girls around him. I think it might be time for me to find out if I can be the king my father would have wanted me to be."

It was all she needed to hear. If he wanted to try, she was ready. Despite his reputation, she'd fallen right back into a peaceful friendship with him. He'd been the old Kash, supporting her when she needed it. He'd asked her questions about her work with the education department and then gave her ideas on how to handle the parliament. He hadn't told her what she should do. He'd suggested, debated.

"I think you'll find me less averse to giving this marriage a real try than you think. I was planning on talking to you about using the Palm Ceremony to begin to explore what we could be as a couple."

He frowned. "I'm not sure what that means. You want to talk? Or have counseling? Because that sounds terrible."

"I was talking about sex, Kashmir. I thought we could use this time to see if we're sexually compatible."

He popped up out of his chair like an eager puppy. "Yes. I think that is a brilliant idea. We should start now. Don't worry. I intend to be gentle with you."

She didn't move at all. "Like you are with your lovely flowers?"

"Women deserve a man's care," he said quietly. "Day, I can't erase my past."

"I don't want you to." He misunderstood her problems with

his statement. "But I do need you to understand that I'm not one of those flowers. I'm not here to sit at your side and bat my eyelashes in the hopes that you'll buy something for me. I don't work like that. I don't care about your money."

"That is easy for you to say. You're about to have access to all of it, aren't you?"

He had a point. "Even if I wasn't, that wouldn't be why I would want you, Kash. Sit down. We have some things to talk about before we get started." This was the point where she would normally introduce the idea of a sexual contract, but she had to ease him into this. Show him how good it could be to hand the reins over to her in this one part of their relationship. "Come here close to me."

He moved to the chaise she was sitting on, lowering himself down with a sullen frown. "I knew there would be talking."

She was fairly certain his lovely flowers did very little talking, but he would get used to it. "Why did you want me back then?"

"I liked you. I liked talking to you. I liked being around you. I rather liked who I was when I was around you." His expression softened. "I don't think you knew how alluring you were to someone like me. You didn't understand how beautiful you were, so you didn't use it against me. Most women do."

"Well, that happens when you surround yourself with women who are mostly valued for their looks. I don't blame them. They've been told their beauty is the only thing worthy about them. If you want to meet women who don't feel that way, you should probably expand out of models and actresses."

"Well, you would be surprised how many gorgeous, sexy physicists turn me down because I'm not smart enough for them."

Oh, she loved this part. She loved the flirtation, the push and pull of verbal foreplay, and Kash was a master. "Somehow, I doubt that. You're one of the smartest men I've ever met. You could talk about anything. It makes me wonder why you don't still study."

"Well, I have a busy schedule of smiling at the public and waving. Then there's all the ministry meetings I take. I note that you never once asked for a meeting with me."

There had been a reason for that. "You didn't seem interested. Honestly, you haven't been interested in much of anything for the last five years or so. Is it because your secret project was taken down?"

He seemed to freeze for a moment. "It was more than a secret project. It was a passion project. I suppose you know about it from Chelsea. She was there at the time, though I only met her briefly. I lost an entire generation of our most brilliant minds that day. Ten of the smartest engineers and scientists in Loa Mali. I did that. Is it any wonder I haven't gone back? You know if I'd reconnected with you, you could have been on that rig that day. I would have asked you to help me with the project."

So guilt had sent him on a half-a-decade bender. "Kash, it wasn't your fault. You weren't trying to hurt anyone."

"I would have hurt the oil companies."

"Including your own," she pointed out. "You weren't doing anything but attempting to push our country forward. Would you have kept the technology for yourself?"

"Of course not. It would have belonged to Loa Mali. I was doing it because someone will. I want to be the first. Our oil reserves won't last forever. Our country is in the unique position to move in a direction others can't. That's why I did it. To put my country on the cutting edge and honestly, so that I could patent the process and make money for us, money to keep our standard of living high."

She reached over and put a hand on his. "A noble cause and one only a man of your intelligence would even understand to pursue. Do you know why I was attracted to you?"

His lips curled up. "I do not have the same false impressions of my own beauty that you do."

Such arrogance and yet she found herself laughing. "Your masculine beauty was the least of your attractions. I liked how smart you were, how passionate you were about making a place for yourself in the world. I wanted to be a part of that. I wanted to support you and yes, I wanted to advise you. I loved how you never seemed intimidated by me."

"I wasn't intimidated. I wanted you. I wanted to get my hands on you and show you how hot you could get."

She was already heating up, but this wasn't going to go the way she feared his other encounters went. "You do know I'm not a virgin, Kash."

His gorgeous eyes rolled to the back of his head in a pure expression of disgust. "Of course you're not. You're thirty-five years old. I would worry if you were." He reached out, putting a hand on her knee. "But you don't have my experience, either. I have to remember that."

"And what kind of experience is that?"

"You know what I mean. I've slept with many women."

"But you haven't slept with me. You don't know what I want or what I need to get hot." She wasn't about to tell him that simply being near him was getting her hot. "I want you to forget about all those other women. I'm unlike any from before. Learn how to please me. Let me teach you how to make love to me."

She saw him still, his eyes heating. "All right. How do I start?"

"Show me what you have to offer me."

His lips curled up in a decadent grin. "Are we going to play games?"

Only the most important one of her life. "It's for pleasure, Kash. I enjoy some games. I find them relaxing, and they help us get to know each other better. If you would rather we simply went to bed, I can do that, too. You should know that I was going to run from you today."

"At the ceremony? Of course. It's part of the ritual. The beautiful bride is unsure of the king. She tries to flee, but he catches her."

She shook her head. "I was going to run. I was going to make you chase me. I was going to make you work for me, and in front of all those people. I would have struggled in your arms until you let me go, fearing you'd hurt me. And then and only then would I have placed my hands on either side of your face and brought my lips to yours. I would have touched you and found you worthy and allowed you to take us both away."

"You would have run from me?" He asked the question in an icy tone, but she couldn't miss the fact that his cock was already hard and straining against his pants.

She didn't move from her chaise. Already, her heart and soul were moving into top space, a place where she was in control, where she could relax and have her way. He would accept her or not. "I cannot be that queen from long ago who allowed herself to be kidnapped and taken away. The choice will be mine. The choice to be queen. The choice to have you. I will make these choices not because I'm about to be royal, but because I am a woman and that is what I do. I will not play that game with you, love. I won't give over and then protest that I had the choice taken from me. I will choose and accept the consequences. I wanted to show them who they are getting as their queen, not some gentle flower who will stand by her man and wave, but a woman who will fight for them as I fight for myself. As I would fight for you."

"You want to see what I have to offer you?" The chill was gone from his voice. His hands were on the medallion around his neck. He took it off and placed it on the table to the side of her chair. "I wonder what will please you. I don't think you're impressed by the palace I'm offering you."

She gestured to the room around her. "That's not yours. It belongs to the people. In essence, they're offering me this magnificent space."

"A hard woman to please," Kash mused. "How about wealth? By marrying me, you'll never worry about money again."

"All your money comes from oil," she replied, enjoying the fact that he was playing along. "Again, that belongs to the people. I should thank them with my service to them."

"Service you can only offer because of me."

"Is it you or your mother? Because you had no idea I still existed. So I have to ask you, Kashmir, what exactly are you offering me?"

He stopped and for a moment she thought he would laugh and give up the game. Instead, his hands went to the drawstring of his pants. His chest was already on display, each and every muscle beautifully defined. The man was sheer perfection physically. He shoved his pants down and he wore no boxers. No, when he shoved those pants aside, he was standing in front of her, proudly naked. "I can offer you my body."

She sat up because he was getting closer. "I have a body of my own."

His jaw tightened, but she saw the light of competition in his eyes. He might be frustrated, but he was also intrigued. He put his hands on his hips, perfectly comfortable with his nudity. "All right, my future queen. Let me tell you what I can offer you. I can offer you the touch of my hands on your flesh, skimming every inch of your body. I can offer the heat of my mouth, my lips and tongue exploring you, tasting your essence. I won't stop quickly because you're complex. I'll have to taste you everywhere, nipping and licking and sucking until I know you by heart." His hand went to his magnificent cock. "And I can offer the pleasure of my cock. I can offer you everything I have, every trick I've learned to bring you joy in bed."

She stood and closed the space between them, her eyes on him. She took in every gorgeous inch of his body. Like those delicate flowers he'd spent so much time with, so much of Kash's self-worth was wrapped up in his handsome face and perfect body. He was celebrated the world over for being beautiful. How many magazine covers had he graced? Likely more than she could count. She needed him to believe in more than his own looks. "Hold still and let me look at you. Don't move. And let go of that cock if you're offering it to me. How can I touch it if you've got it in those big hands of yours?"

He immediately let go, his cock bouncing slightly. He stared forward as she took him in, as though he knew instinctively that this was a moment for him to submit.

"You offer me a lot, Kashmir. Certainly you come in the most beautiful package I've ever been offered. You're the single most stunning man I've ever seen, but I need more." She ran a hand over his chest, letting her skin enjoy the warmth of his, the smooth touch of flesh against flesh. "I need that brilliant mind. I need your intellect. But I also need you to need me."

"I need you, Day," he said with a laugh.

She continued her slow exploration. She couldn't punish him, though later on such sarcasm would be dealt with if they signed a contract. He would probably enjoy the discipline. "Not yet. Right now you think I'm nothing more than another pretty female body, but you'll learn I'm going to be more."

He finally looked down at her. "Fine. What do you offer me, my almost queen? I've laid it all out for you. Tell me what I get."

She sighed as she moved around to his back, enjoying the play of his muscles as she continued to stroke him. He was a massive panther and she wanted to see if he could purr for her. She also liked that he'd asked the question. It made her more certain than ever that he was right for her. She didn't want a man who followed her blindly, even inside the bedroom. Certainly not outside of it.

Now she had to discover if she was right for him, if she could give him what he needed. What he might not even know he needed.

She ran her hands over his broad shoulders, enjoying the shiver that went through him. "I offer you the warmth of my hands on your body, the feel of my skin against yours, promising companionship and comfort. My hand in yours when you need to know you are not alone. I offer you the joys of my mouth. My lips and tongue tasting you, but more than this, my words will lift you up, will always be kind. I offer you my body for your pleasure, so that we can be one with nothing between us, no space, no lies, no heartache, only joy. I offer you my body to grow whatever children we're blessed with. It will be yours while I'm young and vital, and yours when I'm too old do to anything but hold you in my arms. This is what I offer."

"I need you, Dayita." His voice was hoarse.

This time, she believed him.

"Then we can begin."

Chapter Five

Kash gritted his teeth and felt his cock stiffen. He'd only thought he'd had the erection of a lifetime, but when she'd said those words—*then we can begin*—he reached monumental proportions. Any thought of this being some sort of test run was over. He wasn't thinking about anything but pleasing the woman in front of him.

His queen.

The last fifteen years of his life had been about the world revolving around him, being the ultimate authority figure. But here and now, he realized she could be his sun.

She could be his secret. She would never have to know how weak he was, how dark his wants were. He could pretend to indulge her and steal something for himself.

She would never know that all those "lovely flowers" were nothing more than a way to pretend he didn't want what he wanted. A way to pretend he was more of a man than he actually was.

She put her hand on his chest and he could feel his own heart beating. "I think I'd like to join you. You may take my dress off. Carefully and slowly. When you're done, I want you to fold it and put it on the counter. You may touch me, but only as I've touched you up until this point. Do you understand, love?"

He understood that her thick-as-honey voice was doing things to his cock. He couldn't breathe he was so hard and he hadn't touched her yet. He should take control. He should put them on a proper footing, but he couldn't. The words wouldn't form in his mouth. There was only one word that he seemed capable of speaking. "Yes."

She turned and offered him her back. The dress she wore had no zippers or buttons, merely two elaborate ties. She'd told him what she wanted. A long, slow adoration of her body. He didn't have to move quickly and plot out how to bring this woman to pleasure. She was giving him a map, offering him the secrets of her desires, allowing him to indulge his own.

He drew her hair up and swept it to the side, his fingers luxuriating in the silken cloud. How long had it been since he took his time, since sex was something to sink into and not some drunken nightcap to end his day? Maybe never. Maybe because this was more than sex.

He carefully undid the first tie, revealing the golden skin of her shoulder. She leaned her head to the left slightly, allowing him access to that first, precious patch of skin. He touched her, letting his fingertips play over the warmth of her flesh. He skimmed from the curve of her neck down to her shoulder and along her arm.

The worries of the day were floating away and all that mattered was learning her, discovering her every curve and hollow.

"May I kiss you?" The question came naturally.

"Yes. Gently. We're just starting out. This could take us all night."

He leaned over, letting his lips find the spot where her neck and shoulder met. He brushed them there, aware of the way she shivered. "Given that I've waited fifteen years for this, I think a full night is what I need."

"Did you only wait fifteen years?" He could hear the smile in her voice. "I think I waited a lifetime."

He ran his mouth along her shoulder, breathing her in. "You're right. It has been a lifetime."

He moved to the other knot, easing it apart and pulling the fabric free. The instinct was there to toss the clothing aside, but that wasn't what she'd asked him to do. She'd asked him for patience, and he intended to give it to her. His cock wouldn't rule with this woman. He carefully folded the dress, his focus on the task at hand, and yet somehow it made him even more aware of what was to come. His hands ached to cup her breasts, to spread her thighs and get his mouth on her.

Not until she was ready. Not until he was insane for her.

She turned and he saw her naked for the first time. His queen. His. He was vitally aware of the possession that sparked through him. He didn't want to share her with his people, but perhaps he could view it differently. She would be theirs when she was buttoned up and properly dressed. And when her hair was flowing around her like a silky cape, when her breasts were upthrust and begging for attention, when her pussy was on display, that was when she would be his queen. Only his.

And he, her only servant.

"You're beautiful, Day."

She smiled at him. "I'm glad you think so. I want everything you offered. Kiss me, Kashmir."

He moved in, eager to get his mouth on her and yet a bit disappointed the play seemed to be over. Not that she would call it play. Not that he would tell her why he wanted it.

He was the king in all things. No weaknesses.

He reached for her, but she put a hand between them.

"I wasn't talking about my mouth, love."

He frowned. "Then we should go to the bed. I'll lay you out and eat that soft pussy of yours like it's the finest treat. I'll lick you and suck you and fuck you with my tongue, but first we should find a comfortable place."

Her eyes turned steely. "Or you can get on your knees for me and do all of it right here. Can you do that for me? Get on your knees and show me the pleasure of your mouth."

On his knees? He hesitated, longing warring with what he'd been taught all his life.

"Don't think, Kashmir." Every word out of her mouth was velvet seduction. "Do as I ask. You don't have to be the king in this room. You can be whoever you want to be. When we're alone, we can throw off all the ideas of who and what we're supposed to be and let ourselves flow. Get on your knees and worship me. Show me what you can offer me and I'll reward you."

It was a game. Play, as his kink friends would call it. They didn't have to acknowledge anything. His bride was a bit kinky and that was something to welcome.

She didn't have to know how much the idea of worshipping

her fed his soul, how throwing off the heavy mantle of responsibility, tossing away his crown for a brief moment, tantalized him and energized him.

He made all the decisions, bore all the cost. What if he could find one place where he didn't have to? No one would know. No one but him and Day. Their secret.

He dropped to his knees, embracing the possibility. "Tell me I can lick you. Tell me I can suck you and run my tongue all over you. Tell me I can make you come for me, my queen."

Her eyes were hot as she stared down at him. Those gorgeous breasts of hers were close, so close to his mouth, and yet he held back, waiting for the words he wanted to hear. He didn't have to decide. He only had to follow her lead in this.

She cupped his face. "Do you have any idea how happy you make me? How much I want you? Only you. Touch my breasts. Lavish my nipples with affection."

He let his palms find her breasts, cupping them and holding them. Her nipples were hard points against his hands and he could feel the way she breathed out, a low moan coming from her mouth. He teased her nipples, rolling them between his thumbs and fingers. Finally, he leaned over and licked one, the tip of his tongue running around the edge. Her skin smelled like the ocean, breezy and pure. He tasted the salt of her flesh and sucked the nipple into his mouth. He let his arms go around her and surrounded himself with Day. He sucked and played with her, letting himself take his time.

He moved to the other nipple, feeling her hands in his hair. Her fingers tangled there and she guided him where she wanted him to go. He loved the rough feel of her tugging at his hair, lighting up his scalp. He needed to please her, needed her soft moans of acceptance. Every sound that came from her mouth seemed to have a hard line to his dick.

He was going to die, but it would be a good way to go.

"Look at me." The words sent a sizzle through his system. Her hand in his hair tightened, gentle pressure showing him where she wanted him to go. "I want you to trust me. I want to be a safe place for you. Do you understand?"

He didn't. Not entirely, but he would have said yes to anything she'd asked in that moment. "Yes. I trust you."

He did. Certainly more than any woman he'd cared for before. Even all those years ago, he'd known Day was different. He'd known instinctively that she would be worth working for. Now he was caught in a trap, and suddenly that didn't seem such a bad thing.

She leaned over and her lips captured his. He gave in, letting her take control. It felt natural to give her sway. Her tongue came out, running along his lower lip and sending fire through him. His tongue played against hers. Finally she rose up over him, looking primal and gorgeous. A sea goddess looking to mate with a lowly sailor. She would bless him with her body and he would worship her forever.

"Carry me to the bed. I love how strong you are," she said.

He was on his feet in a second, leaning over and lifting her up. In this she was delicate. She weighed next to nothing and felt perfectly right in his arms. "You're so lovely, my queen. I like calling you that. My queen."

"Show me how good it is to be your queen." She stared up at him as he lowered her to the bed. She pulled him down, bringing their lips together once more. "Kiss me properly."

He rather liked her idea of a proper kiss. He moved down her body, touching and caressing as he went. She was a prize and he'd won. He settled himself on his belly as she spread her legs for him.

He could show her how he worshipped his queen. Her pussy was a perfect, ripe peach. Golden and succulent. Already he could see she was aroused, sweet cream softening her. He breathed in her scent, letting it wash over him before he leaned over and ran his tongue between the part in her labia.

"That's right, love. It feels so good. Your mouth feels so good. More. I need more." She stiffened around him.

So responsive. She responded so beautifully and held nothing back from him. He found her praise intoxicating, her willful lust addictive.

He fucked her with his tongue, spearing up inside and coating his lips with the taste of her. He let his finger find her clitoris, rubbing in a soft circle as he explored her.

"Stop," she commanded.

He didn't want to stop. He wanted to make her come and then

thrust himself inside her until he was completely spent.

"I said stop." She tugged on his hair and her voice had gone deep.

Damn it. What had he done wrong now? He rolled off her, frustration threatening to overwhelm the lust of before. He stared up at the ceiling. What did she want from him? He'd done everything she'd asked and now she wanted him to stop?

He groaned as he felt heat on his dick. He looked down and Day was inspecting his cock, her mouth hovering over him. So close. So fucking close.

"I want to taste you, too." She leaned over and teased at his cockhead with her delicate tongue. "Hold on to the headboard. If you let go, I'll stop what I'm doing."

His hands floated up as though they were smarter than his brain and knew when to obey the lovely queen currently giving him head. Her hair spread out around her, tickling his skin and surrounding him with her. He gripped the slats of the headboard as he watched her work. Her tongue came out, licking at the slit on his dick and lapping up the pre-come she found there. She scraped her teeth lightly around his erection, the sensation making him stiffen and grasp the slats with desperation.

She was going to kill him. She was an evil queen, trying to take his crown through sexual frustration. Every time he was sure she would take him deep, her head would come up and she would be right back to teasing licks.

He groaned as she cupped his balls and rolled them gently in her soft hand.

His toes were curling, his body prepping to go off.

And that was when she got on her knees.

He groaned in frustration.

"I'm letting you off easy this time, love. Mostly because I can't wait either." She reached for the box of condoms he'd placed on his bedside table in a spark of optimism.

She wasn't leaving him hanging. She wasn't playing some cruel game. He relaxed as he realized Day wouldn't do that. She'd enjoyed playing with him, exploring him, and now she would bring them both to pleasure.

He gripped the headboard tight and she rolled the condom

over his cock. He watched as she straddled him like a stallion she was about to ride.

Heat rushed through him as she began to lower herself onto his stiff dick. It took everything he had not to hold on to her hips and force her down. She moved over him, taking him inch by inch. He would feel her sink farther and then draw back up, every second a brilliant mix of pleasure and maddening frustration. No woman had ever made him want her the way this one did. No woman made him want to bow before her, to offer up everything he had.

Day settled herself on him, taking every inch of him, and he could hear her sigh with pleasure. She rolled her hips and he groaned, his eyes nearly crossing as she gripped him tight. So small and sleek and soft. He watched as her breasts bounced while she rode him.

Over and over again she rolled her hips and worked him. He watched as her mouth came open and he heard her keening cry. She dropped down and looked up at him.

"Now, love. Take me hard and fast. Make me come again."

He had her on her back before he could take another breath. He was off the leash and he didn't think about anything but doing her will. There was no gentle flower here. He didn't have to treat her with delicacy. She was his match and she could take him. He spread her legs, loving how wild she looked with her hair flowing around her, her arms coming up to grip him. He thrust inside her, one long hard motion of his body.

Instinct took over and he growled as he felt her nails scoring his back. Yes, he liked that. He wanted her mark, to carry it on him and feel the ache so that long after, he could remember how good it was to fuck his wild cat.

He fucked her hard, grinding down on her. He felt her tighten around him and her climax forced his own.

His spine bowed with the force of his orgasm. He gave over and let it take him.

Finally, he dropped down, rolling to the side and taking her in his arms.

She cuddled against him, her head finding his chest. "You are perfect, love. No king ever worshipped his queen more. Thank you for the gift."

He held her until he sensed her breathing slow and steady as sleep took her. Kash stared down at the woman in his arms and wondered if he hadn't gone over the edge of a cliff he could never climb back up.

He'd loved how she'd taken control, but would she see him differently? Would he be less of a man for allowing her to use him like this?

He held her through the night, his body pleasantly tired but his mind troubled.

Chapter Six

Day looked out over the ballroom and wondered where her bridegroom had gotten off to.

"You look lovely, Your Majesty." Rai gave her a proper bow.

He and the other guards had done a wonderful job on the wedding. It had gone off without a single hitch. Between McKay-Taggart working security and the lord chamberlain running the wedding, she'd had to do little except wave and say the words that bound her to Kashmir and the Loa Mali throne forever.

Which was good because it seemed her Kash had a never-ending need for sex. Since that first night, he'd been voracious. He was sweet and so willing to please her when the doors closed and they were alone. There wasn't a doubt in her mind that this was the right thing to do.

They fit together, and tonight she was going to talk to him about more exotic play. Tonight, she was going to discuss punishments and rewards.

She wouldn't ever top another man again. Only her dashing husband.

"You practically glow with happiness," Rai said, his eyes looking out over the dance floor.

"Thank you." She felt happy. Maybe truly for the first time in her life, she felt at peace. Always there had been this nagging question in the back of her mind about whether she could find someone she loved who could accept her as she was.

Now that question had been answered. Kash had answered it

when he'd said "I do."

It was funny how the more he gave her in the bedroom, the less she felt the need to be aggressive outside of it. She'd found herself compromising more and more, especially with him. When he wanted to sit in on her meetings with parliament, she didn't question it. After all, he never forced his opinion on her, but he did give wise counsel.

She was rapidly falling head over heels in love with him once again.

She turned to Rai, wondering if she could help her brand new husband out a bit. She knew he missed this man. They'd been friends for years. She didn't understand the nature of what had caused them to break. "I think Kash would dearly love to have you on his detail again. He misses you."

A bitter smile crossed his lips. "Somehow I doubt that. Or perhaps not. Perhaps he's simply so arrogant and self-centered that he doesn't understand how he hurts the people around him."

Or maybe that would be a terrible mistake. "All I've seen is his kindness."

"Then you haven't been watching, Your Majesty," Rai shot back. "You wait. Give him a month or two and he'll be right back to his old tricks. He'll crawl into the bed of any woman who will have him. And some who don't want him at all."

She stepped in front of him when he started to go. "What exactly are you accusing my husband of?"

Rai's jaw formed a stubborn line. "Nothing at all, Your Majesty. After all, what woman wouldn't want to bed the great Kashmir Kamdar? What woman would say no to him? Certainly not my own wife. If you'll excuse me."

She let him pass with a sigh. So that was what had happened.

"If it makes you feel any better, I believe Kash slept with the young Lia before her marriage to Rai." Hanin stepped up next to her, looking out over the ballroom with a keen eye.

The lord chamberlain hadn't been particularly friendly, but then he'd been under a bit of pressure. A royal wedding in a few weeks wasn't an easy thing to accomplish. Day was happy he seemed to be calming down. "Rai didn't find out until after the wedding, I suspect."

"Yes. He married the girl hastily. From what I understand, Rai discovered Kash had been his wife's lover. You know how palace gossip is. No one can keep a secret here. Kash should have immediately told Rai, if you ask me. No one ever asks my opinion, much less follows my excellent advice. If they did, their lives would all be the better for it." He turned to her. "Rai was right about one thing. You do make a lovely queen. Hopefully now that we will have a sovereign in residence full time, the country will be more stable. The king can wander as he may and we shall have your wise hand to guide us."

"Well, I think you might find that the king is much happier staying home now that he's married. I think he'll take his duties more seriously than he did before." She felt comfortable that Kash's wanderlust had more to do with guilt than anything else. She would gently start pushing him to restart his project. He'd come so close, and he had a true passion for innovation.

The lord chamberlain's lips pursed as though he was thinking about what he would say next. Or thinking about not saying anything at all. "I should hope so. Nevertheless, I hope you find me helpful. Anything at all that you need, I shall be more than happy to provide it for you. This is your household now. It's up to me to make sure it runs according to your desires."

"And the king's."

He bowed his head. "Of course. When he is here, I shall surely take him into account. When you return from your honeymoon, I hope we can sit down and plan the next few months."

"What do you know that I don't?" She wasn't going to beat about the bush any longer.

The lord chamberlain shrugged, an elegant motion. "I know he's planning a trip to Hong Kong a few days after you return from your time on the yacht. He's going to be gone for a week or more and he told security that you would be remaining behind. He's planning a series of trips and I do believe he intends to take them solo."

That couldn't be right. Hanin had simply misunderstood. Kash wouldn't leave her behind right after their honeymoon. If he had something he needed to do, surely he would have spoken with her about it.

She looked back over the ballroom floor where couples were dancing. The ballroom was glittering and elegant, but Kash was nowhere to be seen. She did, however, note that Jesse Murdoch was standing at the edge of the ballroom, his back to the hallway. He guarded the door that led to the more intimate gathering areas. There were several rooms in this wing that the royals used to entertain heads of states. They were cozy rooms, perfect for a talk with her husband.

She would ask him calmly and he would explain that it was all a mistake. Then they could start their honeymoon early. She was ready to leave the pomp and circumstance behind and focus on Kash. He'd had a long day. He would need some play to alleviate the stresses. She'd seen his forced smile, the stiff way he'd waved to the crowd on the balcony.

"Thank you, Hanin," she said politely. "I would love to sit down with you and plan everything out. I think we shall have a busy schedule."

Hanin nodded. "Excellent, Your Majesty. And let me know if you need anything to make this evening even brighter."

Because they should be heading off to bed in a bit. They would stand together and greet their guests and then retire while the party went on. It was custom.

So many customs. She stepped out onto the floor and was forced to smile and greet people whose names she barely remembered. Her brand new social secretary was across the palace, meeting with the photographers and helping the queen mother select the right photos to be published in the morning.

Where was Kash? He'd kissed her on the cheek and then frowned as he'd gone to dance with yet another guest. He'd been dancing all night long and only once with her. Kash had spent the evening charming all the ladies, and she missed having all that masculine attention to herself.

She worked her way through the crowd, trying to ignore the chatter around her.

"I don't know. I hope she's doing this for the right reasons."

"Such a beautiful wedding. He's so dreamy. She's pretty and all but I'm surprised he would marry a commoner."

"I don't know. I expected more from her. She's a bit on the

plain side for a man who could have any woman he wanted."

"The right reason being money and power, since she's not going to be getting any fidelity from that man. Imagine actually marrying Kash. Not that he isn't exquisite in bed. I enjoyed my time with him, but the humiliation would be terrible."

"Who wants to bet how long it is before he's right back to his playboy ways? As soon as she's pregnant, he'll find a way. I've heard he's already seeing that actress again. She showed up at his wedding. What gall."

Day stopped.

"I can't believe he walked out with her. Everyone could see the way he was touching her. The poor queen. Not married more than a few hours and her husband is already cheating."

"Ah, well, we all know he married her because his mother forced his hand. He'll get her pregnant a few times and then he'll be done with her."

She could feel her cheeks heat, humiliation swamping her.

"Don't listen to them," a low voice whispered.

She turned and Phoebe Murdoch was standing beside her. Someone had figured out the new queen was walking among them and the gossip was now being whispered instead of openly talked about. She felt a hundred eyes on her and she steeled her spine. She'd stood up to professors who didn't think she had a place in their world, to parliament members who laughed openly at her suggestions. She wasn't about to crumble because a few people said some nasty things about her marriage.

Day gave them her brightest smile. "I hope you're all having a lovely time. His majesty and I are so glad to be surrounded by such supportive friends. I will let him know how much you care about him."

She caught sight of a few men and women who paled at her words, but she was done with them. If Kash had walked out with a woman, there was a good explanation. She knew something the others didn't. Kash didn't have a reason to hide things from her. He'd been given a clear choice. She would have accepted a marriage without the relationship. She would have been friends and partners with him. He'd chosen and she had to believe he meant to honor the choice.

Phoebe walked beside her. "You are really good at that. I'm fairly certain some of those people peed a little. You know they're always going to talk about you. You have to be able to separate Dayita from the queen."

It was an excellent point and one she would take to heart. She stopped at the edge of the crowd and reached for her new friend's hand. "Thank you. I will try to remember that. Do you know where my husband went and who he was with?"

Phoebe didn't pale exactly but she did frown. "I think he's trying to avoid a scene."

"With a woman?" She was starting to understand what was happening.

Phoebe looked over at the place where her husband was guarding the door. He had a steely-eyed glare that turned away even the most avid curiosity seeker. He caught sight of his wife and they seemed to have a whole conversation with gestures and raised eyebrows. Finally Phoebe turned back to Day. "Apparently one of Kash's ex-girlfriends managed to get through our security. She snuck in as the date of one of the ambassadors. Before we could figure it out and toss her on her rear, she managed to get to Kash. I think he's trying to convince her to leave quietly."

So at least Day knew where she needed to go. "He'll struggle with that. He'll view her as something delicate and weak, and if she's got half a brain in her head, she'll manipulate him."

"I don't think he's trying to do anything but get rid of her," Phoebe said.

Day turned. She wanted to make something plain. "I never thought for a moment that he was. I believe in Kash. I trust him, but he won't understand how to deal with a woman like this. He needs me."

She strode to the double doors that led to the hallway. Murdoch touched his earpiece and muttered something she couldn't understand.

"Your Majesty." Murdoch nodded her way. "Is there something I can do for you?"

"Yes, Mr. Murdoch. You can stand aside and let me get to my husband, who is likely trying to ward off some bimbo."

Murdoch frowned his wife's way. "Seriously, baby? I told you to distract her, not tell her everything."

Phoebe shrugged. "Sorry. I thought that was your 'hey, you should help out your new friend' raised eyebrow. You should really be more specific. And she's not worried that Kash is cheating on her. She's worried he won't be able to throw that chick out on her rear."

Murdoch winced slightly. "Yeah, I'm worried about that, too. I tried to send Rai back there but he said something about Kash being able to handle anything and walked away. I think it's time to fire that dude, but Kash keeps overruling me. I'll escort you back if my wife will watch this door for me."

"I think I can handle it." Phoebe took her husband's place. Somehow, despite the fact that she was wearing a beautiful, filmy gown and heels, Phoebe Murdoch oozed competence.

Murdoch opened the door for Day and they slipped out into the hallway. The minute the doors closed, the sounds of the ballroom seemed to fade and she could breathe again. How did Kash deal with such scrutiny every day of his life?

"Take a deep breath," Murdoch said. "Not a one of their opinions matter. Get used to being judged and get used to smiling and giving them your happy middle finger. I know a bit about this."

"How so?" She hadn't realized how tense she'd been until she'd managed to get out of that ballroom.

Murdoch started walking down the mostly empty hallway. There were a few of the catering workers moving mounds of used glasses back toward the kitchens, and she could hear someone discussing the fact that they would need to open another case of champagne. "I've been the center of attention before, and not of good attention. I've had people think the absolute worst of me and I decided they were right. It got me into a lot of trouble, but I found a group of people who built me back up."

She smiled his way. "Your wife and friends. That's good. I'm usually all right being the focus of criticism. I've never followed what my father would have called the 'proper' path. I can handle it. However, I'm not allowed to use my happy middle finger. The queen has to be more subtle."

Murdoch whistled. "Damn, I wouldn't have gotten through most things without being able to shoot people the bird. I suspect you'll find other coping mechanisms. He's in that room to your left. I'll be out here and ready to escort you back to the ballroom when you're ready. Be careful, though. There are reporters and they've been using this hallway to move around."

"You don't need to get back to Phoebe? I'm sure I'm safe here in the palace."

He shook his head. "Nah, Phoebe's a pro. She can handle anything those people throw at her."

She strode to the door and heard the sound of a whiny female.

"Kash, we can make this right. All you have to do is divorce her. You don't even need a divorce. You can get this marriage annulled and we can start over."

Ah, she recognized the voice from one of the more popular British soaps. Tasha Reynolds was considered one of the world's most beautiful women and she'd dated Kash for the better part of a year before moving on to one of her costars. She'd been giving interviews in the last two weeks about how she felt Kash was making a terrible mistake with his marriage. The woman had gone on every talk and news show she could, spilling secrets about their sex life and how he'd told her he would never marry anyone but her.

So she was a crazy bitch. Luckily, Day had figured out how to deal with crazy bitches a long time ago.

She opened the door and got ready to save her man.

* * * *

Kash looked out over the ballroom, hoping to catch a glimpse of his wife.

His wife. Dayita was his. He should feel settled and satisfied, but something gnawed at his gut. He was falling in deeper and deeper with her, and he wasn't sure he knew how to swim in these waters. Day smiled as she shook the hand of one of the Swedish royals. So poised and perfect.

"She's truly going to make a wonderful queen." His mother came to stand beside him, her hand coming to his arm as though she needed him to balance her. The last week had taken a toll on her, but she'd shooed away any thought of resting. "I hope you'll forgive me someday."

He looked down at her. "It's all forgiven, Mother. I understand that you did what you felt you needed to do. You found a proper monarch for the country. She will be wonderful."

And he would be somewhat superfluous. Already all the serious people shook his hand, laughed and joked around him, and then asked the real questions of his bride. He'd heard the US ambassador asking her for a meeting about potentially inviting the president to Loa Mali for a state visit, and Prince Harry had spoken with her about sponsoring a new charity. Harry only ever talked to him about polo and beer.

His mother had lost Shray, the true king, and she'd finally figured out that Kash was never going to take his place. She'd found a daughter this time, someone lovely and kind and intelligent. Someone who *could* take Shray's place. He would be nothing but a sperm donor.

Yes, he'd heard someone say that, and now it played around in his head.

"What do you mean, Kash? You're the king. Having a queen doesn't take the crown from you." His mother blinked up at him as though she couldn't quite process his words.

He put a hand over hers. It wasn't a good time to have a fight. Hell, he didn't want to fight with her at all. He couldn't truly be angry with her. She'd given him an out. He could leave everything to Day and spend his time as he wished.

Why did that seem so hollow?

"Of course it doesn't, Mother. You're right, though. She is a perfect queen. The ambassadors are all happy about her." He gave his mother a grin. "They don't have to deal with me now. Of course, they will if I find any of them hitting on my wife again. I swear that Spaniard kissed her hand five times. There's no need to kiss her hand at all. Does he think we're back in the Victorian era?"

"You'll have to deal with the fact that your wife is beautiful and everyone looks up to her." His mother glanced to her right. "Ah, they're calling for me. I need to select the official portraits to go out to the press. I'll be back in a bit."

"Don't overdo it, Mother." He would hate for her to not be able to enjoy the festivities, but he couldn't stand the thought of her crumpling.

She waved the worry off as she started to walk away.

And he was left with the good Scotch and worry in his head that he was slipping into something he couldn't come back from.

The night before, he'd gotten on his knees in front of Day and by the time she was finished with him, he was begging for her. He'd been on the ground, kissing her feet. At the time, it had felt like the perfect thing to do. He'd wanted to please her more than anything. He'd been happy and relaxed in the moment and he'd come like he'd never come before. He'd settled down with her and wondered what it would be like to have her use a paddle on his ass. Would it send sparks through his system? He'd loved it when Day gripped his cock and brought him to just the right side of pain. Could they explore more?

What would the world say about the pervert king who let his wife rule him? His father would be ashamed and he would be a laughingstock.

He had to stop this slow descent. He had to find a way to not want what he wanted. It was perverted. He was the man and she was the woman, and if they played those games, he should be the one on top.

Tonight, he would put their relationship on a proper footing.

Why did the thought make him infinitely sad? It was his wedding night. He cared about his bride. He wasn't sure it was love. Certainly it was lust and possessiveness and a deep and abiding friendship.

Was he falling in love with Day? Was that making him weak?

"I've been hoping to catch you alone."

He stopped, a chill rushing through his system as the familiar voice snaked along his skin. He felt a hand at his back and then he was staring down into big, blue eyes and pouty red lips. "Tasha, I'm surprised to see you here since you weren't invited."

A faint sheen of tears made those eyes a crystal blue. "I had to talk to you. I came as the guest of one of the ambassadors."

"You shouldn't have been able to get through security."

She shrugged. "I used my legal name. That should tell you how important this is to me, Kashmir. I made a terrible mistake, but you made a bigger one. How could you have married her? She isn't even pretty."

Day was gorgeous, but he wasn't about to argue with her. "You don't have to worry about me anymore. I've got a wife to do that."

Tasha frowned. "Yes, I've been looking into your wife. I've managed to dig up some facts about her that might shock you. Kash, please let me talk to you. That woman is using you. She doesn't love you."

Oh, but when he was on his knees in front of her and Day was smiling down at him, it felt like he'd imagined love would. In those stolen hours when they locked the rest of the world out, he was a different person entirely. Settled, happy.

And then she would sleep and he would deal with the storm of regret and guilt.

He glanced around but Weston wasn't in the ballroom. He was probably in the control room, looking out over the palace, trying to catch any threats that would come their way. He hadn't caught the real threat. Apparently, all a woman had to do was find some ambassador and she could waltz right in.

Still, the last thing he needed was a huge scene with Tasha. Despite her aggressiveness, she was quite fragile and needed to be handled with kid gloves. On more than one occasion she'd threatened to harm herself if Kash wouldn't do what she wanted him to.

He would let her say what she felt like she needed to say, and then calmly explain that he wasn't going to leave his wife and she should go back to London and her boyfriend. He could do all of this quietly and solve the problem before anyone realized there was one. He glanced around, looking for the photographers. When he realized they were busy shooting Day, he decided to make his move.

"Come on. I'm not going to do this in public. We'll talk in private." He began to walk toward the west doors. There was a sitting room that would serve as a good place to deal with the situation. He should have taken her calls and gently explained that he wasn't unhappy about the marriage. He'd been a coward not to talk to her, and now he had to find a way to make her understand.

She hurried to keep up with him and suddenly he felt her hand reach for his. She tangled their fingers together and held on tight.

Yes, he had to deal with this and quickly.

Murdoch's brows rose above his eyes as Kash approached the door he was guarding. "Problems, boss? You know I can handle any unwanted guests."

He felt Tasha's hand start to shake. She'd always needed someone to protect her. He had to get her to understand that it couldn't be him anymore. "I can handle her. Please make sure no reporters follow us out."

He slipped beyond the door and led her to the sitting room, closing that door behind them.

Tasha was immediately on him. She invaded his space, her head tilting up and lower lip quivering. "I've missed you so much. I know I was foolish to leave you, but you have to understand that woman isn't good for you. I know everything. I still have friends in the palace. I know you didn't want this marriage. Your mother forced you into it."

He tried to ease away from her, but she simply followed him until his back hit the wall. "Please, Tasha. You don't know her. We were friends for years. Yes, this was an arranged marriage, but I agreed to it."

"Because that woman convinced your mother to do it. I know everything. I know how they've been meeting in secret for years."

He worked hard not to roll his eyes. She did enjoy a bit of drama. "They were meeting because my mother was interested in Day's education programs. They became friends. I assure you my mother needed no prompting. She was sick of me acting like a horny teenaged boy, so she found a wife to help me settle down."

"She's not the right one for you. I understand why you did this, but you've taken it too far." Tears rolled down her cheeks. "I never thought you would actually do it. She's wearing the ring that should have been for me."

He would never have married Tasha. Not in a million years. She would have made a terrible queen.

Had he been thinking about it even back then? Had he chosen women specifically for their unsuitability?

He tried to get a hand between their chests, needing some space. "It was never that serious between us. Don't you remember? We agreed we were only having a bit of fun."

"We said that but then we fell in love. Kash, we can make this right. All you have to do is divorce her. You don't even need a divorce. You can get this marriage annulled and we can start over."

"That is not going to happen. Why are you doing this?" What the hell was he supposed to do? He wasn't the type of man to shove a woman, but she wouldn't let him go.

"Because I finally realize how much I love you."

"She's doing it because her show on telly got canceled last week," a familiar voice said.

His heart nearly stopped. Day was standing in the doorway, a fierce frown on her face.

Kash tried to hold his hands up. "It's not what you think."

Tasha turned around, but stuck close to him, her well-manicured hand clutching at his chest. "It's exactly what you think. He's mine. He's always been mine. I'm sorry, but this was all about making me jealous. He took it too far, but he's got my attention now. I know this will hurt you, but he doesn't love you."

Kash was damn near panicking. What the hell would he do if Day thought he was truly in here conspiring with an ex-girlfriend? "I swear, I brought her in here so we wouldn't make a scene. I didn't bring her in here to do anything but talk to her."

"Of course you didn't. You are not the problem here, Kashmir. It's all right." Day shook her head. "It's obvious to me that this woman is taking advantage of your good nature. Why don't you let me deal with this, love?"

She was using the same voice she used on him in the bedroom, the one that let him know she was taking over. For a second, he wanted to throw up his hands and leave it all to her. He could walk out and Day would deal with the crazy ex.

"He's not going anywhere." Tasha stepped away, moving closer to Day. "He's mine and if I don't get him back, I'll go to the press and tell a story that will ruin this family. Do you understand? I know things."

If Day was intimidated, he couldn't tell. "Really? Well, you should go and tell all. I'm sure it will make for excellent fiction."

"It's not fiction. I had an investigator look into you. I know all about your so-called vacations."

Day frowned. "What vacations?"

Tasha turned back to Kash. "Your sweet new wife is a complete pervert. She's into all kinds of nasty bondage things. But she can't even be normal there. Do you know what she does? She's a dominatrix. She abuses men."

Kash felt the whole room go still. What the hell? Day had done this before? She'd topped men and in a place where people could see her? Could know who she was?

Tasha continued on, every word out of her mouth threatening to make Kash sick. "She would take these vacations and she would go to underground clubs. She was little better than a prostitute."

"A prostitute gets paid," Day corrected as Kash watched in horror. "I did everything I did for pure pleasure."

Tasha shook her head, blonde curls bouncing. "I've got pictures of you. This scandal is going to make Kate Middleton's nude shots look like an innocent day in the park. How are they going to feel when they find out their pretty new queen is a pervert? That she tricked the king into marrying her? They'll know he would never marry a whore."

"Don't think you can use that against us," Day was saying. "We're perfectly fine with the way we are and no one else comes into it. So go ahead and spout all the nasty stories you like."

Tasha's mouth dropped open and she stared at him. "You let her do that to you? You let her tie you up and spank you like you're some kind of...naughty little boy?"

"We haven't gotten that far yet, but honestly it's none of your business. Now you can leave my home or I'll have you dragged out." Day took a step toward Tasha.

"Dayita, don't say another word." He had to take control. She'd lied to him. His gut twisted at the thought of her with other men, with submissive men. Was that what she was trying to do to him? Was she trying to change him into some plaything to be used for her own pleasure? So she could have the upper hand in all things? "You should leave this room and go up to the bedroom. I will deal with you later."

Day's eyes widened. "Excuse me?"

He hardened himself against her. He wasn't going to let her humiliate him like this. "You heard me. I said go up to our room and I will deal with you. Don't you even think about walking back into the ballroom. The evening is done for you. I will handle our guests."

"What are you doing, Kash?" For the first time since he'd found her again, she sounded unsure of herself. Day was always so self-possessed. Now he knew why. She made the men around her bow down, and he'd allowed himself to become one of many.

He knew it wasn't fair. Deep down he realized he was being a terrible hypocrite, but he convinced himself that this was different. He looked at her, a chill coming over his whole body. "I'm going to clean up the mess you made for me. Get upstairs or I swear I'll have the guards take you up there."

"I'd love to see them try." She stood up to him.

He couldn't have that. There would be no backing down. This was far too important. He couldn't allow himself to look weak in front of a woman who could apparently destroy them all. He moved into her space, using his height to his advantage. "Do you want me to humiliate you, Dayita? I'll do it. If you don't walk out of here right now and go to our room, I'll carry you. I'll throw you over my shoulder and I'll slap your ass all the way through the ballroom."

"You wouldn't dare."

"Try me." He leaned in. "After all, that's what you want to do to me, isn't it? You want to turn me into a pathetic creature who licks your boots. I assure you that won't happen, my darling wife. You might have tricked me into this marriage, might have fooled my mother into believing you're some kind of a saint, but the manipulation stops now. If you push me, I'll have every newspaper in the world tomorrow running a photo of you being carried off, and the story the next day will be that I abandoned you. I'll leave and you won't see me until I'm ready to deal with you. Do you want that humiliation?"

She'd paled, her eyes shimmering with tears, but her hands were fists at her sides. "Why are you doing this?" She started to reach for him. "We need to talk about this, love."

He backed away. This was how she got to him. She offered him everything he couldn't have, like Eve offering up that apple of hers. "Now!"

She turned, but not before he'd seen the look of abject horror in her eyes. She held her head high and walked out of the door.

"Well, well, it looks like you always make the right choice." Tasha's satisfied voice made him turn.

"Oh, I don't think anyone in the world would agree with you." Kash stalked toward her, his hands itching to do some violence. He wouldn't, but the need was there. To destroy something. To smash it all into bits until his life was completely unrecognizable and he could start over again after sweeping up the ashes. "After all, I chose to bed down with a snake like you, my dear. Listen to me and listen well. You're going to find out what a king can do. If you tell your trashy story to another soul, I swear to god I will make your life hell. I'll be patient and wait. I won't come after you right away, and you'll never realize it's me coming for you. I'll find a way to ruin your reputation. If you're up for a part, I'll pay the producers to hire someone else. If you find a man foolish enough to marry you, I'll send my people in to let him know what marrying you will cost him. There won't be anywhere you can hide. If you destroy my wife's reputation, I'll spend the rest of my life making yours into a literal hell on earth. Am I understood?"

Tears, real ones now, poured from her eyes. "Kash, please. Please, listen to me."

He was done listening. "I can start right this instant. If you aren't off my property in the next ten minutes, I'll consider our war on. I have far more weapons in my arsenal than you do, so think about giving that interview. If I hear even a hint or a whisper of you spreading this story, I'll destroy you."

She turned and ran out of the room.

Kash followed her. Murdoch was standing outside the door, looking from right to left, as though he wasn't sure what was happening.

"That's the second crying female to come out of that room," Murdoch said. "What's happening, Kash? Day looked like you'd ripped her heart out of her chest. Tell me she didn't find you having sex with that woman. She was coming to save you from that chick with the crazy eyes."

Did everyone think he needed saving? "Tell Mr. Weston we won't need the bodyguards anymore this evening. I don't want to be disturbed. Do I make myself clear?"

Murdoch frowned. "I'm not sure what's going on, but I don't like the look in your eyes, Kash."

"Your Majesty." Perhaps his first mistake was trying to be friendly with people. He wasn't a person. He was a figurehead, and it was past time he used the only thing his position afforded him that was worth anything at all. Power. "You will give me my due respect or you can go home, Mr. Murdoch. I'm going to speak to my bride and I won't be disturbed."

Because he had a few things to work out with her. A few questions that needed to be answered. By the time he was done with her she would know there would be no more manipulations, no more pretending. He would be the head of the household in all things and she would fall in line.

He strode to the secret stairwell the servants used. He could get to his apartments without being seen that way. All anyone would say was that the bride and groom had slipped away to start the honeymoon early.

He took the stairs two at a time, eager suddenly to get this over with. He would smash this whole relationship to pieces and see what they were left with. It had never been real. Not for one moment. Day had lied to him. She'd hidden huge parts of her life from him and he wouldn't take it. Not another second.

He opened the door that led to the hallway of his wing and was nearly shoved back. Simon Weston was sprinting down the hall.

Kash started to yell out to the man that he should be more careful, but that was the moment he realized Weston had a gun in his hand.

"Sorry, Your Majesty. I can't let you go down there." Murdoch had moved in behind him. He put a hand on Kash's arm. "You'll need to come with me. There's a problem in your room."

Day? What had happened to her? He started to drag his arm out of the other man's hold when he saw her being escorted out of their rooms. She was pale, her face tear streaked. She'd been such a lovely bride, but now she looked like a woman who'd seen a ghost.

She was escorted by Rai, one big hand on her arm. He strode down the hallway with purpose.

Kash started to move toward her, the instinct to hold her almost overwhelming. She looked so fragile that all he wanted to do was scoop her up and try to protect her. That was the moment she looked up at him. When she caught sight of him, her gaze turned blank and she moved like a zombie, her feet shuffling down the hall, all of her natural rhythm gone.

She walked past him like he meant nothing at all.

He could have sworn he caught Rai's satisfied smirk.

"What has happened?" He knew better than to go look for himself. One of his blasted guards would choke him out and he would wake up hours later looking like a fool.

That was something he did all too often these days.

Murdoch started to lead him down the hall, back the way Day and Rai had gone. "Apparently, one of the servants likes to sneak a sip of your Scotch at night."

Seriously? All of this over Jamil's nightcap? He stopped, forcing Murdoch to drop his hold. "If you're talking about the old man who turns my bed down at night, I told him he could have a glass when he likes. He worked for my father. He's been here as long as I can remember. For god's sake, don't arrest one of my bloody butlers over a tumbler of Scotch."

"He's dead," Murdoch said, his voice flat. "He died after drinking the Scotch that was brought up this evening. Simon caught it on camera. He tried to get here first, but the queen found him. She's very upset. Someone tried to poison you, Your Majesty. It's time to get you out of the palace for a while."

Kash felt the room go cold. Apparently, his evening wasn't going to end pleasantly.

Chapter Seven

Day sat in the chair offered to her, her whole body weary. Had it really only been twenty-four hours since Michael Malone had shoved her on a private plane? He'd been waiting at the security entrance to the palace to take her from Rai's custody. She and Kash had been taken to the private airfield in separate vehicles, and the plane had taken off before she could quite realize what was happening.

Now she was here in Dallas, Texas, and she felt numb. She'd slept little and spoken not one word to her husband.

Her husband, who'd looked at her like she was some kind of a freak. Her husband, who had made it plain he wanted nothing to do with her.

How easily they'd broken. As if what they had together had been nothing but spun sugar to dissolve in the slightest hint of rain.

"I know you're both tired, but I wanted to give you an update on what's happening in Loa Mali." A man with short brown hair sat behind a rather plain but sturdy desk. He was a large man, his shoulders broad and his jaw square, an all-American type. The name on the office said Wade Rycroft, but the man had introduced himself as Alex McKay. "Ian sends his sincere apologies, Kash. We've got a problem he needs to handle. It's a family situation."

Apparently the bodyguards had decided to ship them to home base.

"I don't care about Taggart's family issues. I would like to know exactly what's going on. I've heard nothing. We were given no choices, McKay. I will not be treated like some prisoner." Kash stood up. It was obvious none of his anger had fled over the course of the day.

"You're being treated like a man who was damn near assassinated," McKay replied, his voice even, but the narrowing of his eyes made his irritation clear to Day. "This is what you pay me for. You pay me to ensure your safety and the safety of your wife. More than that, you pay me to keep your monarchy safe. My employees did exactly what they should have done. They got you out of a dangerous situation. They shipped you somewhere no one will think to look, with the absolute best security you will find in the world. Two of my most experienced men are working to figure out who wants to kill you and also to keep the assassination attempt out of the press. If you find anything wrong with my plan, there's the door. You're free to go."

Kash turned and walked toward the door. He hadn't read the same body language she had or he simply didn't care.

Day stayed in her seat. One of them had to be reasonable. "I thank you for your quick service, Mr. McKay. My husband is going to act like an ass now. Let him. I would appreciate any update you could give me. Did they find out what kind of poison was used? Has Jamil's daughter been informed? She needs to know she'll be given his full pension."

"Jamil had a daughter?" Kash stopped at the door.

Naturally, the man had been sharing a Scotch before bed with Jamil for years, but he didn't know about his servant's family. In the few weeks she'd been living at the palace, she'd made it a point to learn about the family's closest servants. They were men and women who had devoted themselves to the palace for years. They deserved some respect. She kept staring straight ahead. "Yes. He took care of his daughter and her two children. His son-in-law died two years ago and he's the sole source of income while she's taking classes at university. I would like to offer to pay her tuition and to keep up Jamil's paychecks while she's in school."

Kash worked his way back to his seat and slumped down. "Jamil is really dead."

McKay's voice was the tiniest touch more sympathetic this time. "Yes, Kash. We wouldn't have hauled you out of your country for anything but true worry for your life. And as far as your servant's daughter knows, her father passed away of natural causes and the palace will take care of her. It's best we keep this under wraps for now. The press would swarm the island if they knew."

Kash looked infinitely tired as he sat back in the chair that seemed almost too small for his enormous frame. "The press was all over my island already. How do you expect them not to notice that the king and queen have been taken away?"

"I've set that plan in motion. Your yacht was seen launching last night after midnight for the Arabian Sea. Right now it's being captained by a friend of mine, and every now and then two of my employees who look a bit similar to you will be seen cuddling on the deck or taking in the sunset. Believe me, they know how to sell this. As far as the press knows, you and your queen are on a private honeymoon cruise and you do not wish to be disturbed. Rumor has it you've packed enough food and drinks for a full two weeks at sea."

Kash's hand tightened on the armrest. "Two weeks? You expect me to hide out here for two weeks?"

"Hopefully by then Simon and Jesse will have figured out exactly what's happening," McKay continued. "They've already identified the man who delivered the Scotch. He's being questioned right now, but he claims to know nothing."

"It will likely have been a young man named Gilad. I can't imagine he's an antimonarchist," Kash muttered. "His father was once the head of security. He grew up around the palace."

"We're gathering data," McKay replied. "We're going to figure out when the Scotch was poisoned and every single person who touched that bottle. When we know anything at all, we'll let you know. Until then I want to offer you the safety of Sanctum. Kash, you've been here before. You know all the rules. I've closed the club down to everyone but actual McKay-Taggart employees and their partners. We've converted the privacy rooms into suites for your time here. You may use the club, or if you prefer, stay in your rooms. I want you to have some company, if you would like. There's a full bar and a kitchen that will also be staffed while you're here. I thought I would have someone go over how the club runs with your new bride."

"Oh, I'm sure she knows," Kash said bitterly. "My bride is very familiar with all things BDSM. Does she not have a membership here? I'm surprised since she belongs to clubs all over Europe. Was the US too far to travel for your trips, my dear?"

McKay looked between them as though just figuring out there was serious tension there. "No, she's not a member, though she is welcome through your membership. Are you a member at another club, Your Majesty?"

Well, the cat was out of the bag and had been beaten half to death, so she might as well not hold back. She sat up straight, unwilling to allow Kash's sarcasm to bring her low. "I hold a membership at The Velvet Collar in Paris and a club in Berlin called The Tower."

McKay grinned. "Holy shit. Mistress Day." He stood up and held out a hand with what seemed like genuine happiness. "I knew you looked familiar. We haven't met, but I did attend one of your classes a few years back. My wife and I joined Ian and Charlotte Taggart on vacation and we spent a few days at The Velvet Collar. It was fascinating. You taught a brilliant class on suspension play. We use your techniques all the time. I'm so honored to host you."

She shook the man's hand, grateful at least one person in the world didn't think she was some kind of criminal for her desires. "And I am honored to be here. Rene at The Collar speaks highly of your club."

"I'll be thrilled to introduce you around," McKay said, warmth in his voice. He let go of her hand and then turned to Kash. "And if I didn't say it before, congratulations on the wedding. I'm sorry I couldn't make it, but we've traveled so much lately. Ian and Charlotte were sorry to send their regrets as well, but the wedding happened so fast."

"You didn't miss anything at all," Kash replied.

"I'm sure it was lovely." McKay frowned but moved toward the door of the office anyway. "I'm going to make sure the rooms are ready. I can imagine you're tired. I'll be back in a moment."

The door closed and silence hung in the small office.

"Would you like to explain why you're so angry with me?" She had to ask. She didn't understand what had really happened.

He stared straight ahead. "You lied to me."

"I never lied to you. I never told you I was a virgin or that I didn't have a past."

"You also didn't mention that past included being a dominatrix. You didn't think that would be a problem? You didn't think that would open us all up to ridicule? The queen of Loa Mali wears leather and likes to spank naughty men. Some press statement that will make. It's a nightmare and you've brought this down on our heads because you were selfish and manipulative."

"They were private clubs, Kashmir. You've been to them too. It's all right for you to frequent clubs, but not me, is that correct? I would like for you to state your hypocrisy so I can understand its depths." Weariness was starting to be brushed aside in favor of a righteous anger. "Would the playboy of the Western world like to condemn me as a whore?"

He waved her off. "No one cares what I do. They will care about you, and that's merely me being realistic. It's already bitten us in the ass. We've already had our first blackmail attempt. How many more? How many times will I have to threaten or bribe some man you used to punish so he won't out you? My mother is sick. This could push her over the edge."

At least she could answer that particular fear of his. "Your mother knows. I brought it up to her in the beginning. I should have brought it up to you, but honestly, I didn't want to hear about your past. I was letting it go and moving into the future. I thought you would give me the same courtesy."

He finally turned. "My mother knows?"

"Yes, I told her, but she explained that she already knew."

He ran a hand over his hair, messing it up further. "And yet you didn't think to explain to me that you preferred feminine men? You merely decided to change me into one?"

Change him? Was that what he was worried about? "I'm not trying to change you in any way. I like the way you are. There's nothing at all wrong with it. You can be strong and still need to submit. It doesn't make you less of a man."

His jaw tensed, anger making his whole body rigid. "I do not submit. Not to you. Not to anyone. I'm the king."

"I never said you weren't the king. What we do in the privacy of our bedroom, it doesn't change who you are outside of it. And there's no weakness in submitting sexually to a partner who understands your needs and supports you. This is about finding one place in the world where you can give up control, where you know you're safe because your Mistress would never harm you."

He threw back his head and laughed, a terribly bitter sound. "Safe? You don't make me safe, Mistress Day. You want to make me weak and you've already placed my whole kingdom at risk."

Perhaps it was how tired she was or the fact that she'd heard it before exactly how wrong she was for being comfortable with herself and her needs, but she was ready to give him what he wanted. She stood and faced him. Blissful numbness had overtaken her and she couldn't work up the will to cry. She wasn't strong enough at that moment. It would come later, but for now she stared at the man she'd loved since she was nineteen years old. She wasn't strong enough to lie to herself anymore. It had always been Kash, from the moment he'd grinned at her in class and winked her way. Back then, he'd been the one who'd made it all right to be who she was, glasses and impulses and all. The funny thing was she would never have walked into a club, never have studied up on dominance and submission, had it not been for Kash. He'd given her the strength to accept herself and now he hated her for it.

"I'll contact a lawyer after I've had some sleep." There wasn't anything else she could do. She wasn't going to stay when it was so clear she was unwelcome.

"A lawyer? I've already taken care of it," Kash insisted. "This time. But there will be a next. I'm sure of it. My god, even Ian Taggart knows who you are."

She sighed as she walked to the door. "I didn't mean to take care of your ex-girlfriend. I meant to file for a divorce. Or annulment perhaps. We haven't actually consummated the marriage, so it might be possible."

"Divorce?" He said the word like he'd never heard it before.

What exactly did he want from her if he didn't want to end the marriage? "Yes, Kash. Divorce. You're so horrified by the fact that I like to take control during sex. You're horrified that my whorish past might come up, and despite the fact that you've slept with every woman on the planet, somehow this will make you less of a man. You're horrified by me personally. So the simple way to fix the problem is for the two of us to get a divorce. Since I handle everything anyway, I might as well be the one who files. Oh, you can tell everyone it was you, but we both know you'll be far too lazy to call a lawyer yourself."

Before she could open the door, he put a hand on it, holding it closed. "Lazy, am I?"

She shouldn't have said that, but her defenses were down. She shook her head. "We shouldn't talk anymore until we've had some sleep. If Mr. McKay has set us up with only one bed, I'll take the couch."

"Shouldn't the Mistress have the bed? Shouldn't I sleep on the floor like the good lap dog I am?" He seemed determined to see the worst in everything.

"I never asked you to do that, Kash."

"But you would have at some point. You were preparing me to be your boy. I believe the term is grooming. You were grooming me to accept being your slave."

Naturally he would see it that way. "I was trying to bring you comfort."

"I cannot be what you want me to be."

"Hence the divorce. Then you can go back to your delicate flowers and leave your manly wife behind. Perhaps they'll make you feel more like a man with their simpering neediness."

"Or I can go back to them anyway, keep my marriage and my crown, and turn you into what I need you to be," he shot back. "Have you thought of that? I can bend you to my will and then you'll know who the Master is."

There was no way she was taking that. "Or I could save us both an enormous amount of trouble and cut your balls off while you're sleeping and stuff them down your throat so you never threaten me like that again. If you lay a single hand on me, you'll find out how strong I can be."

That seemed to throw him. He stepped back, his hands up. "I wasn't going to hit you, Day. I would never hit you. I...god, I didn't mean it that way."

At least he wasn't about to become an abusive prick. He was simply feeling the stresses of the past few days, the same way she was. "I'm going to find a place to sleep. I can't talk about this anymore today."

He reached out, this time his hold on her arm gentle. "Dayita, I would never hit you. I'm sorry I made you feel that way. But you should have told me before we married that you need something I can't give you."

"You don't know what I need at all. I need to play in the bedroom. I never would have asked you to defer to me outside of there. I thought you needed someplace where you didn't have to be the king, where you could relax and let someone you trust take over. That was all I ever wanted. I wanted for us to explore and find what works for us. I wasn't ashamed of my past. If it gets out, I don't care. I didn't think you would either. I thought you loved me more than you loved your own image. A silly thing to think since this was an arranged marriage."

"We're not divorcing, Day," he said, but his tone was low and weary. "Royals don't divorce."

"Tell that to Charles and Diana," she replied. "Somehow the British monarchy is still around."

She walked out, closing the door behind her, and stepped out into the hallway. Naturally she had no idea where to go.

"Sometimes it's hard to accept the things we need." Alex McKay stood at the bottom of the stairs leading up to what she suspected was the dungeon portion of the club. "Especially those things that run counter to what we've been taught we should need."

"Why do you think I was gently working him toward a light form of submission?" She asked the question with the weary tone of a woman who knew she was about to be judged and found lacking.

"So you were being sneaky about it? You know he's been in this club a few times. He always tries to play the Dom, but it was obvious to me his heart wasn't in it. I actually suggested he scene with one of our Dommes. I suggested that he should do it because every Dom should know what it feels like to be the one on bottom. Most of my tops eagerly embrace the experience because they know it will make them a better Master or Mistress. Not Kash. He utterly refused, and when I insisted I couldn't give him Master rights without it, he left and hasn't come back until today. Oh, he's friendly enough, but I knew then I'd hit a tender nerve. But you did get him to submit, didn't you?"

Had she been wrong to lead him the way she had? She'd never demanded that he do anything. She'd simply gone on instinct. Should she have turned it all into a long lesson about what she wanted from him that would have ended in a contract signed by the two of them? "I don't know that I would say that. I don't need his pure submission. I was only trying to give him what I thought he needed. He's not capable of telling me. You're right about that. It's why I did what I did."

"He has to be able to look himself in the mirror." McKay leaned against the railing of the stairs.

"He did nothing that he should be ashamed of." How could Kash even think that?

"I know that. You know that. I don't think he understands that at all. Sometimes the best play a top can make is to be patient and show some kindness to his or her submissive. Even when they don't really deserve it." McKay gestured to the stairs above. "Your rooms are on the third floor. I opened the connecting doors between rooms two and three to make a suite. My wife, Eve, stocked the rooms with toiletries and clothes. You made her day because that woman loves to buy clothes. There are two beds if you need them, but I would advise you not to make decisions today. I know he's a douchebag, but sleep on it before you dump him. I think he needs time. Two weeks isn't a lot of time to adjust to getting married and to changing his view of himself."

"I don't know that patience will win this war, but I will definitely sleep before I do anything," she replied.

"You'd be surprised how patience can be rewarded. I should know. I wouldn't be married to the most beautiful woman in the world without it. And her kindness. Goodnight, Your Majesty." He nodded her way before he walked back toward the office.

Day started up the stairs, McKay's words playing through her head.

* * * *

Kash sank into the chair despite the fact that his every instinct told him to go after his wife and beg her forgiveness. He wasn't going to do that. He didn't need to apologize. She'd taken what he'd said in the wrong context. He would never hurt her physically.

So what exactly had he meant? Fuck. He had no bloody idea. He didn't even recognize himself anymore.

Here he was married for less than forty-eight hours and his wife was already talking about divorce.

How had he gotten here? Not two weeks before he'd been perfectly happy. He'd been carefree. He'd had everything he could possibly want.

He'd hated his life.

The door opened and Kash forced himself to sit up straight. He wasn't about to lose it in front of Alex McKay. He'd known the man for a few years, but only in a friendly acquaintance fashion.

This man had known more about his wife than he had.

Anger burned through him at her betrayal.

"So everything is set up," McKay explained as he sank back into the chair. "The only people who will be in and out of the club for the next forty-eight hours will be the Dom-in-residence, myself, and your bodyguards. I'll have Michael and Boomer on the daytime shift, and then Remy Guidry will take over the nighttime shift. I've left you dossiers on Wade Rycroft and Remy, so hopefully you'll feel comfortable. While Wade serves as the caretaker for Sanctum, he's also a former Green Beret. He'll back up Remy at night. Then we'll have the club open for select members the day after that. Unless your majesty would prefer to be alone, and then we'll close Sanctum for the full two weeks."

Kash shook his head. He would go crazy if he were stuck here with only his wife. He'd woken up the morning of his wedding certain that two weeks alone and naked with his wife was exactly what he needed. Two weeks where he didn't have to worry about anything but pleasing his queen.

Two weeks where he would have fallen further and further under her spell.

"No, I don't want that. Please tell Mr. Taggart that he should go on as though everything is perfectly normal. I'll be crawling the walls in a few days." Or he would be signing divorce papers.

It was the rational thing to do. He could spend a few days poring over constitutional law and laying out the best plan to remove his inconvenient wife so he could get back to his real life. He'd fulfilled his obligations by marrying her in the first place. There was likely nothing that said he couldn't divorce her.

Why did the thought of divorcing Dayita make him almost as angry as what she'd done to him?

"Kash, do you want me to bring in someone for you to talk to? You've had a rough couple of weeks. Lots of pressure on you."

He'd found out his mother was dying, been forced to marry, fallen in love, been betrayed.

Was he in love with her? Was that why he was so angry? Had any other woman caused him problems, he would have gently ended the relationship. He would have moved on and not thought about her twice. He had the feeling Day would haunt him for the rest of his life.

"We have a man named Kai Ferguson who works in the building next door. You've met him before."

Kash frowned. "Yes, I've met him. I'm not going to sit in some room and discuss my feelings with his man bun. If he wishes to speak with me and have me take him seriously, he can get a haircut."

McKay groaned. "You're as bad as Ian."

He certainly was not, but he also wasn't going to get caught in some ridiculous discussion of what should be private feelings. All feelings should private. All of them.

Smile and wave and never let them see you're anything but happy, son. You cannot allow the press or any of your people to see you as anything less than a king. Kings do not have feelings. Kings have responsibilities, and we do them without complaint. I know your brother acts the fool much of the time, but he's not going to be the king. He can be the clown.

He'd been twelve and Shray almost fifteen. Kash had hidden in his father's study because he wanted, just once, to know what these weekly meetings between his father and brother were like. He was never invited. It was not information for the spare. In the early days, his mother would distract him by playing games with him or suggesting they watch a movie. At the time, it had felt like precious moments he got with his mother. It was only later that he understood she was trying to spare his feelings.

His father had cared for him, but Kash had always known his

place was to be the spare, and once Shray had married and had children, he would be worthless. He would have been nothing but the clown-like uncle, only relevant because of his childhood.

It was why he'd studied, why he'd gone out into the world. He'd wanted to make something of himself. Yes, he would have been the spare—a footnote in royal history—but he would have been a man of learning, someone his father could have been proud of.

How had he still ended up the clown?

"Don't close the club. I would rather have something to do at night."

McKay nodded. "All right. I'll let Ian know. He'll be happy about that. He needs a night at his club, but you should know he was willing to give it up to protect you. He considers you a friend."

"I consider him a friend as well." His stomach was in knots. He stood up. He needed sleep but he wasn't sure he would be able to sleep with her in the room. There must be a bench somewhere. "I know you said you'd put together a room for us, but I suspect you didn't understand the nature of my marriage to Day."

McKay's face was a polite blank. "I've been given a full report on the state of your marriage."

"It's an arranged marriage. It was never for love or feelings. It was strictly to secure the crown." If he started explaining things that way, perhaps he could keep some much-needed distance. He simply had to view his marriage the way it was intended—as a pure exchange of need. He needed a wife. She needed all of his money and power.

Except she hadn't really gone out and spent much. He'd overheard her arguing with his mother that she didn't need a new wardrobe. His mother had been the one to insist that Dayita have what she called a "trousseau." Day had put her dainty foot down when Mother had suggested that she redecorate the queen's traditional apartments. Day had claimed it was lovely and all she would need was her desk from home to make the rooms livable.

"That's funny," McKay said quietly. "That's not what my men observed. I was told you were quite fond of the queen. They said you changed when you met her. You weren't fighting actively against the marriage once you realized who you were marrying."

Somehow things had fallen into place when Day had walked into the room again. His world had seemed brutally cold after realizing his mother was sick. He'd felt alone. And then Day had walked out as though the universe couldn't possibly take away someone so precious without handing him someone else. Day was the one who encouraged him to talk about his mother. He wouldn't talk about it, but there had been comfort in knowing she was there if he needed her.

Why was she there? Why had she done the things she'd done? Taken him down the dark path like some temptress leading him to sin.

Not sin exactly, but certainly something that could lead to his ruin.

"I calmed down and accepted the marriage after I realized my mother was dying." It wasn't a lie. It also wasn't one hundred percent truth.

"Ah, well, Kai could talk to you about that, too. I know you have to be concerned."

Numb was a better word. He still wasn't sure he'd accepted that she was terminally ill. She'd seemed so invigorated by the wedding.

According to Day, his mother had known about Day's past. Did his mother think so little of him that she believed he needed some kind of keeper? That he needed a top to show him the way? How his father would have laughed. Poor Kash, always the clown.

"I'll handle this on my own. I thank you for doing your job." He needed to put a good spin on this. He'd made a mistake by showing his irritation with his new bride. They had to present a united front even when he was so angry he couldn't look at her. He had to think of the crown. Not himself. He had to be the kind of king his father would have wanted. Strong. Dominant in all things. Never wavering. "Now that I've had a few hours to think about it, coming here is actually the best thing that could happen to us. We don't have to pretend we're in love. Day and I can relax and play without fear that someone will go to the press. You need to understand that if anyone goes to the press…"

"What you would do is nothing compared to what Ian would do. Trust me. You're safe here." McKay closed the folder in front of him. "I'll let you know if we hear anything from Simon and Jesse. Chelsea and Phoebe have come onto the team as well. Chelsea is searching around the web to see if she can find a hint of anyone talking about harming the king while Phoebe is sitting in on the interviews. She was Agency for years and she's got excellent instincts. You're in good hands."

He was sure they would find whoever had poisoned his Scotch. He stood up. "Again, my thanks. I'm going to get some sleep."

"Of course. The guards are already here. You're safe." McKay let him get to the door before speaking again. "You know Day had poured herself a glass of that Scotch before she found the body. It's why Simon was running so hard down that hallway. He'd seen Jamil fall and your wife enter the room. Your servant was out of her line of sight when she walked in. I've seen the video. She was seconds away from taking a drink. Luckily she was pacing and found Jamil. If she'd taken even a sip, you would be a widower today."

His stomach dropped at the thought. Day had almost taken a drink? A vision of Day laid out on the floor, her warm eyes cold and unseeing, nearly made him stumble and fall. He'd been the one to send her to that room. He'd been the one to upset her. He'd been the reason she'd reached for the Scotch. She tended to prefer tea before bed. She hadn't been getting ready for bed. She'd been getting ready for a fight.

He managed to nod McKay's way. He'd always hated the fact that palace security required CCTV cameras in the living portions of his suite. His bedroom and the bathrooms were the only parts of the palace where he had some privacy. This was one time he had to be grateful. "Thank you for telling me. She didn't mention it. I'm certainly grateful to Mr. Weston for getting to her as quickly as he did."

He walked out the door. He knew the way to the privacy rooms that would serve as his suite while he was here. He took the stairs two at a time but stopped when he reached the third floor landing.

What the hell was he going to say to her? He wasn't about to meet with a lawyer.

He'd almost lost her.

He was so fucking angry with her.

If this was what love felt like, Kash didn't want it. This was a terrible ache in his gut, a pendulum swinging between anger and insane grief.

He stepped quietly into the room and there she was. Day hadn't bothered to get undressed, though a gown and robe had been left out for her. She'd simply lain down and fallen fast asleep, her shoes still on.

What the hell was he going to do with her?

He shrugged out of his jacket and toed off his shoes. There was another bed in the adjoining room, but he didn't want to use it. Suddenly, despite the fact that he was angry, he didn't want to leave her alone.

Had what she'd done truly been so bad? He was a hypocrite of the first order and he knew it.

Her eyes fluttered open. "I'll go to the other bed if you want this one."

He found himself sitting at the end of the bed, pulling her feet into his lap as he unbuckled the straps at her ankles and eased the shoes off her feet. "Just stay here. Day, I'm…I was surprised by your background. I wish you had told me."

She sighed, a sad sound. "I suppose I knew deep down you would reject me."

Something about the lonely sound of her voice softened him. "I can't live that way. I can't be that way."

For a moment she looked like she would say something, and then she rested her head down again. "And I can't be anything less than who I am."

"Where does that leave us?" He was so tired. He'd been running on anger and adrenaline, and now he was flat out of both. He was a bit hollow, lost as to what he should do.

"It leaves us where we were before. We can divorce and you can find a more suitable bride, or we can be friends. We can understand that we don't work as lovers but we might be good partners. If we're discreet, it could possibly work."

The thought rankled but he couldn't fight more tonight. Today. God, he wasn't even sure what day it was. He only knew he seemed so far from the man who'd held her hand and promised to honor her forever.

"Go to sleep. We'll figure it out." He wasn't sure they could figure anything at all out.

He just knew he didn't have the strength to yell at her anymore. He lay down beside her.

"Kash?"

The bed was soft and he wished he had the right to pull her into his arms. He would be warm if she wrapped herself around him. "Yes?"

"I'm sorry. I never meant to hurt you. I thought I was giving you what you needed."

But he couldn't need those things. He couldn't let himself even want them anymore. Still, as he lay there, all he could see was the girl she'd been. He'd given her up once for his crown. Could he do it again? How much would being king cost him? He reached out and brushed her hair off her face. She was so lovely. Of all the women he'd been with, why was it only this one who'd ever truly moved him, who'd ever fed his soul? "I won't yell at you again. I'm sorry. When you wake up tomorrow, we'll be friends again. All right?"

A tear slipped from her eye but she nodded. "Friends, then."

He watched her until her breathing evened out and she was asleep. Despite the heavy weight of the day, Kash lay there wondering if friends could ever be enough for him again.

Chapter Eight

Day looked down at the magazine in front of her, a deep sadness running through her heart. It had been a solid week since her wedding but seeing herself in that gorgeous yellow sari, Kash standing beside her in all his wedding finery, made her ache inside. For the most part she'd been able to avoid news coverage, but she'd walked down to the women's locker room to use the sauna and someone had left a copy of *People* magazine, with its cover story on the royal wedding, laying on one of the benches.

Had it been so little time since she'd been that happy woman?

"Hey, I was…that's weird. I was looking for that magazine. It's not every day you find the celebrity holding the magazine she's on the cover of. Well, unless you're my brother-in-law. I swear he keeps his own press clippings around at all times so he can pull out some sexy picture of himself and sign it." The woman in front of her smiled. She was a bit taller than Day, with a friendly face and a mass of curly brown hair tied back with a black ribbon. She held out a hand. "I'm Kori Ferguson."

Day shook her hand. She'd been told Kori might be in and out of the club. She and her husband, Kai, ran a clinic next door. They specialized in helping soldiers with PTSD. It was the kind of thing Day would have usually been interested in. She would have asked a million questions and wanted to know about the science behind their therapies. Now she could barely work up the will to return the woman's smile. "Dayita Kamdar."

Kori stepped back, the smile on her face turning a bit

mischievous. "Should I curtsy?"

The Domme in Day recognized what a righteous brat that one would be. The woman in front of her would likely be fun to play with. Of course, she was sure Kash would see her even thinking the thought as a form of cheating. He didn't seem to be capable of understanding that play didn't have to end in sex.

He also wasn't capable of seeing how much he needed.

Day handed over the magazine. "No curtsies, please. I'm trying to be undercover. I don't think Mr. Taggart would take it well if his staff started curtsying to the royals."

Kori snorted lightly. "I'm so not that man's staff."

Naturally, she was offending everyone these days. "I apologize. I meant no offense."

Kori shrugged. "None taken. I'm sure Big Tag would call me staff. Then I would do something mean to his locker. Then he would laugh and handle it super well, and Kai would get all pissy and I would find myself tied up and well, you know where it goes from there. Big Tag is surprisingly good natured about practical jokes. I filled his locker with Jell-O once. Don't even ask. It was a week-long project. I thought he would flip his shit. He laughed hysterically and asked me if I could do it to Adam's car."

It was an interesting place she found herself in. She might have even loved Sanctum had she not felt so deeply alone. "And did you?"

"Still working on it. So, are you coming to the masquerade night?" Kori opened one of the lockers and stuffed the magazine inside. "Kai and I are getting things ready. I was surprised you haven't come to any of the play nights. Kai said you were active in the lifestyle."

She had to go with the united front she and Kash had agreed on. He'd been true to his word. He'd softened his stance and hadn't accused her of being a whore or trying to ruin his kingdom again. They'd sat down the day after they'd arrived and agreed that they could make no decisions and do nothing until they figured out who had tried to kill Kash. While they were stuck here in Sanctum, they'd decided they would work on being friends. After the first day, they'd slept in separate beds, kept up different rooms. They'd been polite, but there was a distance between them she'd never felt before. Not when they were together. Somehow, when they were in the same room, there had always been a connection she could feel. It had been cut now, and she wasn't sure they would ever get it back.

Kash didn't seem interested in finding that connection again. He'd spent his time watching movies in the men's locker room or playing video games with the bodyguards. Day had been left to read or work out, or—worst of all—think.

"My husband and I are going to keep a low profile while we're here," she said simply. "We're on our honeymoon. I think we want to keep things private. You know how newlyweds are."

Kori whistled. "Dude, you have to get your stories together. Kash is telling everyone that this is nothing more than an arranged marriage and the two of you have an agreement. He's planning on playing tonight. One of the things I brought in was a set of leathers for his royal deludeness. Sorry about the dude, Your Majesty. I dude everyone."

Kash was planning on playing? Was he kidding? "My husband requested that you bring him a set of leathers?"

Kori's eyes went wide. "Whoa. Okay, I believe it now. I didn't before. When they said you were in the lifestyle, I thought it was kind of like Kash was in the lifestyle. Like you played around a bit, but you would be more of a delusional tourist than anything. I apologize for the rudeness, Mistress Day."

She was well aware that she'd likely turned on a dime, but something about Kash going behind her back to play rankled. "I appreciate your acknowledgment, but it isn't necessary. What is necessary is your honest answer to my question. Did my husband request that you bring him a set of leathers because he intends to play in the club this evening?"

"Yes, ma'am. If he doesn't intend to play, then he's going to be walking around your private suite in a full-on mask tonight. He's the one who requested the masquerade theme. Everyone wearing some form of costume means there can be a full play night."

"There have been several play nights already." Not that she'd attended them.

"Yes, but the club hasn't technically been open to the full membership. It's only been open to a close-knit group."

"Why would that…" The answer hit her square in the gut. "Are they all couples? No single submissives?"

Kashmir would want a sub. He would want some delicate thing to blink her eyes at him and never complain so he could feel like a man. It wouldn't matter that the delicate flower couldn't give Kash what his soul craved. All her husband cared about was his image.

Kori sighed and sank down to the bench. "Yes, it was all couples the last few nights. I think Big Tag was trying to make you more comfortable. He admires you as a top. Apparently some dude in France likes you, and Tag likes that dude, so there's a mathematical equation in Tag's mind that adds up to you being one of the good ones."

"I'm well known at The Velvet Collar. I believe Mr. Taggart is good friends with Rene, the man who owns the club. He's also a friend of mine." And one she should have listened to. "I was trained by Rene. One of the things he taught me was that I can't change a submissive who doesn't want to change. I should have listened to him."

A leopard didn't change his spots, and Kashmir Kamdar would never be faithful. Certainly not to her. He was probably keeping her quiet and focused until the moment that he could break ties with her. He would know a compliant wife was better than one actively fighting him. Hence his decision to stop haranguing her. He'd made his decision and now he was surviving as best he could until he could spring whatever plan he'd come up with on her.

Until then, if he could quietly have his fun, he would do it.

"Please excuse me." She started to turn to go.

"Arguing with him won't solve the problem," Kori said suddenly.

Day turned, arching a brow and then realizing what she was doing. They weren't playing. They were in a club, but the roles weren't rigid here. She was tense and upset and slipping into the one role where she felt in control. It wouldn't help her. It would only serve to cause her more trouble. "I wasn't planning on arguing. I was going to talk to him. You're right. We do need to get our stories straight."

"But it will end up in an argument, you know. Look, I'm not trying to overstep… Okay, I am, but it's totally what I do.

Overstepping is kind of a hobby of mine. If you go find Kash, you'll get into an argument, and that won't solve anything. He's too stubborn to give in and you gave him an out. Is it so surprising that he took it? Kash has been fooling himself for years."

"An out?" Now she was confused.

Kori shifted on the bench, gesturing for Day to join her. "Kash talks when he drinks. He wasn't playing so Tag gave him a free pass to the bar. He came down to the club last night and after a couple of shots, he started talking to my husband. Oh, in the beginning it was all about how Kai should cut his man bun. Don't you underestimate the power of the man bun. Anyway, after another few shots, he told Kai that you lied to him and tricked him into a D/s relationship."

She couldn't help but roll her eyes in perfect disdain. "That's ridiculous. I didn't trick him into anything."

"So you outlined what you wanted from him?"

There it was, that creeping, completely unfounded guilt that seemed ready to overwhelm her at any given moment. This was why she hated all the time she'd spent "thinking." "I gave clear instructions and they led us both to incredible encounters."

"So you didn't work up a contract with him?"

And the wave was cresting. "It wasn't like that. I knew we wouldn't have that kind of a relationship."

"But you wanted one." Kori leaned in. "Mistress Day, you don't have to talk about this, but I know you're not talking about it with Kash and I don't think you have made friends here. You've been through something stressful and I understand pulling back. But talking can help. It's helping Kash."

He did seem happier. He'd had breakfast with her this morning and spoken more than a few words. They'd had a lively discussion about an article he'd read in a scientific digest. It had almost made her feel normal.

What would it hurt to talk to Kori? From what she'd heard from Kash, this woman and her husband were in some ways the mom and pop of the club. Big Tag and his wife were the king and queen, but Kori and Kai were the ones many of the members talked to when they had a problem.

"If I had sat him down and explained that I was a Mistress and wanted him to submit to me sexually, he would have run as fast as he could. Kash thinks submitting means he's weak. He can say he understands the lifestyle all he likes. He doesn't."

"I don't know about that. I think he does understand much of it. The thing he doesn't understand is himself, and tricking him into something he's not ready for wasn't the best plan."

"I wasn't tricking him."

"I understand that, but that's how he'll see it. Why didn't you tell him you had experience?"

How much had Kash talked? Little hypocrite. He'd told her they should show a united front and then turned around and given up their every secret. "I didn't hide it. I simply didn't talk about it. I didn't want to hear about Kash's conquests."

"But you knew about them."

She couldn't avoid it. "Everyone knows about them. His escapades are legendary."

"While yours were private. You knew much more about him than he knew about you. Doesn't that put him at a disadvantage?"

She caught hold of her anger. There was nothing in Kori's demeanor that indicated she was being judgmental. She was the wife of a therapist, and Day would be surprised if she hadn't picked up a few of her husband's techniques. It was a bit like a science experiment. She'd put forth a theory—that Kashmir had been "tricked." Now it was up to Day to prove or disprove the theory. Kash believed it. By examining her own actions with Kori, she could find a way to change his mind.

Or she would decide she owed her husband an apology.

"I don't view relationships as a game. I don't seek to have an advantage over him. I wasn't trying to trick him. I was trying to form a connection with him and it worked. When we were alone together, he responded to everything I asked of him. He enjoyed it."

"Until?" Kori asked.

"Until the moment he figured out someone knew about my background as a Domme. We were perfectly fine until he realized it was possible someone could find out."

"Interesting and not unsurprising. I did hear that Ian and some of the others were working to ensure your privacy," Kori explained.

"I'm fairly certain after they're done, you won't have to worry about the press finding out."

"That's the real problem. I never worried. I didn't care. I'm not ashamed of myself. I take pride in who I am and what I can do. I've helped many submissives learn about discipline and to find their inner strength. There's nothing wrong with it."

"No, but it is seen as abnormal by many in society."

"And it always will be if we all hide."

Kori shook her head. "It can't be you. You gave up that right when you chose to take the crown, Your Majesty. You get to stand up for people who don't have a voice. You get to do amazing things for the needy people of both your country and the world, but you don't get this. The minute you decided to become Loa Mali's queen, you ceased being able to take that part of yourself public. I'm not saying there's anything shameful, but you have other fights to fight. Bigger fights. You can be whoever you want behind closed doors, but you belong to the people otherwise. That's what Kash has to deal with."

It hit her forcibly. Somehow she'd known it in an intellectual way, but she hadn't fully grasped what it all meant. Kash's life had changed that day fifteen years before. He'd gone from coddled spare son with all the choices of his life open to him to a man whose path was laid out before him with no exit ramps.

She was now trapped with him and Kori was right. She had to be realistic. There were many ways she could help the people of her country, but she couldn't do anything at all if she was so controversial a figure that no one would listen. She wasn't a pop star who could say whatever was on her mind and still expect to collect a paycheck at the end of the day. She wasn't even a politician. She represented the people of Loa Mali.

Kash had been submissive for fifteen years. Submissive to his crown, to his people. His sexuality was one way he could have some form of control. Still, even he couldn't walk into a BDSM club without causing a scandal. They had to keep that part of their lives private.

It wasn't going to work. Sadness replaced her anger with him. Anger would solve nothing. She'd been naïve to think she could show him how good it would be to submit to her, that he needed to submit.

"He isn't capable of giving himself what he needs," she said softly. "He won't ever give in. Not fully. That's why he was going to travel after our honeymoon. He needed distance."

"If it helps at all, I think you're right. I believe he would find great joy in having a place to submit to a strong top. It would help him realize he doesn't always have to be the king, but I fear he's spent too long with a crown on his head to be able to change his mindset. It's one thing for him to be known as a manwhore, something different for him to be seen as sexually submissive."

He wouldn't be able to do it. She could see that now. He'd indulged himself, but even right before their wedding, she'd felt him pulling away. He'd always intended to pull away. He'd been trying to stave off that moment when he would have to tell her he could never be that way again.

Had he dreaded it? Had Tasha showing up that night actually been some form of a relief for him?

"I should let it be." Talking to him wouldn't change a thing.

Kori frowned. "Oh, I didn't say that."

"You were right. Arguing isn't going to get us anywhere. I understand his position. I was wrong to try to be sneaky. I should have been upfront with him. It would have saved us both a lot of time and heartache and potential lawyers' fees. No, I'm going to give him the space he needs. I'll try to talk to him about what we need to do, let him know I won't fight him. I think that's what he's afraid of. He's afraid I'll cause trouble, but that's not my intention at all. I want to make this easy on him, and definitely easy on the queen mother."

She wasn't sure what made her sadder, the idea of losing Kash or that for a moment it had felt like she'd had a family again. For a few weeks, she'd felt like she belonged.

"I agree you should go easy on his mom, but you should totally give him hell. It's the only way they ever learn. Look, you're the Mistress. I get that, and you all have rules and shit, but sometimes a bit of bratty behavior goes a long way." The smile that lit up Kori's face let her know she played the brat a lot. All the more fun for her Master. "Sometimes you've got to change the game on a man to get him to see things in a different light."

That sub was probably so much trouble, but then again, she also seemed smart as hell. Day wasn't sure what she was thinking, but maybe it was time to change the game. After all, the rules had been stacked against Kash since the day he'd been born.

"What are you thinking?"

"You know what they say, Mistress. What's good for the goose…"

Was good for the gander. Ah, she understood. Perhaps it was time to start over, but with no secrets between them. He would likely still reject her, but if there was any chance at all, she would take it.

"I'm going to need some help."

* * * *

Kash stepped into the lounge with an uneasy sense of guilt. He'd told Day that he was going down to the conference room to play some video games. He'd then changed as quickly as he could and left via the back door of their suite, praying she wouldn't see him. He was dressed in the leathers the group had been kind enough to supply. He wore leather pants and boots, a thin leather vest, and a mask. With his hair pulled back in a tight queue and the mask covering half his face, he was certain no one who didn't know he was here would recognize him.

Would Day recognize him like this? Would she respect him like this?

He'd lied to her. Damn, why had he done that?

The lights had been turned on and heavy industrial music thudded through the club. It looked like Taggart had gone all out since there was a heavy layer of smoke running across the dungeon floor. It gave the space a hypnotic, other-worldly feel.

This was what he needed. To be out of his own head for a while, outside the world and the places where all the responsibility weighed him down, where he could be someone other than the king.

But wasn't that exactly what Day had been trying to offer him?

He shook off the question and jogged down the stairs, moving quickly toward the lounge section of the club. Guilt followed him.

It kept pace with his movements, giving him not a moment's rest.

She was trying to be his friend and he was plotting against her. She thought he was going to give her some happy-ass divorce, but he couldn't. He fucking couldn't, and that pissed him off, too.

He needed this evening. That was what he told himself. He needed a night to prove to himself that the thing with Day had been an outlier—an experience that varied from the norm. He wasn't the man who sighed and kissed his woman's feet. He was the top.

There would be no sex tonight. He couldn't. He...he was married to Day, and he felt that deep in his soul. But perhaps if he found a sub to top, the world would shift back into place.

Then he would be able to sit down with her. He might be able to deal with the situation rationally. When he really thought about it, he was doing this for the two of them.

If he could figure his own shit out, perhaps she would understand. Perhaps she would fall in line and he could be strong enough for the two of them.

Kash made it to the lounge area, where most of the group would start their evening. Some people were already out in the playroom area and some had scenes going in the dungeon, but he needed to find a partner.

To top. Because he was the top. He was the Dom. That was how it had to be.

"Are you serious? Dude, what is wrong with you? Is that a wig?" Taggart asked a man with long hair that very likely was a wig.

Taggart sat on one of the lounge chairs, leaning back and looking like a king holding court. Well, if the king of Sanctum also happened to be a long-haired rocker with a red bandana around his forehead.

Apparently the group had taken the whole masquerade theme seriously. Kash had thought they would all just wear masks, but some of the group were in full-on costume. Charlotte Taggart wore red thigh-high boots and a Wonder Woman costume that would certainly fall off her the minute she started taking out the bad guys. Although it could be effective. She had lovely breasts. She could distract her enemies with those.

"I'm not going to apologize, Axl Rose. Khal Drogo is a badass," the other man said.

"He's also about five feet taller than you," Taggart returned.

The other man shrugged. "I have about a billion dollars more than he has so I think I win. Also, my sun and moon is even prettier than the one on TV. Hey, gorgeous."

A lovely woman stepped into the lounge wearing a flowing white gown and a wig with platinum blonde locks. She looked at the man who would probably have made a better hobbit and sighed, her hand over her heart. "And you look amazing, my love. Don't let the big bad wolf tear you down. I'll set some dragons on him."

Taggart grinned. "I got Wonder Woman to shield me."

The man with the fake swords at his sides stepped up and put his hands on the woman's hips. "I've got a billion dollars on Big Tag, too. Don't you worry about my ego. I can handle it. You ready to handle me?"

"You know I am, baby," the woman replied and then her eyes took on a steely look. "How do you greet me?"

To Kash's surprise, the man fell to his knees, his hands on his thighs as he offered himself up to his Domme.

The woman put a hand on his head and accepted the offer with a smile. "Come, my love. Let's go play. It's been a rough week. I think you need some serious discipline."

His face turned up and he was grinning. "Yes, after that last board meeting, I'm going to need a little something something, if you know what I mean."

She reached out a hand, helping him up, and then led him away toward the play area.

"That is one happy tech guru," Charlotte said with a smile on her face.

"I remember when he was all uptight and grumpy." Serena Dean-Miles took a seat. She was dressed in a schoolgirl outfit complete with pigtails and Mary Janes. "Hey, Ka… I mean, hi, Sir. We're calling him Sir tonight, right?"

"He's undercover, though I wouldn't have agreed to any of this if I thought he was in real jeopardy," Taggart explained, his hand on his wife's knee. "Every single person in this club knows the rules. No one is going to talk to the press because they know they would have to deal with me. And Mitch. He's a bloodsucking lawyer. He's like a giant tick. Once he settles in, it's really hard to get him out.

Ask Laurel. One unplanned pregnancy and she's saddled with the man for life."

Charlotte shook her head. "Don't believe him. They're incredibly happy. And now Serena and I are going to help the Mistress set up for her demo. I've heard Harrison nearly had a heart attack when he found out a Domme was going to be doing a ropes demo tonight. He had a rough case this week and he's sure he can avoid the heart attack he sees coming his way if he can get in a good, long session."

"Harrison Keen? The attorney?" He'd met the man briefly when he'd been at Sanctum the year before. Keen had been on the board of a charity Kash funded. Harrison Keen was an all-American man who commanded attention when he walked in a room. "He's going to help this Mistress with her demonstrations?"

Taggart laughed, the sound booming through the lounge. "No. He's going to beg the woman to tie him up and beat his ass red. Keen's a big old bottom. Oh, don't get me wrong. He's the alpha male in the courtroom, but when he's in the dungeon, that man is all about kissing some dainty Domme feet."

"We talking about Keen or Milo?" a new voice asked. Adam Miles strode up. He was dressed in a perfectly pressed suit, his hair slicked back and a briefcase in his hand.

"Keen," Tag replied as his wife stood up. "Milo's lost his damn mind. I swear, the nerds are taking over. Between Milo's dragons and Phoebe and Jesse's weird wand fetish, it's getting sketchy around here. Now Adam's come dressed as Simon. It's a crazy fucking world, man. You know it's not normal for your wife's fantasy guy to be another team member, right?"

Miles shot Tag his middle finger. "Fuck you. Si doesn't have a copyright on three-piece suits. I'm not dressed as him. I'm a professor and that's one naughty schoolgirl."

Serena stood and cuddled up against her husband. "You know I am, professor. Very naughty. I didn't do my homework. I suppose someone's going to have to punish me."

"I think we can work something out, you bad, bad girl. Look at that pout." Adam growled down at his wife and then his entire demeanor changed. "Hey, babe, don't let me forget. We're out of wipes. Jake used nearly a whole box yesterday."

Serena nodded. "We're calling it the Great Poop Incident. I've never seen a baby poop so much. Jake was overwhelmed. We can steal a box from the nursery when we pick up the kids."

"I heard that," Taggart said with a frown.

Serena shook her head. "Nope, Axl Rose is an outlaw. He would totally agree with my decision to move to a life of baby wipe thievery." She looked back up at her husband. "I'll see you later, professor. I'll try to stay out of trouble, but you know how naughty I can be."

Miles smacked his wife's backside, eliciting a squeal from her. "I've got a paddle with your name on it. Now go and do what you need to do. Jake'll be up in a bit and then you'll have to deal with two angry professors."

Charlotte kissed her husband and the two subs were off to help set up the scene.

Miles sank into the chair opposite Taggart. "I sent you the report on the masked one's latest threat."

Kash sat down with the two men. "What do you mean latest threat?"

Taggart had his phone out, pulling up files. "You ran down where they would have gotten the poison?"

"Of course," Miles shot back. "I'm a genius."

"What was the poison?" Kash asked. "It had to be fast acting. There are only a few poisons that could be used that would act so quickly. Was it cyanide?"

"It was a conotoxin," Miles replied.

Taggart was shaking his head. "Dude, I am never going to Australia. Everything wants to kill you there. Even the flipping snails. I do not get it. Charlie wants to go for vacation, but I think it would be one long attempt at survival."

"Snails?" He didn't need Taggart's sarcasm.

"There's a marine snail, native to Australia," Miles explained. "It's called a cone snail and it's one of the most venomous creatures on the planet. Unfortunately, Tag's right about Australia. Everything wants to kill you there. Have you ever seen a real kangaroo? They can punch and shit, and they are not unfamiliar with fight club."

"Where would the assassin have gotten this venom?" Kash

needed to keep them focused.

"Probably from a pharmaceutical lab." Tag nodded. "Yep, there it is. A small lab working on the coast reported a break-in, and someone stole a small supply of the venom. They're studying it to see if it can be used to treat epilepsy and a host of other disorders."

"I need to check travel records, but I'm getting some pushback," Miles said. "They don't know why some firm in Dallas wants to invade the privacy of a bunch of Loa Mali's citizens. Perhaps if the king could call?"

"I'll do it in the morning. My cousin can get you all the information you need." Someone had tried to kill him. It still wasn't something he'd entirely processed. "So you think someone traveled to Australia, stole some of this toxin, and came back to use it to kill me. Why not use something simpler?"

"Despite what *Murder She Wrote* will teach you, it's actually hard to get your hands on a poison that works so quickly," Miles explained. "Most agents require time and will sicken the victim before killing him. Cyanide works well, but you have to have enough of it and it's highly controlled. I'll figure out who went to Australia shortly before the robbery and we should have a suspect pool."

"Australia is quite close." He didn't want them to think this would be easy. "We have an excellent relationship with them. We don't require visas coming into or out of the country. It will be a large pool. It's winter break back home. Lots of people on holiday."

He glanced out over the playroom and caught sight of the *Game of Thrones* couple again. That was when it clicked. He'd seen that man before. He'd met that man before. "That was Milo Jaye."

Taggart barely looked up from his phone. "Yep, that's Milo. Thanks, Adam. Did I punch your face for that lately?"

Adam's eyes rolled. "Sure, bringing one of the wealthiest men in the country into your circle of influence is a punchable offense."

"I already filled the tech guru nerd spot. Case married into a family of them," Taggart argued.

"Yeah, well, the Lawless clan has yet to accept your offer to come to Sanctum," Adam shot back. "And you know how the old saying goes. You can never have too many ridiculously wealthy tech gurus on the team."

"But he's one of the most powerful businessmen in the world." Kash didn't understand.

Taggart's eyes finally came up. "Is that a declarative statement or a question? I can tell you he's a smart fucker. I wasn't going to let him in. He found the weakest link in my chain, sued Adam, and voila, now he's happily getting his ass slapped by his girlfriend. They were pretty dumb in the beginning though. Milo thought he was the top."

Adam snorted a little. "That was pretty funny to watch, and I'm so not the weakest link. If you see Jake, tell him I'm in the conference room trying to trace a couple of flight manifests down, and that if he starts our scene without me, I'll kill him."

Adam strode off toward the stairs.

"Why so interested in Milo Jaye?" Taggart asked.

It was odd to be having such a personal conversation with Axl Rose, but he did have some questions. "He's not the type of man I would see as a submissive. As a matter of fact, I wonder about the other one, too. The lawyer. He seems to be so masculine."

A brow arched over Taggart's left eye. "How does masculinity come into this?"

He should stop talking right here and now. This wasn't a conversation he needed to have. "You know how it is. The woman submits to the man. That's how it's supposed to be."

Both of Taggart's eyes widened, and he looked around like a man who'd just realized something was about to kill him. "Dude, you do not say that bullshit in this club. Like seriously, not even outside of it. The subs have ears. They have ears everywhere, and those ears are attached to faces that have mouths, and those mouths talk, and then my wife hears that I was in a conversation where she and all womanhood was subjected to the patriarchy or some shit. She'll have a really long political term but what it really means is I sleep on the couch."

He should have known all he would get out of Taggart was sarcasm. "I'll try not to speak of the patriarchy around your wife."

"Hey, don't be so touchy." Taggart relaxed back and studied him for a moment. "You really think being Dominant or submissive has something to do with gender? Because in my experience, it doesn't. It's more about the psychology of the person and the way he or she deals with the world around them. It can be something as simple as a woman or a man was once in a position where he or she was out of control. Especially if that situation involved something sexual. They might need to be in control during sex. I control who plays in this club. I'm not going to allow a submissive in who is actively seeking to hurt himself. I would connect that person to Kai or another therapist. There's no room for self-hate here. It can be too dangerous. I deal with those people more magnanimously than the other side of it."

"The other side?"

"The ones who truly want to cause pain without pleasure, who seek to control their submissives in a way that is not healthy for the sub. It's why almost none of my friends in the lifestyle are twenty-four seven. Even the ones who started that way tend to ease up over time. You can cross the line into abuse if you get the wrong Dom and sub together. Don't get me wrong. That kind of a relationship can work, but it's rare. The submissive must be as strong as the Dominant for a relationship like that to work."

"I thought the whole point was that the Dom was the strong one."

"That's because you don't take any of this seriously. When I try to talk about the fundamental ideas of the lifestyle, you tend to take another shot and talk about spanking girls. The only reason I let you in here is because I trust you not to hurt the subs. Also, you tend to have terrible taste in women. I thought I might be able to save you."

"I do not have terrible taste in women." He'd been with some of the most beautiful women in the world. And many of them were horrible human beings.

"Dude, you can't even tell a supermodel from a spy. Hint, the spies are the ones who try to kill you."

He would never live that down.

Taggart leaned forward, his voice softening. "I like your wife very much. I have to wonder if she's not the reason you're suddenly asking questions."

"I know you've met her before."

"Have I met Dayita Samar, or Mistress D? I've certainly met the latter. She's a friend of a friend and she's considered one of the finest Dommes around."

His stomach clenched at the thought. He was trying to forgive her for not telling him. He was trying to see things from her point of view. "That is good for her and for whomever she chooses to top."

"Kash, she's a serious sexual top. From what I understand, it's merely a part of her personality. The same as it is mine. No damage or trauma forced it. Some of us are simply born this way. Like Harrison and Milo are bottoms. They gain great pleasure from serving their lovers in certain ways and from being served in the way only a top can."

"Yes, I understand this much. They enjoy having their backsides smacked and kissing a woman's feet."

Taggart's icy blue eyes narrowed. "Okay, that was judgmental, but I think you're new to this so I'll keep talking. There's more to it than getting spanked. I've gotten spanked. It doesn't do anything for me. I think if one of the male subs were here, they would tell you that what they get is a place where they don't have to be in control. Hell, the female subs would tell you that. There are some strong-as-hell boss ladies who grace this club. They come from all walks of life and they seek to relax, to have those few hours a week where this other part of their personalities gets to come out. They can indulge that piece of themselves. Humans are complex. Well, Adam isn't. Adam's a douchebag, but for the most part there are these whole other people who live inside us and never get to come out unless we're brave enough to explore. I might be the top here, but don't you doubt for a second that I wouldn't get on my knees in front of my Charlie. There's nothing weak about that. I love that woman. She gets every piece of me, with nothing held back. And you know what, she's the reason why I found that softer side of myself. She and our kids. I'm a completely different person without them. Colder. Alone. Some might have called that strength, but it was really fear." Taggart shoved his phone back into his pocket. "Have you talked to your wife about this? About how to move forward?"

"How do two tops move forward?" The words felt stubborn, but he couldn't admit the truth. He couldn't simply say what he wanted.

"I have a married couple here who are both tops, and they enjoy themselves mightily. And before you start talking about cheating, they don't sleep with their submissives. They give their expertise to the subs they top and then go at it like a couple of angry rabbits. Seriously, those two know how to tear up a bed, but then you go to hand them a bill and they get all legal on a man's ass. Note to self, no more fucking lawyers. We've got enough damn lawyers."

Jacob Dean strode in, wearing a suit that was only slightly less perfect than his partner's had been. "Hey, Tag, you seen Adam? I got stuck in traffic. Stupid 75."

Taggart nodded. "Yeah, he's working on a case. Said he'd be a while and you should start without him."

Dean gave him a thumbs-up. "Excellent. I'll go get our girl warmed up."

"You're an asshole." Kash watched as Dean strode away.

"It's all a part of my charm." Tag stood up. "I think the demo is going to get started soon. I'm going to go watch. Also, it'll be fun to watch Adam and Jake fight when Adam realizes Jake got that first piece of pie."

He wasn't sure what pie had to do with anything, but he followed Tag into the play space. All around him the members of Sanctum seemed to be embracing the idea of a masquerade. He caught sight of the ridiculously wealthy Milo Jaye and his girlfriend. Milo was on his knees in front of her, his eyes soft and a smile playing on his face. His girl lightly ran the tip of a cane down his chest, and it sent a shiver through the man's body.

Why did the image have to tighten his groin? Why couldn't he be normal?

What the hell was normal?

"So your wife didn't want to come down and play?" Taggart asked as they moved toward the largest of the stages. "She's more than welcome, of course. I have no problem giving her full Mistress privileges here."

"But I am given merely probationary privileges?" Naturally Day would be able to oversee him if she'd come down. She could stop him and instruct him if she thought he was doing something incorrectly.

Taggart nodded. "Oh, yeah, she's way better than you. You could learn a thing or two. I don't know why you wouldn't. She's a badass."

"In my country, women are not supposed to be badasses. They are supposed to be partners, to be helpmates to their husbands." Had he honestly just said that? What the fuck was wrong with him? He didn't believe that. He fought against that kind of backward thinking. When he'd been running his lab, he'd made sure to bring in all the brightest minds, male and female.

And now the only use he had for anyone was to bring him his next drink, be his next body in a bed.

How had his life gotten so damn shallow?

Taggart slapped him on the shoulder, one of those American male gestures that let a man know he was both stupid and tolerated. "Maybe that's why you couldn't tell the difference between the chick who wanted to kill you and the ones who were in it for your cash. As for me, give me a badass chick every day of the week. You say you're looking for a helpmate? Badass chick will not only cook your breakfast, she'll take care of the assassins trying to kill you, give you the best blow job of your life, and scare off all the people you don't want around. You can keep your delicate chicks. Give me a Russian mob princess. There's a class of women who know how to treat a man right. Conversely, they also know how to cut a man's balls off if you don't hold up your end of the bargain."

"That being?"

He smiled, a bright, open expression that Kash wasn't used to seeing on Taggart's face. "Complete and total dependence. I'm joking. Though that is what I feel when she leaves me alone with the kids. Sometimes I think that's her way of letting me know what hell on earth is like. I'm ready to drop to my knees and beg her to never leave me and all she did was go buy groceries. Yeah, that's a clever plan of hers. That's my girl. She's always plotting. So you didn't tell me why Day didn't want to come down and play. You've been here. Why hasn't she?"

Because he'd made her feel so terrible about their situation that she mostly sat around the room like a prisoner waiting for her execution. She read a lot, used the gym when she was sure no one was around. She'd taken to sitting in the small alcove that contained the basketball net. He'd caught her sitting in the sun, her face turned up as though she missed the warmth. She'd been so stunningly beautiful in that moment that he'd wanted nothing more than to take her hand and lead her upstairs.

"Do you think a woman like Day could be happy with a vanilla relationship?"

"Why should she have one?" Taggart asked.

How did he make him understand? "It's not seemly. If we ever got caught…"

"You get caught all the time, dude. There are pictures of your junk pretty much everywhere. You know you have your own YouTube channel, right?"

"That's different."

Taggart stared at him for a moment. "How? Because you're a guy and you're supposed to fuck around, and she's female and should remain pure until she gets to marry the guy who's fucked around?"

"I don't think like that. I don't have a problem with the fact that she's slept with other men."

Taggart stopped, settling himself on an unused bench. "Good, because that would make you a really heinous hypocrite and I might decide you need assassinating."

They were in a scene space that had three walls around it. It looked a bit like an exercise room, except the barbells were alongside a number of paddles and crops. He understood why Taggart had chosen this space for his impromptu conversation about hypocrisy. Kash could hear him easily over the music, but they could still see the large stage.

"Would Day get to stay queen if you died?" Taggart asked, his eyes narrowed.

He had the sudden suspicion that only the truth might save him. Taggart often believed he was smarter than anyone else and that the world should work according to his rules. "No. That would be against the rules of our primogeniture. My cousin Chapal would become the king."

And then they would have the problems of succession because Chapal would be stubborn about divorcing his husband and marrying a female simply for procreation. A female who would be required to provide a son. He and Day could have ten daughters but if one son was born, he would supersede all his sisters.

Why was that the rule? Because some asshole a thousand years ago decided men were more important than women? That a man— any man—could lead better than a woman?

He had a sudden vision of a young girl. She would have her mother's silky hair and serious eyes. She would love science and she would be told to study housekeeping. She would be taught to wave and smile and defer to her younger brother because he would be king.

He'd made progress. He'd been the one to push for women to get their degrees. It had been in his coronation speech. He remembered writing it even when his father's advisors had told him not to push. He'd done it for Day. He'd done it because he'd been in love with a girl who'd wanted to discover the secrets of the universe.

And then his lab had blown up and the guilt had eaten away at him for five long years. He'd turned away from truly leading, and a whole group of nasty old men had gained power in his absence. They'd tried to turn the country back, tried to tell all those little girls who they should be.

The only person fighting them had been Dayita.

While he'd been off drinking his guilt away, she'd been quietly fighting for the next generation. So that both boys and girls received everything their country could give them. So when they became men and women, all were strong.

"Besides, dude, you're like the king and shit," Taggart pointed out. "What the hell does it mean to be the king if you can't tell everyone to fuck off about a couple of things? I get it. You can't behead people anymore, but you have some power. You can protect your wife. Unless you think your wife is wrong because she's not a simpering flower who needs you to protect her from everything life throws at her. Unless you think she's wrong for needing what she needs and being strong enough to ask for it."

Kash clung to the one thing he could be righteous about. "Ah, but she didn't. She didn't ask for it."

Why had he said that? He'd bloody well outed himself.

If Taggart was surprised, he didn't show it, which led Kash to wonder if this hadn't been the point of his conversation all along. "She tricked you into submitting to her?"

"Yes."

Taggart thought about that for a moment. "How does that work? Did she get you drunk? Blackmail you?"

"No. She didn't tell me what she was doing."

"She didn't give you instructions?" There was a suspicious tone to the question, as though he didn't really believe he had asked one at all. As though it all should have been obvious. "Because those are usually the norm in a D/s relationship. In vanilla relationships you sometimes fall into bed together and one partner naturally takes the lead, but you can usually tell who that is. Did she fight you for it?"

Nope. He'd lain down the minute she'd turned that sexy-as-hell voice on him. "It wasn't like that."

"Did she tie you up when you were asleep or something? You know that's assault and we should really talk about that."

Taggart was twisting his words, the bastard. "No, she didn't do that. And yes, she gave me instructions."

"She asked you to get to your knees? She asked you to let her take control? How was this confusing to you?" Taggart asked in a rapid-fire interrogation.

"I understood the instructions."

"And it seems as though you followed them," Taggart surmised. "Did she tell you she would stop the sex if you didn't obey her? Is that how she blackmailed you?"

He hadn't even thought to ask the question. He'd been so enthralled by the way she took control, by the relief he felt at the idea of not being in charge for a few fucking minutes in his day. "I did what she required. It didn't seem wrong at the time. But she didn't tell me about her past. She didn't tell me what she wanted from me."

"Did she require your submission outside the bedroom? Did she manipulate you into giving in to her when the subject wasn't sex? Women can use any number of manipulative techniques to get us to submit to their evil wills."

He had the feeling Taggart was making fun of him. It made him think though. She hadn't tried to manipulate him. She'd asked if he was going to come to her meetings with parliament, that he sit back and allow her to handle things, but that was her job. She understood it far better than he did. He'd spent the whole time getting hot because of the way she masterfully handled those men, but he'd also realized that she was competent.

They hadn't fought until that last day. They'd found a familiar friendship that had filled some place inside him he hadn't realized was empty.

"No, she hasn't tried, but that doesn't mean it wasn't part of her plan. She was grooming me." It sounded stupid even to his ears.

Taggart's whole body buckled under the force of his laughter. He was red in the face when he came back up. "Kash, man. That is the best. For a hot minute there I thought you were serious. Oh, you got me good. That was hysterical."

He was deeply appreciative of the fact that his face was covered with a mask because he could feel his cheeks heating. It was ridiculous. "Yeah, I thought it was pretty good. You know me, I am an incredibly funny man."

Taggart gave him a wide smile. "I was worried there for a minute. She's an amazing woman. Your girl is kinky and she'll keep you on your toes for the rest of your life. You totally could have done worse. You should thank your momma for picking a wife who's badass enough to be your queen. And Kash, it's time to let go of all that other shit and get the hell back to work."

"What are you talking about?" He feared he knew. Taggart was one of the only men on earth who knew what he'd been working on and how wrong it had gone.

"You've been hiding from that project for years. It wasn't your fault some douchebag decided to kill your project, and it's not your fault that your people died. And this time around, you'll have me working security, and I've heard that queen of yours is pretty smart, too. You've fumbled around for years. It's time to do what you're supposed to do."

"What's that, Taggart?"

Taggart's eyes went to the stage and they lit up as the lights came on. "Well, well, there's some manipulation. I should have wondered why Charlie was so hot to help set up. See, not all plots are bad things. Some end up leading to happy endings. You wanted to know how it would work with two tops, you can find out tonight. Or you can play with your girl and be happy and tell anyone who thinks it's wrong to go straight to hell. It's your choice."

Taggart started walking away. Kash put a hand on his shoulder to stop him. "You didn't answer my question. You said there was something I was supposed to do."

"Yeah, man. Some asshat who's no longer alive thanks to a badass babe set you back. Now it's time to step up again. Time to change the world. The world needs visionaries. You can't be a visionary if all you do with your life is worry about what other people think. Be brave. Be the fucking king, my man."

He glanced up and saw what Taggart had seen. A gorgeous woman wearing a black catsuit that clung to her every curve was walking onto the stage. Walking? That woman didn't merely walk. She strode. She owned the ground she walked on. A black mask covered her face, but there was no question of who she was. Between the long, midnight black hair that nearly reached her waist and those gorgeous lips of hers, he knew his wife. Although he'd never seen her look so confident, so secure in who she was than that moment she walked onto the stage.

Day was done waiting for him. She was here in the dungeon and she would move on.

Charlotte Taggart took the stage as Day looked over the ropes that had been left for her. Charlotte stepped up and looked out over the small crowd. "Thank you all for joining us tonight. We've got a special treat. A friend of ours is here in town for a few days. She's considered an expert at both bondage and suspension play, and she's going to give us a demo tonight. She's going to show you that with proper technique, a tiny Domme can handle her big, burly sub."

Was that what all that rigging was for? There was an elaborate system of ropes and pulleys connected to an apparatus obviously meant to suspend something in midair. It looked like she would be suspending a man there.

"Please welcome Mistress D."

There was clapping and shouts of hellos from the couples around him. They were all shapes and sizes, all colors and ages. There were men with women clinging to them and women with men resting at their feet. Some of the couples were same sex, and then there were the threesomes. Not a one of them seemed uncomfortable.

No one cared here. They were all seeking the same thing—to be happy.

Day took center stage. She didn't need a microphone to be heard. "Thank you so much for having me here tonight. I love rope. I love how it feels in my hands and how creative I can get when using it on a partner. I love suspension play as well because when my lovely sub is trapped in my web and suspended off the ground, he is completely vulnerable to me. There isn't a part of him I can't torture and touch, no ground beneath him to keep him from me. Of course, I prefer submissives who enjoy the sensation, and not all do. As with any play, this should be consensual and kind...even when it's quite cruel."

Because the cruelty was nothing more than a game. Because Day wouldn't want to hurt anyone. She merely sought to give her partners a space to explore their fantasy selves, to be someone different than they were in their daily lives, to give up control and feel free for a few hours.

Why should that be forbidden to him?

He saw what could be their lives flash before him. If he chose to stick to this path, they might very well find some friendship, but she would need this. If he forced her away from this lifestyle altogether, a piece of her would be lost, hollowed out. Or if he allowed her to play quietly, she would eventually find a man who wasn't intimidated, who wouldn't allow some societal norm to take away his choice, to define his masculinity.

What right did anyone have to choose who he would be?

He was the fucking king.

"I want to show you some of my techniques," Day continued. "I know the big Doms of the room have no trouble at all suspending their dainty subs, but I prefer my men with muscle. I want to show you how a smaller top can safely suspend and play with her bigger, heavier sub. Can I get a volunteer?"

Three other men held their hands up, one trying to crowd the stage as though willing to physically block out the other men.

He could sit back and watch. He could think this through and make a rational decision.

"I volunteer. Me. And if any one of you touches my wife, I swear I'll kill you where you stand, is that clear?"

Taggart gave him a big thumbs-up as he moved toward the stage.

Chapter Nine

Day frowned as she watched the man shove his way through the crowd. She hadn't been able to hear exactly what he'd said, but she'd gotten the gist. He was selecting himself and taking the choice from her.

He was about to find out she didn't play that way.

She looked over at Charlotte and Kori, who were standing off to the side, waiting to see if she needed any help. Serena Dean-Miles had been assisting until her big gorgeous brute of a Dom had explained that she had a meeting in the principal's office.

"I want that man taken out of here," she said to Kori. "Do we have bouncers?"

Kori nodded. "Sure we do, but I think they're going to make you take care of this one."

It wasn't her club, but this was her scene and she meant to make things clear. She was in charge and she would select her volunteer. It certainly wouldn't be some mouthy brat of a beast with no manners.

Oh, god, it was Kash.

She turned and there he was, stepping up the stairs. Another man put a hand out. She'd been introduced to Harrison Keen only moments before. She'd thought she would probably use him as her test subject. He was a lovely man, six foot with plenty of muscle. He was perfect to show her techniques off on.

"Hey, the Mistress gets to decide, asshole. Have you ever been in a club in your life?" Harrison was asking.

"Have you ever been thrown into a damn hellhole of a prison because you touched a powerful king's wife? I have this prison. Well, they might have turned it into a tourist attraction, but I can build a new one."

"What the hell are you talking about?" Keen shook his head.

That was her Kash. He could make some of the oddest threats she'd ever heard, and he didn't mind going medieval on people. Was he here to haul her off the stage? When she'd agreed to do the demo, she'd chosen to do it for herself, to have some fun and relax. Not to give Kash the middle finger. She'd thought about it and decided she wouldn't do it for revenge. Only for herself. She'd suspected he wouldn't even realize she was here. She'd thought he would have found some delicate sub and settled in for the night, and seeing them together would finally make her understand that her marriage was over before it had truly begun.

Of course, she might find out her husband was here to treat her like some child who couldn't make a decision for herself.

Kash hoisted himself up onto the stage, his body moving with the elegant grace of a panther. How could he seriously think that a tiny mask could hide his beauty? Anyone who knew him would know the brilliance of his eyes, the straight, square line of his jaw, those sexy broad shoulders.

She put her hands on her hips, completely unwilling to give up her space. He could reject her, but he wasn't taking this from her. She leaned in, making sure she couldn't be heard. "Kash, I'm not hurting anyone. I've got my mask on. No one knows it's me."

"I know it's you. I'll know it if you play with another man, and then I think our cover will be blown because I will kill the man. I have diplomatic immunity, but it could still cause problems and Big Tag would be upset. No one is getting topped by you but me." He loomed over her.

She wanted it more than anything, but how could she believe it? "You'll hate me when it's over."

His jawline softened. "I could never hate you."

She wasn't so sure about that. "I think it's a mistake. We don't have a contract. You were right. I should have sat down with you and explained everything."

"That seems dull. If you had tried that, I would have gotten bored. I am easily distracted these days and it's all my own fault. I've let my mind go to waste. I know it's an easy thing to do when you're in a body this beautiful, but it's been pointed out to me lately that I let the world down when I don't also exercise my gorgeous brain. I will stop playing so many video games and join you in your morning reading."

She shook her head. "Kash, everyone will be watching you."

He frowned. "Of course they will. Have you seen my body? It's stunning. I am a man in his peak physical condition, and more than that, I am a king, blessed with the body of a god. I've been told I have a glow about me."

Who the hell was this? This was the Kash she remembered, the Kash who joked about his own arrogance. The Kash who'd been such a good friend, who'd caught her heart. Still, he couldn't have changed overnight. "I can't go through that again. I'll go up to our room and we can talk about this. It's what we should have done the first time."

He shook his head. "I don't want to talk. I won't understand that way. I have to see a thing, to feel it, to experience it. I might get angry later, but I won't be angry with you. I'll be irritated with myself. I wasn't raised to be comfortable with something like this, but I don't want to take this from you. Let me be your submissive tonight. We're among friends, and none of them will talk. I don't have to be the king. I can be someone else, someone who can give you what you need."

It was all she could ask for, but she still found it hard to trust. "Why are you really doing this? You know I'm not going to have sex with another man."

His lips curled up ever so slightly, and he stared at her with something akin to wonder on his face. "Because I never thought you would look so beautiful, so sexy as a Domme. Because I want to be what you need, even if it's only for an hour or so. I want to pretend we're not fighting and that I can let go for a while."

There was a tension to his shoulders that told her he was still worried about it, a stiffness to the way he held himself that let her know the fight wasn't over. But if they never tried, if she didn't let him bend because she was so afraid he would break, they couldn't possibly know if it could work.

She could go easy on him. After all, this was merely a demo. She wasn't about to lead him into some crazy sexual sadism. She was teaching other club members how to safely secure their subs. She didn't need to make him kiss her feet or to slap his ass.

She turned to the crowd. "Thank you all for your patience and thank you to all who were willing to volunteer. This lovely man will serve as my submissive this evening. Let me start by showing you how I've set up the rigging. Darling, you can kneel in the middle of the stage and wait for your turn."

His eyes tightened as though the command rankled, but he turned and took his place. Kash dropped to his knees and she began.

Four hours later, she walked through the dungeon, her mask off finally. It was funny how when she'd taken it off in the locker room, she'd barely recognized the woman looking back at her from the mirror. That woman seemed to have aged a bit, her glow dulled by regret.

She should have stayed in her room, given him more time.

The club was closed and the space quiet now. She wondered if Kash had changed and gone back to his room. He'd been quiet, too. Contemplative. During the demonstration, he'd been completely compliant, offering her nothing but his obedience, but she hadn't felt any joy from him. There had been no relaxing into the moment. He'd been an automaton, easy to use, but there had been no connection between them.

She stopped at the stage where she'd briefly had some hope. It was gone now, and she had to ask herself some hard questions.

Could she live without this the rest of her life? Could she give it up and truly be happy? Could she be happy without Kash?

"You didn't change."

She stopped, taking a deep breath because he'd startled her. She'd thought she was the last one left downstairs. "I was down in the locker room talking to Kori and her friend Sarah. I didn't have clothes down there. I changed up in my bedroom. I didn't think it would be seemly to walk around the club in nothing but a towel."

"Some people walk around here perfectly naked. I don't think anyone would mind." He was sitting on one of the spanking benches. The whole place had been cleaned by a group of efficient submissives and one or two tops who helped supervise them. Even when they were cleaning, they'd still played with the tops, offering up saucy comments that led to playful swats.

This was a place of happiness, and yet she felt so damn hollow.

"It would feel odd after-hours. There's something magical about the club when it's all lit up, something that lends itself to fantasy. Now it's back to reality." Back to figuring out what to do about their marriage. "Do you want to walk up with me? I can change and make us some tea. We should talk."

He was silent for a moment, his head hanging low. "I didn't like it, Day."

Her heart constricted. There was no anger left inside her, only a deep sense of loss. She moved toward him, putting her hands on his shoulders. "I know. I'm so sorry I put you through it. I shouldn't have. I pushed you. That's why we need to talk."

He groaned and swung his legs, jumping down from the bench. "You people talk too much. I've decided to forgive you for not talking to me about this in the first place, Day. You were right. I hate the talking."

She held her hands up. "All right. I won't mention it again, but we have to make some decisions and soon."

He stood in front of her. "What kind of decisions? Whether or not you leave me? Why do you need this so much?"

How to explain it to him? "It's a part of me."

It was a part of him, too. She was so sure of it, but it couldn't work if he never let himself be.

"I was embarrassed. I didn't like all those people watching me like that."

"Yet you don't mind having five or six sex tapes on the Internet at any given time." The words slipped from her mouth. Maybe she was still angry.

He shrugged as though none of it bothered him at all. Not the sex tapes. Not the million and one articles about his rampaging hormones. The only thing that bothered him was the one thing she needed. "The sex tapes are normal."

Frustration welled inside her. "This is normal, Kash. You use that word like it has meaning. And unless you've got the last name Kardashian or make your living off porn, I assure you having a bunch of sex tapes out in the public domain isn't something most people do."

He stared at her for a moment. "You're jealous."

She shook her head, ready to end this blasted evening. "Believe what you want to believe, Kash. I'm going to bed."

"I was embarrassed," he said quietly.

Which was exactly why this could never work. She stopped. The last week suddenly seemed so much longer than a mere seven days. "Like I said, I won't ask this of you again. I didn't ask this of you tonight. You volunteered."

"Because I was jealous."

She sighed. She'd known it at the time, known better than to allow it to continue. But the idea that he was willing to try had been far too tantalizing. "I told you I wasn't going to have sex."

He leaned against the bench. "Then what's the point? Explain it to me. I've been sitting out here for hours trying to figure it out. I don't want this, Day. I don't want a wall between us, but I can't seem to find a way around it. I tried tonight."

He had. She'd watched him struggle with it, completely unable to come up with a way to connect to him. When she'd tried stroking him, he tensed up. When she'd softened her words, she got the same response. "I know and it didn't work. It's not your fault."

She was fighting against years of ingrained belief that he couldn't be a man and show weakness. Oh, he could show drunkenness or promiscuity and still be a man. He could act like an idiot at a party, but this was forbidden. To show this kind of vulnerability was not something he could do and might never be able to accept about himself.

Was she willing to live without a piece of herself? Could she take that part of her soul and wrap it up and put it in a closet somewhere, never to be taken out again? She wasn't at all sure she could.

"I don't want you unhappy," he said quietly.

She reached for his hand. "And I don't want you unhappy."

Kash brought her hand to his chest, placing it over his heart. "Do I let you go? I don't want that, either. If we divorce, I'll be back in the position of giving up my throne. Maybe that's for the best. Maybe we should think about abolishing the crown altogether."

And give the power over to a group of men who thought women should stay in the house and not make waves? Who argued with her over whether or not girls should be educated? "Why are you questioning this? You're a good king."

"I haven't been good for five years," he said, his tone weary. He let her hand go and started to pace, his body moving with a restless energy. "I shut down after my project blew up. I told myself it was all my fault and I gave up. That's what I was thinking about tonight. I tried to clear my damn head, but I couldn't because I knew everyone was watching me."

Was that really what the problem had been? He'd never shown any issues with their play before, but then they'd always been alone. It was only when Tasha had threatened to out them that he'd flipped out and lost his damn mind.

What would one of the world's most famous men need to relax, to center himself? Would he need one thing for himself? One piece of his life that was utterly private?

"Kash, stop pacing. Sit down, for a moment, please." She eased behind him as he lowered himself to the bench, the expression on his face still and sullen. "Can you give me a few minutes? I want to try something. This isn't sexual play. This isn't me being your top. Just for a few moments, let me be your wife."

"I don't know what that means, Day."

She needed to show him. She eased the leather vest off his shoulders and put her hands there, stroking out and away, as though she could brush the tension from him. "It means whatever we need it to mean. It means that sometimes I need you to stop being the king for a while and let yourself be a man."

"I don't get to be a man. I can be a celebrity. I can be a king, but I can't be just a man."

That was where he was wrong. She started in on his shoulders, finding the pressure points and easing them. And perhaps this was where she'd gone wrong. She hadn't given him true aftercare because the scene had been so stilted and rushed. Day leaned over and kissed the back of his neck. "Who told you that?"

He breathed deeply and she could feel him starting to relax. "My father. He didn't tell me. He told Shray. He told me I could be anything I wanted because I didn't matter, though he didn't use those words, exactly. I got the gist."

She worked her way down one muscled arm and toward his hand. "I doubt he meant it like that. I know he loved you."

"Did he? Perhaps then, but I know I wasn't the one he taught to be king, and I screwed everything up."

"Because of what happened at the lab?"

He nodded slowly, but already she could see how much easier he was breathing, how he'd started to let her lead his body. "I should have been more careful. I should have known."

She massaged down his other arm. Sometimes he was like a giant tiger and he needed to be petted or he roared and roared. He needed to be eased into real intimacy because he distrusted it so. "I should have known someone would steal my car last year. I should have known that walking in that parking garage late at night would be a mistake. It's my fault he stole my purse, too."

Kash moved quickly, turning and catching her hand. His eyes were cold as ice. "Who?"

Another mistake. She leaned over and kissed his forehead. "He knocked me down and took my car. The police found it on the beach two days later. They never caught the man. Was that my fault, Kash?"

He frowned but eased up on her wrist, turning and offering his back again. Such a touchy tiger. "Of course not."

She smoothed her palms down his back, sending a shudder through him. "Should I have not driven again?"

"No. You should not have. Had we been married at the time, I would have escorted you everywhere. Your lovers were quite lazy if they did not. Nor should you have been allowed to walk alone at night, and I will ensure that you have all the bodyguards. Women, of course, fierce women who would slaughter anyone who dares to look at you."

She groaned but wrapped her arms around him. She loved him. So much. This was the Kash she adored. Why couldn't he see that he could be anything he wanted to be when they were alone? "I didn't have a lover at the time. And don't change the subject. What happened wasn't your fault, but how you reacted to it was."

He leaned back into her. "You're not the first person to point that out to me." His head rested back, bringing their cheeks together. "I don't want to think right now. I want you touching me. I want you needing me."

Longing rushed in again. How easy it was to turn the tide. "I always need you."

"Tell me what you want me to do." He whispered the words. "Tell me how to please you. I won't think anymore. I won't think about eyes being on me or my past sins. If you tell me to stop, I can do it now. We're alone."

"Are you ashamed of how I make you feel?"

He sat up straight, letting go of her hands, and she could feel the distance between them. "We should go to bed. You were right. We have to talk about this. We have to find a way to work through our differences because I need you to understand that we can't go on like this."

She wanted so badly to reach out to him, to have not ended the moment, but the thought of something sacred to her being a dirty secret for him wasn't manageable.

"Your Majesties," a deep voice said, and the bodyguard on duty stepped into the space. Wade Rycroft was a huge man with a slow Texas accent. She'd spoken to him a few times, enjoying his stories of living on a ranch with five brothers and more cattle than one could count. Now, though, his usually jovial face was set in deep lines.

Kash stood, stepping in front of her as though the man was going to hurt her somehow. Or perhaps he was embarrassed by the way she was dressed. "Yes?"

"I've been informed there's a problem back in Loa Mali," he explained. "Your mother has been hospitalized. We've got a private jet waiting to take you back."

His hand was suddenly in hers again. Though his face showed no expression at all, he tangled their fingers together. "Of course. We'll be down in a moment."

She followed him silently upstairs, wondering what the next few days would cost her husband.

Chapter Ten

Kash stood outside his mother's room, shaking his head at Simon Weston. "What exactly does that mean?"

Weston looked like he hadn't slept in a couple of days. The strain of taking over the household security, dealing with the press, and trying to find a killer had likely worn on the man. He'd probably thought this would be a cakewalk, a fun job that would be almost like a vacation.

Kash had fooled him.

"It means that I found a vial of the poison in your former guard's room. I had an anonymous tip come in that Rai's new bride had been to Australia recently."

"Her mother lives there."

"When I searched the room he used here in the palace, I found the vial."

Kash shook his head. "No. Absolutely not. Rai hates me because of something I did before he got married. Namely, his wife. He might cut my balls off if he had the chance, but he would never try to kill me. Not like that. He might do some froufrou historical duel thing because he watches far too much Masterpiece Theater, but he would never poison me."

Simon's expression didn't change a bit. "I understand that it seems convenient, but I did have him arrested. At this point he's being detained for possession of an illegal substance, but to hold him further, the police have to be able to announce the real charges. That's why he's not being held at the police station. He's in a guarded room here in the palace. I wanted to get the okay from you to go public so I can have him moved to the city jail."

He wasn't about to have his best friend slammed into a jail cell. "No. There will be no charges. He didn't do this. Have him released immediately and let him know I want to talk to him. If I know Rai, he's got his own theories. And tell him not to punch me. It's been a long day. He can punch me later."

Actually, that wasn't a half bad idea. He was sick and tired of missing his best friend. He should allow Rai to beat the shit out of him, admit to having a tiny penis that couldn't possibly have pleasured Rai's wife, and see if they could move on.

Or he could ask Day what she thought he should do. She might be able to get him out of a beating. He didn't really care what anyone except her thought of his penis. Only Dayita needed to know it was a glorious beast that brought pleasure to its queen.

"Kash, as your acting head of security, I have to tell you that this is a mistake," Weston began.

"No, tossing Rai in jail when it's obvious he's been set up is a mistake," Kash shot back.

"Or we're making the real culprit feel like he's gotten away with something and giving ourselves some time to figure this out."

And allow Rai to hate him even more? "No. I want him released within the hour."

Weston's jaw tightened. "This is a mistake."

"It's my mistake. I won't allow him to rot in jail for something I know he hasn't done. Look in other places. CCTV showed nothing?"

"We believe the Scotch was brought in with the poison already inside."

"Then whoever this is has his conspirators. It's someone familiar with how the household is run, but not familiar with my habits."

Weston seemed to stop, as though that statement brought on some new idea. "Yes, you're right. Your own men would have known that Jamil typically joins you for a drink. They would have known he could potentially ruin everything. I see what you're saying. I have an idea."

"As long as your idea gets Rai out of his hellhole prison." One day Rai would forgive him for deflowering his bride—before she was his bride. But there would be no forgiveness if Rai himself was deflowered by some rough and tumble prison love.

"I'm calling now. And I'll set up a meeting that might be interesting." He pulled out his phone. "And Kash, she's not as bad as your lord chamberlain made her sound. I'm sorry for that. He told me she was on death's door, but the doctors claim she could be back on her feet in a few days if she'll rest. She's responding to the medication well. She's quite the survivor, your mother."

Hanin had always been a drama queen.

Kash shook Weston's hand and nodded to Michael Malone, who was standing guard outside his mother's room. He was relieved that she was better than he'd expected, but he'd seen her asleep in her bed, looking so pale and fragile.

He closed the door behind him. His mother was still sleeping and he didn't want to disturb her. Like Day was sleeping. He'd carried her out of the car and up to his room. He wasn't sure why, but he'd passed her own room by completely, choosing to settle her into his bed.

The two women who meant the most to him were sleeping and he couldn't. He was restless and wanting, and he wasn't even sure what he wanted.

Kash stared out the window of his mother's room, the slow sound of the monitors forming an odd rhythm. Each beep was another second of life, another breath, one more heartbeat. How many beeps would his mother get?

He stared out over the beach where he'd played as a young child, where he and his brother had built sandcastles and then pretended they were monsters destroying grand cities. And their mother would laugh at their antics. His father would usually be at some meeting or other. After Shray was old enough, it had been only Kash and his mother playing on the beach.

He'd run from that life, a pendulum swinging as far from his father's regimented existence as he could. As though he had to choose. The king or the playboy. Nothing else. Nothing in between. No compromises. He had to be a king like his father or a rogue so full of himself he never, ever cared about criticism.

Did he have to be one or the other, or could he find his own path, one informed by his father's love but free of his prejudices? One where he could be both king and man. Both sovereign and husband.

"What do you see when you look out there, son?"

He turned and moved to her bed, sinking to one knee in front of her. "Should I call the doctor?"

She shook her head. "No, I'm fine. I'm feeling better. I caught a terrible cold. It settled into my chest, but I'm breathing better now."

And any secondary infection would be made worse by the cancer. She would be weak and unable to fight off something Kash could easily handle.

"What do you see? While you've been gone, I've been thinking so much about your childhood. I wonder how you see it when you look back. Everyone asks you questions. I try not to bother you with them because I know how often you're surrounded by reporters and advisors and politicians, but I need to know. I worry we don't see the same things."

He glanced back toward the window. What did he see? He saw sand and sun and rolling waves. He saw ghosts. "I see the beach where I played with Shray when I was young. I see the beach where you would take me to play long after Father took Shray under his wing to teach him."

His mother frowned. "To teach him?"

"To be king. When Shray was a teenager, Father told him he couldn't play with me at the beach anymore. He had to be better than me because he was going to be king. Father never came to the beach. He never played."

His mother's eyes softened, a sheen of tears forming. "Oh, my darling, how can you say that? Your father played with you many times when you were young. Look through the pictures I keep. Go and get them. They're in a box in the bottom of the dresser."

He started to argue with her, that she needed rest, but he could see how desperate she was so he strode to her dresser like a dutiful son. He needed to smile and tell her everything was all right because she was sick and his own misery would only bring more to her. He needed to agree that his childhood was beautiful and everything was perfect.

He'd seen the pictures of his childhood. They were mostly taken by state photographers and again, they'd been interested in Shray. Kash hadn't minded because the thought of sitting still had been mind-numbing at the time. He opened the bottom drawer and found a metal box. He pulled it out and turned back to his mother.

He rushed back because she was struggling to sit up. "Mother, stop."

She frowned up at him. "I will stop when I am dead, and as that might be soon, you will leave me to make the decisions. There's a proper queen now. I can become the old bat who says and does whatever she likes. You see, you thought I brought in Dayita for you, but it was really for me. Where is she?"

"She was exhausted. She didn't sleep at all on the plane. I put her in bed about an hour ago." Likely because she was worried about everything, because he was giving her hell and causing her to question their marriage because he couldn't bring himself to bend even a little.

Are you ashamed of how I make you feel?

He could still hear the question, hear the small tremor in her voice. Day was always so steady, so strong, and yet in that moment, she'd sounded small.

He'd made her small.

His mother shifted on the bed, leaving a space for him. "Good, she needs her rest. Now come and let me show you. It's easy to forget, you know."

He sat down next to her. "Forget what?"

"That the truth of our lives changes given our perceptions. That time and experience can make things hazy. You weren't in a good place with your father when he died. I think that colored everything about your relationship with him. I can't let that go on, Kashmir."

He huffed, forgetting for a moment that he'd promised to be good. "So you think some photos you kept will change my perception of my childhood?"

"This isn't my box, love. This was your father's. This was precious to him."

Kash looked down at the rather plain metal box. It was the kind of thing people kept important papers in, sturdy and weatherproof. It had a piece of tape on the top with a single word written in neat, masculine script.

Kashmir.

He touched the box. "Why would he have a box with my name on it?"

"Open it and find out," she urged. "After he died, I found both of your boxes, yours and Shray's. For a long time it was hard for me to think about Shray's, but recently, I've enjoyed going through it and remembering how close our family was. This is what you've forgotten, what you have to remember before you have children of your own. He loved you."

He hated the fine tremble to his hand as he opened the box.

Inside he found a mass of photos, but not the kind taken by the press. These were personal pictures taken by an amateur hand, pictures of himself and Shray smiling in the surf, their faces splashed with the waves, of himself as a giggling baby held in his mother's arms, of his toddler self hiding beneath his father's ornate desk. In that photo he was grinning ear to ear and reaching up to whoever was taking the photo. This wasn't the picture of a child afraid to interrupt his father's work. This child knew he was the center of the world.

He took a deep breath, the sweetness of his childhood washing over him. Had he forgotten? He'd run through the palace like a little monster, and eventually he would be scooped up in strong arms and tossed into the air, giggling and begging for more.

He could feel it, feel how he'd flown up, the thrill rushing through him. He'd put his arms out and tried to fly, and never once had he thought about falling because his father was there to catch him.

His father. He would scoop him up and take him to the kitchens for coconut ice cream.

"Why did he stop coming to the beach with us? Why did he take Shray and forget about me?" Though it was easy to see he hadn't really. While the pictures seemed to stop around the time he was thirteen or fourteen, they were replaced with newspaper articles and report cards. There was a birthday card Kash had made tucked inside.

His mother's hand came out, so frail and delicate on his own. "When you were almost fourteen, your father was diagnosed with Parkinson's disease. He was taking some medication that made it unwise for him to spend too much time in the sun."

Kash felt like the world had shifted. "What? Father had Parkinson's?"

His mother nodded. "Yes. In the beginning he worried he would die very soon or be incapacitated. He needed to get Shray ready. He didn't want you to worry. He wanted you to enjoy your childhood. He always told me that he was lucky you were his second son and not his first."

"Because he thought I would be a terrible king."

"No, because you were so smart, so brilliant when it came to science. He was so proud of you. He said a mind like yours shouldn't be wasted on politics. He said a mind like yours could change the world, and that was so much more important than being a king." Her hand gripped his, holding him. "He was worried during those years. He thought if the parliament found out about his diagnosis, they might seek to abolish the monarchy on the grounds that his heirs were too young. I remember he would remind himself that a king must be strong."

He couldn't help it a moment longer. The world was a blurry place and yet he finally understood. His father hadn't been talking about him. Or perhaps at times he had been. Perhaps it didn't matter that his father had been a king. All that had mattered was he'd been an obnoxious teen, and they would have clashed no matter what.

What mattered was that his father had loved him, that his father had believed in him, that his father had been more than a king. He'd been a man.

A man with flaws and fears.

A man with love and regrets.

A man who could love his wife and children and make mistakes. He could follow in his father's footsteps and have a life filled with loved ones, with a woman who knew him as more than a king. A woman who loved him because he was her husband.

And maybe, just maybe, if Kash was brave enough, he could be a man who changed the world.

He leaned into his mother, holding her gently. "I'm sorry for staying away for so long. I'm sorry I didn't remember."

"He wouldn't let you see. I argued that he should tell you," she whispered. "But he wanted you to have as normal a life as you could. He saw how it aged your brother. He couldn't do it to you. And I was so lost after he died that I kept his secrets. You should know that I left you a letter detailing all of this in case I died. You have to know that the illness might be hereditary, though the likelihood is still low. You'll have to watch your health carefully as you get older. Your father was significantly older than me. He was sixty when he was diagnosed."

"Hush, we don't have to talk about that now." He wasn't going to worry about something that might or might not happen. He needed to focus on the now. Every family had something in their medical histories to worry about.

His mother looked up at him. "I don't want us to end the same way, with you angry with me. I made these mistakes, but I love you. I love you and I ask you to forgive me."

He shook his head. "There is nothing to forgive. Nothing, Mother. I love you. And things will be different now because I love my wife. I think I've always loved her but I was afraid to show it. I'm not going to be afraid anymore."

He made the choices. And if anyone found out that he liked to submit to his gorgeous, dominant wife, well, they could go to hell because they didn't understand what a woman like Day could do to a man.

No one got a say in his marriage except him and his wife.

He held his mother, the truth of his life sinking in and finally filling a place that had seemed hollow. "I don't want you to die. I command that you not die."

His mother smiled up at him. "Give me something to live for. You know I'll hold on for a grandchild."

He sighed.

"What is it?"

"I've screwed up so much with Day, I fear she won't forgive me, Mother."

Her hand slid over his. "Tell me."

He grimaced. "Much of it is sexual, Mother."

"Well, of course it is. It's you. You know, Kashmir, the one thing I thought you would get right was the sex stuff."

"Well, didn't I prove you wrong?" Perhaps his mother could help. She'd already given him the perfect woman. Now it was up to him to figure out how to keep her. "I think I've messed up with Day."

"Of course you have. You're a man. You can't help yourself. Tell me what's going on."

According to Day, it wasn't like she didn't already know. He was about to tell her everything when there was a loud shout from the hallway.

Startled, he slid from the bed. "Wait here, Mother. I'll be right back."

"Kash, you fucking bastard!"

That was a familiar voice. Weston had gotten Rai out quickly. Kash stepped out into the hallway where Rai was straining against the much larger Boomer. It was good to see Rai couldn't do everything. His best friend often seemed far too competent to be believed, too fit and perfect. Now he looked silly because Mr. Boomer had put a hand on his head and easily held him at arm's length.

"Uh, he wanted to go in without an appointment," Boomer said. If holding back the other man was any strain on him at all, it didn't show. "Si told me no one sees the queen momma without an appointment. Now, he didn't leave me an appointment book or anything, so I think what he was trying to tell me was that the queen momma needs her sleep and no one should see her except her son. I don't think he's her son."

While he found Mr. Boomer quite charming, he didn't want to piss off Rai any further. "It's fine. Please let him go so we can handle this here and now. And, Mr. Boomer, if he does hit me, let him. Unless he goes for my face. My face really belongs to the whole country, so you need to protect that."

Boomer moved his hand and Rai nearly fell to his knees.

"Damn you, Kash," he began.

"I would have thought letting you out of jail because I know, despite all evidence, that you would never harm me might put you in a better mood."

Rai shook his head. "Not mad at you. Need to tell you. It was never you he was after. I figured it all out a few minutes ago. It's Hanin. He wants to kill Day. He was always after Day."

Fear flashed through Kash and he took off running for his room.

Nothing mattered if Day wasn't alive. Nothing at all.

* * * *

Day came awake to the sound of a door creaking open. She sat up, her head still cloudy from sleep. She glanced at the clock, the digital light shining, and realized her head was actually cloudy from lack of sleep. She remembered falling asleep in the car after the plane had landed. That had been a little over an hour and a half before.

She glanced around and realized she wasn't in her room. Her suite was done up in light, airy colors, and this place was a darkened tomb.

Kash's room. Had he brought her here? She suspected so.

She yawned and forced her body to move. Something was going on in the outer room of the suite.

She sat straight up in bed as her brain started to function, remembering exactly why they'd made that ridiculously long flight.

Her mother-in-law. Her sweet, lovely mother-in-law had taken a bad turn and they'd needed to get home in time to potentially say good-bye to her.

Day's heart constricted. How would Kash handle losing his mother? He tended to shut down when things got too emotional. He'd been alone for so long and here she was sleeping while he was facing one of the hardest moments of his life.

Some partner she'd turned out to be.

She scrambled to get out of bed. How far was it to the hospital?

She moved to the doors that led to the outer rooms of the suite, opening them and finding the cause of the noise she'd heard previously. A group of neatly dressed servants were busy setting breakfast up on the table in the living area. It was the table where she and Kash typically shared their morning. Michael Malone stood inside the door, dressed in an all-black suit, an earpiece in his left ear. He nodded her way.

So she had her guard back. They'd been much more subtle at Sanctum. She'd barely seen them, though she'd known they were there. Now that she was home, there would always be a guard on her door.

How much longer would she be here at the palace? How much longer would she have this family?

"Coffee, Your Majesty?" one of the maids asked.

Day sought her name. She was trying to learn them all because they were important to the family and needed to know they weren't mere cogs in the wheel. "Elissa, yes, please, but could you put it in a cup to go? I need to get to the hospital as quickly as possible."

"Why would you need to go to the hospital?" The lord chamberlain walked into the room, looking resplendent in his three-piece suit. "Is your majesty ill?"

She shook her head because all the servants had stopped as though the thought of her being sick was beyond what they could handle. "No. I'm fine. I need to go and see the queen mother. I assume that's where my husband is. I need to go and be with him. Can someone update me on how she's doing?"

Hanin shook his head, his eyes on her. "Now, now, Your Majesty. I can update you. You know how I adore the queen mother. I've worked for her and her family all of my life. I apparently overreacted. I was in a panic when I contacted the Americans to bring his majesty home to see her. I'm so sorry. At the time I truly thought she could die on us."

"And now?"

He moved across the room, picking up the silver server and pouring her coffee with an expert hand. "She's recovering in her room. Queen Yasmine is one of the strongest women I know. It's from her breeding, you know. She comes from a good family. That's important."

Relief spilled through her. The thought of losing Yasmine had nearly crushed her, and what it would have done to Kash... She didn't want to think on it. "I'm glad she's all right. Is my husband with her?"

"Of course." Hanin brought the delicate china cup to her.

"Have something to eat, Your Majesty. When I saw them last, they were having a lovely conversation. There's nothing at all for you to worry about. After you've had some fortification, I'll take you down to her room myself."

Her hands were shaking. How long had it been since she'd eaten? She walked over to the table and set the coffee cup and its saucer down. Her stomach was a little touchy. Perhaps pouring acidic coffee on it first thing wasn't the best play.

"Elissa, do we have any tea? I think coffee might upset my stomach today. And perhaps some toast. All this looks lovely, but I need something simple. It was a long flight and I think all the stress is wearing on me."

Elissa nodded. "Of course, Your Majesty. The lord chamberlain didn't order tea for you, but I can pop down to the kitchen and be back in no time at all."

"Thank you." She glanced up to see Hanin frowning. Naturally she'd upset him. The lord chamberlain seemed to take offense easily. Kash had talked about pensioning the older man off when his mother was no longer with them, and Day was starting to agree with him. It was obvious the man had deep ties to Yasmine, but he didn't seem to like the younger royals much. When the time came, she intended to ask Chapal's husband, Ben, to take the role. He would have the palace running in a proper and modern fashion. Until then, she needed to get along with Hanin. "Thank you so much for the update and for this lovely spread. It's all beautiful, but it's too much for me this morning. I'll have a spot of tea and go join my husband."

They'd barely talked on the plane. Kash had sat in his seat, a beer in one hand, while he'd stared out at the night sky even as it had turned into day. She'd tried to sleep, but couldn't stop thinking about what had happened.

Was he ashamed? She couldn't overcome shame. She could handle him being shy, needing to go slow. She couldn't handle being his dirty secret.

"Your Majesty?"

She glanced up and Hanin was still standing in the room. The other servants had all gone, but he had stayed behind. "Yes?"

He glanced back to where Malone stood. "Might I speak to you privately, Your Majesty? It's palace business and I'm afraid it can't wait."

She couldn't think of what he needed from her that her guard couldn't hear, but she wasn't going to argue with him. He ran the palace and there were certainly plenty of secrets to be kept. She nodded. With her mother-in-law out of commission, she was in charge. "Of course. Mr. Malone, would you mind?"

"I'll be right outside. I'll knock when Elissa gets back and after you've eaten, I'll escort you to Queen Yasmine. She asked about you earlier." He stepped out and closed the door behind him.

"Are you sure you won't have some coffee? I can get you some cream and sugar, if you like," Hanin said, his hand on the ornate silver pot.

She shook her head. Tea sounded so much better. "No, but thank you."

"You don't mind if I pour some for myself, do you?" He was already reaching out for another cup.

"Feel free. Now, what is the problem, Hanin?"

He was silent while he poured the steaming hot coffee. When he turned around there was a frown on his face. "The problem is one of perception. I'm worried that when certain stories come out, and they will eventually, your past will bring down the royal family."

She stilled because the whole room seemed to chill. "What are you talking about?"

"Do you think Kashmir's whore of a girlfriend is the only one who knows about your past?" Hanin asked, his tone dark and nasty. "I have been the queen's right hand for years. I helped her investigate you."

"And I assume you disapproved."

"Of course I did. You're common. Worse than that, you're not even a proper female. You argue with your betters."

"My betters being men, I suppose." Oh, her mother-in-law was going to be disappointed, but Hanin was leaving the palace today. He would not be allowed back, but she was interested in seeing how far he would go.

"I'm sick of this generation of women not knowing their place. The queen has always known. She didn't argue with her husband or her son, and her son is an idiot."

"I assure you the queen had control. She might have done it in a sneaky way, but Queen Yasmine did not sit back and allow the men around her to run things. She simply didn't take credit for her work. My generation doesn't have to dissemble." She stood up. Maybe she wasn't so curious. She was ready to go and be with her family.

She was ready to start the fight for Kash's heart because he was worth it, and she needed to tell him that. In plain English. Hanin was right about one thing. Her husband could be an idiot at times. Especially when it came to his own emotions.

"Your generation will bring down this monarchy with your disgusting need to expose yourselves, your every emotion, your wants and needs," Hanin continued. "No one cares about them. Society can't work when everyone is an individual. Can't you see that? We need the crown and the crown needs true royalty."

She held up a hand. "You're dismissed, Hanin. I don't want to see you here again."

He gripped the coffee cup like it was a lifeline. "You can't do that. You can't fire me."

"I can and I did. My husband will back me up, and once my mother-in-law has heard how you've spoken to me, she'll be on my side as well."

"The queen won't believe you."

Day gestured up to the camera that covered the living room. "She'll see you. She might not hear things, but there's no doubt you're being less than gracious right now."

His mouth turned up in a nasty smirk. "Oh, but I cut that camera out of the feed. With all the new security, it was easy to explain that the king wanted more privacy. No one questioned it. So we really are alone right now, dear, and I truly wish you'd tried the coffee."

That chill she'd felt before went positively arctic as Day glanced down at her own cup. "You poisoned the Scotch."

"I was watching the ballroom and I saw when Tasha hauled Kashmir off. I saw when you strode in and made a spectacle of yourself. I'd been watching for days and knew you liked to play the man. I knew you had a glass of Scotch with the king. So when he sent you up, I sent up Jamil with the special Scotch I'd had prepared. I knew you would get there first, and like the weak slut you are, you would need that drink. You almost took it. I almost had you."

She'd come so close to falling into that trap. "You could have killed Kash."

"It was a risk I was willing to take, but I planned to rush in and save him. Then we could have found a proper bride." He stared down at the cup in his hand. "I didn't know Jamil was a thief."

"He wasn't a thief. He was the king's friend." She started to back up, trying to put some distance between her and the man who'd tried to murder her only a week before.

"The king must be taught that he is above us all. He can't be friends with the help. He must be the king, exalted and revered. That's what we're missing. I believe a bride, a pure royal bride, could teach him this. Or at least she could have his child and we could start over again."

How long had Hanin been planning this? The idea chilled Day to the bone. "You advised the queen to arrange the marriage."

"Yes, but then she wouldn't listen to me when it came to selecting a bride. She'd found those letters you sent and decided it had to be you. She couldn't see you for the whore you are. Even after she knew about your sexual perversions, she couldn't understand that you were wrong."

Because the queen mother understood that a person was complex and that sexual differences didn't mean anything as long as a man and woman were in love.

She loved Kash. They could work it out. They just had to believe they could. They could get through anything as long as they held on to each other and promised to never let go. That was how a couple in love got through life. They simply held on.

"I'm going to leave now, Hanin. You should probably run." Would Malone hear her if she shouted out? The door was thick and the walls well insulated. How many steps before she could put a hand on the door and throw it open? Her guard would be there.

She backed up, slowly, unwilling to take her eyes off the snake in the room.

That snake slowly reached into his pocket and pulled out a gun. It was a shiny revolver. "Run? Why would I run? This is my home.

It has been for as long as I can remember. Don't move another inch, Your Majesty, or I'll be forced to put a bullet in you. I don't want to. It could make for a much more salacious story for the tabloids."

She froze because there was nowhere to duck, nothing to hide behind unless she could get to the entryway. There were two columns on either side of the door that might offer her some protection. "I'm not going to drink your poison, Hanin. You're crazy if you think I'm going to do your work for you."

"So you're willing to let me kill Elissa when she returns? When that door opens, I intend to shoot whoever is standing there. I'll know my game is up. I'll shoot her and then you. I'm willing to die for my cause. I've served this crown with everything I have. I'll give my life to protect it. I will not allow a whore queen to take it all away from me."

He also wasn't as strong as he thought he was. Already she could see his hand shaking. Elissa would be back any moment, but she couldn't let that fact push her into obedience. She didn't want Elissa to get shot, but she wasn't about to help her would-be murderer.

Of course, he couldn't know that. He was crazy. He could likely be led to believe any number of things.

"You'll have to bring it to me. Bring me the cup you made for yourself."

He stared at her, his eyes narrowed. "Drink the one I made for you. They'll both work. It's right there. Hurry. Elissa isn't slow. She's good at her job. She'll hurry because she wants to please her queen. She's young and can't see you for what you truly are."

Which apparently was a whore. Very original of him. "I'm too scared. What if you shoot me? I can't. I can't think."

Better to let him believe she was far more scared than she was. It was odd, but the fear seemed to be in the background, as though she'd moved into survival mode and nothing else mattered.

Unless Kash was the one who walked through that door. If Kash took the bullet, she would want her own. She would want to curl up and go wherever he was. He would need her.

Hanin stood there, his hands starting to shake, and she wondered how much of Hanin was really there. "You ruined everything. Everything."

The cup in his left hand started to rattle and she saw her chance. She sprinted for the door. He might shoot her, but it was better to have the chance. The minute that shot rang out, Malone would come in.

Day screamed as she dove for the pillar.

The door blasted open and she caught sight of the one thing she hadn't wanted to see. Kash rushed in, his big body a massive target. He caught her in his arms and shoved her behind him. Rai was there along with Malone, all three men running into the room.

"Stand down!" Malone ordered.

"Hanin, you're caught," Rai explained. "Put the gun down."

The gun clattered to the floor. "It wasn't loaded. I couldn't risk hurting the king."

Kash still stood in front of her. "But you would kill my queen?"

The cup and saucer rattled, the sound jarring. Day had to peek around her husband to get a look at Hanin.

Hanin's eyes were wild as he spoke. "She's unfit to be queen. She isn't royal."

"She's my wife. She's royal now," Kash returned.

"And when they all find out what she does?" Hanin spewed his bile. "How she dominates men? Does she do these things to you, Your Majesty? Is that how she caught you? You're in her web."

Day's stomach tightened. It was the one thing Kash couldn't handle. Someone knowing.

Rai and Malone had heard that accusation. It could kill Kash.

"Let her go," Hanin insisted. "No one will follow her, Your Majesty."

"That's where you're wrong," Kash replied. "She already has one devoted servant. She has me. I'll see you hanged for this."

"No need." A hollow look hit Hanin's face. "This isn't my home anymore. This isn't my world anymore."

He brought the cup to his lips.

Day started to yell out, but Kash turned and caught her, his arms going around her. Even as he started to haul her out the door, she could see Hanin falling.

Kash rushed her out, taking her from the sight. He strode to her room, opening the doors and charging in. He turned briefly and yelled down the hall at his guard. "If that wasn't poison he drank, Rai, let me know so I can kill him myself."

"He's quite dead, Kash," Rai replied as he followed. "Malone is calling it in and staying with the body. Who could have guessed snails would be so poisonous? It's how I figured out it was him. He has a cousin who works at a lab in Western Australia."

Kash set her down. "And how did you know it was Day he wanted to kill and not me?"

"Because I heard him talk about how she would ruin the crown," Rai replied. "I thought it was idle gossip until I put together he was the one who had poisoned the Scotch. He was in the booth with me that night. He watched you send her away. We all heard that conversation."

Then the guards knew? Her hands were shaking.

Rai reached for one of them, pulling it up. "Your Majesty, you should know that the guards all take an oath of silence when it comes to the family we protect. You should also know that I've long believed Kashmir needed a woman who could spank his ass silly, and I'm glad to hear he found one. Not a one of my men sees you as anything less than the queen and Kashmir as anything but one incredibly lucky man. Well, they do worry that our lovely and intelligent queen has been strapped with such an ignorant ass for her husband."

Kash was standing beside her, looking down at her hand. "Thank you, Rai. Thank you for wanting to save her."

Rai kissed her hand and then let it go, turning back to Kash. "Of course I wanted to save her. You, on the other hand, I would have let drink all the snail venom in the world. I hate you."

Kash was grinning. "But you'll come back to your job."

Rai was already moving for the door. "Yes. I'll return to work but only because I love my wife and this pays better than anywhere else."

"Rai, I'm glad to have you home."

He stopped at the door, not looking back. "And I'm glad to have a friend who believed in me even when all the evidence was against me. Even when I behaved like an ass. Stay here. I'll post a guard on the door, but I don't think we can keep this out of the press. I'll try, but two bodies in a week is a lot to cover up."

The door closed behind him and Kash wrapped his arms around her. He hugged her close. "I'm so sorry."

She held on to him and hoped this wasn't the end.

Chapter Eleven

Hours and hours later, Day closed the door to her room with the full knowledge that none of this was over. Hanin was dead, but there was still such distance between her and Kash. Who would have guessed that the attempt on her life would have been the highlight of her day? Now she had to sit down with Kash and figure out what to do with the rest of their lives, with their marriage.

She looked back into the room. He was sitting on the couch in her sitting area, staring into space. Her bed was not more than ten feet away. How lovely would it be to sink into her comfy mattress and drift off to sleep?

Perhaps they should put this whole conversation off. The day had been tiring. "I think I should go to bed."

He didn't look her way. "No. We should talk. We can talk here. There are no cameras. We can't go back to my room. They're still working in there. In the morning the press will be swarming and we'll have to admit to everything. We'll also have to announce that Mother is ill. Tomorrow will be a long day."

"All the more reason to get some sleep." And to put off the moment where they would have to decide whether to even try to make this marriage work.

"Day, I can't go on like this. I want this over and done with tonight. I want to walk into that press conference tomorrow knowing I don't have anything further to announce. I want my world peaceful again."

Wow. That felt like a kick in the gut. One little demo and an assassination attempt and he was ready to blow up the marriage. Still, he was the one who'd been forced into it. She couldn't hold him to a marriage he hadn't truly wanted in the first place. "I understand."

It was going to be a much longer night than she'd planned. They would have to draft a statement and figure out how to deal with the constitutional crisis dissolving their marriage would trigger, but perhaps it was for the best. She wasn't sure she could stay married to him if they weren't going to try to have an honest marriage.

She was in love with him.

"I don't think you do understand, and that's what we need to talk about," Kash replied. "I've figured out what went wrong with the demonstration the other night at Sanctum. We can't go to clubs. It doesn't feel right. I'm not an exhibitionist. At least I'm not now."

What was he talking about? "Kashmir, I'm sorry you didn't enjoy the demonstration. I wish you had, but at least we know."

He stood up, gracefully moving toward her. He'd been stiff for hours and still seemed anxious. He shrugged out of his jacket and kicked off the loafers he'd been wearing, getting more comfortable. "Yes, we know that I don't like the thought of other people seeing me like that, but I have some reasons why I feel that way, why I might never be comfortable sharing that. I know there's nothing shameful about it, but I'm not there yet. I might never get there. I have to know if you need the crowd."

She wasn't sure what he was talking about. "The crowd?"

He moved to her closet, disappearing briefly inside. Kash walked out carrying a small leather bag and she winced.

Her kit. Not that it was actually her kit. That was packed away in the deep recess of a storage closet, along with most of her belongings from before her marriage. The brown leather satchel was the one Kori had put together for her back in Dallas. It was nothing more than a few hanks of jute rope, a paddle, some binder clips, and impact toys.

He walked over to her four-poster bed, setting the bag down. "Yes, the crowd. Do you require the crowd to fill your needs or is this something you'll be happy doing alone with me?"

Hope lit inside her, a tiny flame praying to be stoked. "Kash, what are you saying? I need you to be plain."

He turned to her, the look on his face so serious. "I know I didn't please you that night. I thought about it all the way home, trying to find some excuse. There isn't one. There's merely a preference. Let me try again. Let me try while no one is watching. Everyone watches me. Every minute of the day. I play into it. I use it to my advantage. But while I was with you that night, I hated that other people were watching. For the first time in my life, I truly needed something that was private, something that belongs only to me."

"I don't need the crowd. I don't need it at all." She needed him. Only him. If he could need her, that would be all the fulfillment she would require. He was telling her he was willing to try. Another need rose, hard and fast and nearly volcanic. She'd tamped it down before and maybe for the same reasons. Maybe because she was evolving. "Take off your clothes, Kash. I want to see you naked. No one's here except the guards, and they won't leave their stations. It's you and me and I want to play."

"Ah, there she is. Do you know when you lower your voice like that, I can feel it in my cock, Day?" His fingers were on the buckle of his belt, working it free. He shoved his slacks and boxers off his hips, freeing his cock. His shirt hit the floor an instant later.

His cock obviously liked her Domme voice. It stood tall and proud, almost coming up to his navel. He didn't have any problems with exhibitionism now. A thrill sparked along her spine. There was no playing now. No candy coating. No gentle easing in. He knew what she wanted. He knew she was the top and he'd done as she'd asked. The question now was how far could she push him? How much control could she get him to give into her hands?

"Was it only the crowd you didn't like, Kashmir?"

He stilled as she moved around him. "Yes. It made it hard for me to relax. It's been a rough time. I need you to help me be out of my head for a while. I want to be alone with you. I don't want to share you."

Given how often he'd shared lovers, she was taking that as a win. "There's no sharing now. You're all mine and I want complete and total submission from you. Can you give me that?"

"I don't know. I have to figure out what I can and can't give," he said, his eyes down.

She could handle that. That was exactly the point. "All you have to do is tell me no. If you say no, I stop everything and we go back to the start and there are no recriminations. I want to try this with you but I need you to understand that if it doesn't work, I'll choose you."

His eyes were suddenly on hers. "You would give this up?"

She'd thought about it for a long time. What was the scale on this question? How did it balance out? She knew what Kash's issues were and they ran deep, childhood deep. They were ingrained in his personality. Was she willing to give him up over what was only one piece of their relationship? She'd lost him to his responsibilities before. Could she do it again?

"I would give this up if you need me to. If this is a choice between you and having this in my life, I'll choose you."

His shoulders relaxed, that tense look around his eyes softening in an instant. His hand came out, brushing against her cheek. "I will never ask you to, love. I'm sorry I acted the way I did. If I can't give you what you need, we'll make accommodations, but I think you'll find I can learn over time."

"You haven't learned much if you think this is how you greet your Mistress." She gave him her best stare, the one that was sure to have every sub in a mile radius dropping to his or her knees.

Kash's lips turned up and he gracefully fell to the floor. "Not Mistress. I don't like the term."

So he was already attempting to push her buttons. "You think this is about you then?"

"I know this is about me." Confidence rolled off him. "I control this. This might be the one thing in the world I truly control. Everything is responsibility and politics, and those offer only the illusions of control. It's what I thought about while I was hanging in suspension that night. I thought about the fact that my life is a series of choices that are forced on me. This isn't forced. This is offered. I can take it or leave it and the world won't come to an end. No one goes hungry because I made this choice."

It was precisely why so many powerful men and women chose this way to play. They did it because their actions affected so many in the real world. They could choose to be a bit selfish for a few hours, to let go and allow themselves to relax and hide away for a while. To let that part of them that needed to be soft and submissive have some sway.

She opened the kit and picked up the crop Kori had purchased at her behest. It was a nice one, flexible with a soft leather tip. She could control it, her strength and the angle of impact determining how much pain she inflicted. Of course, it could also be a tool. She slapped it against her hand, bringing Kash's eyes up to hers.

"Spread your knees wide." She let the soft tip of the crop find his belly, running it up and over his muscled abs and perfect chest, all the way up to his chiseled chin. "Spine straight. Now tell me what you think you should call me, if not Mistress. This is my fantasy, too. If you want to spend some time being worshipped and adored, then I want to feel powerful. Needed. I want to spend a few hours being someone more than merely Dayita."

"You are always powerful," he whispered. "Always. You don't need a crown on your head to be a queen. That's who you are. You are my Queen and I do want to worship you. Show me how powerful you are, Your Majesty. Show this lowly servant what a queen is."

Every word that dripped from his mouth seemed to race through her veins, lifting her up and taking her higher. She looked down at her "lowly" servant, taking in every inch of his gorgeous flesh. She took her time, inspecting him carefully. She let her hands run through his raven dark hair. He kept it long and it had a natural wave to it. She tugged on it, pulling it to the point that he would feel the sizzle along his scalp. A shudder went through him and she watched his cock twitch.

Yes, that was what she wanted to see.

"Did you like it when I tied you up?"

His head was back, giving over to her hold. His eyes were on hers, as though he couldn't look anywhere but exactly where she wanted him. "Yes, but I couldn't relax because everyone was watching me."

She should have thought of that, should have realized that Kash tended to overcompensate for his flaws, for his fears. He would smile and play the fool in the press because he didn't think there was a way out. Every lover he'd taken before had been with him for the purpose of being seen. This was a chance to have something secret, something that belonged only to the two of them.

"Then I should reward you for being such a good servant. You did so well. You let me show our friends exactly the techniques I wanted to show them. I thank you for that and I honor you."

"What would you have done if I didn't mind being seen like that?" Kash asked.

"Like I've told you, I didn't have sex with most of the people I topped."

"But if I had merely been a submissive coming to the glorious Mistress Day, if I had been some random man who needed a bit of play, who let you tie me up and suspend me off the ground, what would you have done?"

He wanted to be different. Of course, he was, but he needed the words. He wanted some dirty, filthy fantasy? She could give him that.

"If you had walked into my dungeon, all of my rules would have flown out the door. I would have looked at you and known that you were everything I had been waiting for. I would have tied you up. I would have used my ropes to bind your arms and legs. They would cling to your body and you would feel them as an extension of myself, of my will. You would feel me all around you." She sighed and moved on, letting the crop trace the line of his spine as she continued. "You would be wound up tight and then I would suspend you. You wouldn't be able to fight me or to do anything at all but take what I give you. I can give you pleasure or pain and it's all my choice. You would swing in my trap, your body both heavy and light at the same time. You would be secure. You would know I would never, ever let anything harm you, that I would work my hardest to ensure your safety so you could enjoy the ride. Did I say I would wrap my rope everywhere? Because there would be one place I left untouched, open and vulnerable." She completed her circle, moving in front of him again. "Can you guess which part of you I would have left out? Which delicious piece would be dangling like ripe fruit for me to enjoy? Can you show me?"

His body had tightened, but not in a bad way. He reached down and gripped his own dick, stroking himself with a rough hand. "This part."

She slapped the tip of the crop over his hand, a gentle sting which had him releasing himself. "No touching what belongs to me. You're my servant and that means your cock is mine, a treasure of the royals like my crown or my scepter. You wouldn't like what happens to thieves."

Or he would, because it would lead to an insanely pleasurable round of torture.

The hint of a smile crossed his face before he schooled himself again. "No, Your Majesty. I wouldn't want to find out what happens to thieves. I apologize. Please continue your story. It was just getting good."

"I would suspend you so you were looking down, so you could see me moving underneath you. Did you like my rig?"

"It was perfect. I did love how you used science and engineering to such kinky ends. Our professors at Oxford would approve."

Likely not, but she had used their methods. "With my machine, I can move you easily up or down, and I would move you into the perfect position where I could touch your cock. Like I said, it's ripe fruit and I would pick it. You would be utterly helpless while I played with your cock."

She reached down, gripping him as he'd touched himself. Kash liked it rough. A growl went through him, but he managed to stay in his position. She eased down on her knees in front of him, holding that magnificent cock in her hand.

"You're going to kill me," he whispered, his jaw tight.

No. Just torture him a bit. "It's my right to play with you however I see fit. Rigging you up without someone around to help me if something went wrong would be unwise and would put my precious servant in potential danger, so I can't do that tonight. But I can give you a little taste of what it would have been like. Would you like that, my servant?"

"I am here to do her majesty's bidding," he replied, his voice thick.

She stroked his cock, loving the feel of him hardening in her hand. She could barely get her fingers to meet around the stalk. With a little twist that made him hiss, she got back to her feet. "Go to the bed and lie down, facing up. I'm going to tie your wrists down."

He grimaced, but managed to get to his feet and place himself where he needed to be. Kash laid himself out in the middle of her bed, on display for her pleasure. It would be easy for her to do what she needed to do, to initiate him into honest play.

"Place your wrists above your head, hands toward the posters." She'd already found her rope, playing with the length in her hand. Kash moved his arms to form a V from his body. Such strong arms. She slid the rope along his right arm, letting him feel the fabric and how heavy it was. She snaked the jute around his wrist, watching him shiver. She tied one end around his wrist and the other to the heavy post that held up the canopy of the bed. "Let everything else go. I want you to concentrate only on what I'm doing to you. How do you feel? Concentrate on your body and the responses to my stimuli. How did you like it when I touched you with the crop?"

His eyes closed and he breathed out, his body relaxing again. "I liked it. I liked the way it felt. I liked how unsure I was whether you would caress me with it or if you would slap that tip against my skin. And then when you struck, the pain flared, but it was good. It felt like my skin was alive."

She worked the rope over and around his wrists. "Did your cock respond?"

"Yes. It got harder. I wanted more."

She secured his right wrist and moved on to the left. "How does being tied down make you feel?"

"Oddly safe." He pulled gently at his right wrist, as though to check to make sure he couldn't go anywhere. "I feel like I'm laid out for a feast. You're going to eat me alive, aren't you, Your Majesty?"

Then he'd already figured out what her game was. Though he might not know all her moves. She tightened the left wrist, not so much he would lose circulation. Just enough so he could feel it, know he was caught and he wasn't getting away.

"I'm going to take what's mine. I'm going to feast on everything you have." She tied his left wrist down and was ready to begin.

* * * *

She was going to kill him. He was going to die and Kash was perfectly fine with it. This was everything he needed. He needed her dirty and dominant, needed to feel like every bit of that glorious brain and stunning body was focused on one thing and one thing only—him.

Dayita wasn't thinking about what he could do for her, what his position could buy her. She craved his body, his private soul, and he suddenly realized that he'd only felt this wanted once before in his life.

That day by the river when she'd told him to hold still so she could kiss him. She'd been dominant then, too. It had been the exact quality that had drawn him to her. Day had known her mind and believed in herself. She hadn't needed a man, but she'd chosen him anyway.

He pulled at the bindings, not to try to get away, but because he liked the sensation of being so vulnerable. There was something dark and forbidden.

A king is never weak.

He forced his father's words out of his head. His father hadn't meant them as anything but a mantra, and he understood that now. His father hadn't seen him as weak. That had been Kash's own insecurities, and they had no place here. He wasn't a king in this place. He was a servant. He was Hers.

It was a good place to be.

She had the crop in her hand again. His whole body tightened at the sight of her. She was sex on two legs, pure feminine willpower. The blouse she was wearing had come open, showing the tops of her golden breasts, and he longed to see her nipples, for her to offer them to him so he could suck and lave them with his affection. The black silk of her shirt looked perfect against the golden tone of her skin. For all the tough trappings of her persona, her face was still soft and feminine even when she barked orders his way.

"Bring your knees up."

He moved them up so his feet were flat on the bed.

"Feet further apart. As far as they can go." She snapped the crop against his inner thigh, showing him what she wanted.

The pain flared and then sank into his skin. He was certain if he hadn't been so aroused, the damn crop would hurt, but now his dick threatened to explode every time she swiped it against his flesh.

He didn't think about it. He simply moved his feet until the crop came off his thigh. Wide. She'd spread him so wide. His cock was there, open and vulnerable to her. To his queen.

He gritted his teeth as she ran the crop along his inner thigh again, brushing over the little red spot where she'd flicked him. The leather tip ran along his sensitive flesh and then found his cock.

He was not going to come. He was not going to come. He was going to last.

"Stay right where you are." She put the crop down and he watched as she unbuttoned her skirt and let it drop to the floor. She slowly undid the buttons on her blouse until all he could see was the lovely green bra and lacy panties she wore underneath. And all that gorgeous skin of hers. "You're so beautiful, Kashmir. I love how hard you are. Your cock is lovely and look, it's offering me a gift."

Day reached out and swiped her finger over his cockhead, gathering the drop of pre-come that had pulsed out.

He watched as she sucked her finger into her mouth, eyes closing as though she was concentrating on her treat, as though she loved the taste of him.

He stared down his body, unable to take his eyes off her. When he was in charge, he simply fucked his partner until she came and then he would have his pleasure. Never had he spent such decadent amounts of time on the sensations of touching each other, of being vulnerable to another human being. She could call it play all she liked, but this was something more. This felt sacred to him, something he could only ever do with her because she was the right woman, the only woman for him.

The only woman who could conquer the king and let him be a man.

"You taste so good, my servant." Her nipples were hard points outlined by the silky cup of her bra.

"There's much more where that came from, my Queen. All for you." Only for her. From this moment and forever more. Only for her.

He loved the arrogant smirk that hit her lips. "I can only imagine. I think I'll have to take you up on that. I find I'm very hungry."

She ran her hands up either leg, brushing the flesh there as though inspecting every inch of her possession.

"Then the queen must have her feast. Is this what you would have done? Would you have placed me naked in your web with nothing but my cock exposed for your pleasure?" The vision tightened his gut, arousal pulsing through him. He wasn't a man who had to wait for pleasure, but now the anticipation was a form of joy. He didn't have to worry that Day would leave him like this. She wouldn't ever leave him at all.

She climbed onto the bed, her limbs moving with the sensuous grace of a cat. "Yes. I would have lowered you so I was able to easily torture your cock. A lick here. A caress there. And when you thought I would walk away and leave you wanting, all trussed up and desperate, that's when I would suck you into my mouth. That's when I would work you to the back of my throat and milk you dry."

He was not going to come. He was going to think about baseball or a sport he actually knew something about, and then he would survive her torture. "Now I wish I'd been a bit more brave."

Her nails scored lightly down his torso as she loomed over him. "Bravery has nothing to do with it. This is all about finding what works for the two of us. Privacy works for you. I'll be honest; I'm not much of an exhibitionist when it comes to sex either. I'm happy to have you to myself, happy to keep you from the lustful gazes of all those other women. And men. Many of the men were looking at you, too. They should know better than to look at the queen's property. Don't they know what happens to those who even think to take what belongs to the queen?"

Something bad because his queen was a badass. Yes. She wasn't some delicate flower who sat in the sun all day, waiting for someone to bring life to her. She fought. She worked. She protected.

She was precious.

"No one would dare and you should understand that if anyone tries to hurt my queen, I will be her warrior."

She leaned forward, her body brushing against his. "And what a warrior you are. So strong. Let's see how long my warrior can hold out on his queen."

Her mouth hovered over his, the cups of her bra sliding on his skin. He could feel the intoxicating mix of silk and warm, soft flesh. Then all that mattered was her tongue against his bottom lip. She dragged it over him and he felt the sizzle down his spine. She deepened the kiss, urging his mouth open. This he could do. He might be totally under her control, but his tongue could match hers, sliding in an intimate glide that had them both panting. Over and over she kissed him, her body pressed to his. She'd made a place for herself between his legs, and her pelvis rubbed against his dick, threatening to push him over the edge.

No. He wasn't going to give in. He wasn't going to give up. Not until she'd had her pleasure, not until she'd taken him deep inside her body and ridden him like a racing stallion.

She kissed her way down his body and he bit back a groan. She was determined to make him insane. He was sure of it. It was there in the way she kissed along his jawline, ran her tongue over the flesh of his neck. Those dainty fingers of hers found his nipples, rolling them at first, and then giving him a hard tweak.

He held on to the ropes, his only lifeline in a sea of pleasure. He had to stay focused or he would let his queen down. She was the important one, her pleasure the goal.

And that was why it worked, he realized. Day was thinking the same thing. How many times had he heard Taggart and his friends talk about the "exchange"? BDSM, he'd been told, was an exchange, and it only worked when it was one of equality, when each partner brought his or her unique gifts to the relationship, offering them up with generous hearts. Kash had laughed inside because he'd seen it as an exchange of orgasms, and wasn't that really the point of all sex?

This was more. While he was concentrating on pleasing Day, she was focused on pleasing him. While her happiness was the goal, his was also her goal.

When both partners put aside all selfishness and concentrated on the needs of the other, that was when the exchange worked.

God, he'd thought Taggart had been talking about sex. He'd

been talking about love. He'd been talking about how to build a marriage.

The king and queen would always have to think about their country, but he was more than a king. He was Kash and she was Day, and they could find their own path, their own rule, their own ways to love each other.

His father's way had been to keep all his precious memories in a lockbox and try to show everyone how strong he was. Kash could find a different way.

Day's mouth hovered over his cock, the heat nearly frying his brain. He wanted to shove his pelvis up, forcing his cock inside those luscious lips, but he held still. This was her time and he was her prize. He wasn't going to take that from her. Instead, he stared down the length of his body as she leaned over and her tongue darted out, swiping across his cockhead.

His hands tightened on the ropes, holding himself in place under the sweet lash of her tongue.

"Don't you come, my servant." The words hummed against his sensitive flesh and he could feel her lips there, smiling as she tortured his cock. Her nails brushed against his heavy balls right before she cupped him. "You won't like what happens if you displease me. We'll see how my servant feels about a cock ring."

She squeezed his balls to brush along the right side of pain.

His eyes rolled to the back of his head, and he bit his lip to stop himself from blowing then and there.

"Do you know how beautiful you are right now?" She sucked the head of his cock into her mouth, heating his body until he was sure he would burst into flames. She whirled her tongue over and around and then gave him the barest hint of her teeth. "I love watching you dance on the edge. I love watching you control yourself so you don't go over too fast and ruin the pleasure."

He shook his head. "Not about the pleasure. Want it to last because of you. Want to stay here with you. That's why I fight. I don't want this to ever end."

He wanted the moment to stay suspended, forever right here with her. It couldn't. He knew that, but he could draw it out. He could make it last so the memory would feel like days instead of hours.

"I don't either. It doesn't have to. This place where we can be whoever we want to be, it never goes away, it's merely hidden for a while. But each and every time we're alone, you'll have all of me, Kashmir. And when we're not alone, know I'm waiting for you. Even when we're not alone, know that I will be your queen, your wife, your love. However you need me, that's what I'll be for you."

He didn't need her to be anyone but exactly who she was—his perfect match, the one who could bring out the other side of him, the only woman who could make him whole.

"Be mine. That's all I need."

The smile that crossed her face was glorious. "Only yours. I only need one servant."

"And I only need one queen."

She unhooked her bra and her breasts bounced free. She palmed them, teasing him with the sight and the fact that his hands were still tied down. They twitched to hold her, but she merely gave him a show, rolling her nipples and rubbing the satin of that patch of underwear over his cock. He could feel how wet she was, the fabric damp and slick with her arousal.

It was torture, but the best kind.

"Kash, are you sure you want this?"

"Yes, I'm sure I want this orgasm. I will take it over my next breath. If you don't hurry, it might be my last breath ever, my Queen."

She laughed, the sound magical to his ears. "That wasn't what I was talking about. I was talking about our marriage. Are you sure? Because I was thinking maybe my servant would like to help me out. My kingdom is in desperate need of a prince or a princess."

He groaned again, having to bite back the harsh shot of arousal her words sent through him.

He was going to have a family with her. He was going to have children who ran through the palace, children who laughed and played. Children who he could teach to be the one thing they needed to be—happy.

"There is nothing I could want more than to serve my Queen in this way." He stared up at her, needing her to know there was nothing playful about this. "I love you, Dayita. I'm sure. There's no one else for me from now on. It's you and me and our family."

"Just us." She leaned over and brushed her lips against his. "And the world, but mostly us."

She shifted her hips and he felt the thin crotch of her undies slide to the side as his cock finally found her pussy. Day got to her knees above him, taking him with the bold, aggressive nature he'd come to crave from her. She lowered herself onto his cock.

Kash couldn't stand it a moment longer. He tilted his pelvis up, feeling her sink onto his cock.

"I should punish you for that, my naughty servant." She moved above him, rolling her hips and taking him as deep as he would go. "But I can't help myself either. I need you. I love you."

"I love you, too, my Queen." He needed her more than he could possibly say. He worked with her, letting her ride him. Her body moved over his, taking what she needed and giving him back everything she had.

It couldn't last. When Day's head fell back and he felt her clench around him, he gave up.

The orgasm was a flash fire, running through his system and leaving him scorched. Day fell forward, her head finding his chest.

He could still feel the pulse of the aftermath when she looked up at him.

"Don't think we're done yet, my servant."

He wasn't done serving her. Not even close. He was ready to spend the rest of his life doing exactly that.

Epilogue

Ten months later

Kash stood looking out over the site that would shortly be his new world. It was nothing but a few acres of ground right now, but once the plans were finished and his contractors had brought to life his vision, this place would be filled with all the world's greatest scientists. It was a place for them to gather, to work, to research and share their ideas. It was a place he hoped could change the world.

"I thought I would find you here."

He turned, a smile on his face because there was nothing he loved more than the sound of that voice. Well, he'd also become partial to the sound of his soon-to-be-born daughter's heart. The hummingbird thud they heard when the doctor came to visit always made his heart clench. "Two more days and we break ground. I've already got meetings with some researchers who are interested in my challenges."

She joined him, her hand slipping into his. It felt natural to be connected to her. "Medical or tech?"

"A couple of doctors who don't want to work with big pharma. They're interested in my drive to cure Parkinson's." He'd put out the call. He and a few other billionaires had pooled some of their resources and offered the world's great minds money and labs and housing in order to solve the problems humanity faced.

He was going to change the world. And if anyone thought they could stop him, they would have to think again. This time he would fight. He wouldn't stop because soon he would give this world to his children, and he never wanted them to think he didn't care.

"Excellent. I heard we also recently received a hundred million dollar grant from Milo Jaye to study pollution solutions," she said with a smile. "You can thank me for that. I gave his wife all the plans and specifications for my suspension tools. They're all about suspension play right now."

"As long as you didn't give them any of our toys." He pulled her close. It was so much easier to be himself now. Something had settled inside him and the world seemed like a different place. A softer, more welcoming place.

His wife still argued with the parliament, but he'd noticed lately that the women of his country seemed to be louder than before, more sure of themselves. They showed up regularly, standing behind their queen, standing up for their daughters.

"I never would. How else would I take care of my favorite servant?" Her voice had gone dark and deliciously deep.

He felt that tug in his groin. Somehow, even though she was almost ready to give birth to their child, she was still the sexiest thing on the planet. She could still make him want to drop to his knees and beg to worship her. "I think I'll be the one taking care of you for a while, my Queen. You have another monarch to give birth to."

He'd successfully argued and won his battle to abolish the antiquated rule of succession that preferred sons over daughters. His daughter, the one who slept inside her mother now, would never worry that she wasn't enough. She would be queen unless she decided she did not want to be. As his firstborn, the choice would be hers to make.

She squeezed his hand. "I think that is going to happen sooner than we think."

"Is she kicking a lot?"

"I'm pretty sure I've been in labor all day," she said, as though talking about the weather. "We should probably go back to the palace and call the doctor. I think your mother will get to meet her namesake tonight."

Yasmine. Their daughter. Oh, god. He was about to become a

father.

He was a father. He was a father and a son and a husband. He was a submissive and a king.

He could be all of those things because he was also Hers.

But first, he needed to get her home so their first child wasn't born on his construction site. He wanted his mother there. She'd defied all the doctors and was still holding on. Though the queen mother moved more slowly these days, she seemed happier than ever, ready to welcome her granddaughter into the world.

"Rai! What are you doing allowing your queen to wander around when she's about to give birth?" Kash asked.

His guard, his best friend, smiled as he stepped from behind the tree where he'd been discreetly waiting. Kash knew the man would never leave him alone. He would always be there, even when he acted like an ass. "Have you tried to tell the queen what to do?"

Day was shaking her head. "Walking is good for the labor. Stop being so overprotective."

He took her hand and started for the Jeep. When she winced, he scooped her up. "There is no such thing. I am exactly the proper amount of protective."

"Really?" she said with a grin, her arms going around his neck. "Who says that?"

"I do. And I'm the king."

After all, the king was never wrong. Kash carried his wife back to the palace and into their future.

* * * *

Also from 1001 Dark Nights and Lexi Blake, discover Dungeon Games, Adored, and Devoted, Close Cover, Protected, Enchanted, and Charmed.

Sign up for the 1001 Dark Nights Newsletter
and be entered to win a Tiffany Key necklace.

There's a contest every month!

Go to www.1001DarkNights.com to subscribe.

As a bonus, all subscribers will receive a free
1001 Dark Nights story
The First Night
by Lexi Blake & M.J. Rose

Turn the page for a full list of the
1001 Dark Nights fabulous novellas...

Discover 1001 Dark Nights Collection Four

Visit www.1001DarkNights.com for more information.

THE BISHOP by Skye Warren
A Tanglewood Novella

TAKEN WITH YOU by Carrie Ann Ryan
A Fractured Connections Novella

DRAGON LOST by Donna Grant
A Dark Kings Novella

SEXY LOVE by Carly Phillips
A Sexy Series Novella

PROVOKE by Rachel Van Dyken
A Seaside Pictures Novella

RAFE by Sawyer Bennett
An Arizona Vengeance Novella

THE NAUGHTY PRINCESS by Claire Contreras
A Sexy Royals Novella

THE GRAVEYARD SHIFT by Darynda Jones
A Charley Davidson Novella

CHARMED by Lexi Blake
A Masters and Mercenaries Novella

SACRIFICE OF DARKNESS by Alexandra Ivy
A Guardians of Eternity Novella

THE QUEEN by Jen Armentrout
A Wicked Novella

BEGIN AGAIN by Jennifer Probst
A Stay Novella

VIXEN by Rebecca Zanetti
A Dark Protectors/Rebels Novella

SLASH by Laurelin Paige
A Slay Series Novella

THE DEAD HEAT OF SUMMER by Heather Graham
A Krewe of Hunters Novella

WILD FIRE by Kristen Ashley
A Chaos Novella

MORE THAN PROTECT YOU by Shayla Black
A More Than Words Novella

LOVE SONG by Kylie Scott
A Stage Dive Novella

CHERISH ME by J. Kenner
A Stark Ever After Novella

SHINE WITH ME by Kristen Proby
A With Me in Seattle Novella

And new from Blue Box Press:

TEASE ME by J. Kenner
A Stark International Novel

FROM BLOOD AND ASH by Jennifer L. Armentrout
A Blood and Ash Novel

QUEEN MOVE by Kennedy Ryan

THE HOUSE OF LONG AGO by Steve Berry and MJ Rose
A Cassiopeia Vitt Adventure

THE BUTTERFLY ROOM by Lucinda Riley

Discover More Lexi Blake

Charmed: A Masters and Mercenaries Novella

JT Malone is lucky, and he knows it. He is the heir to a billion-dollar petroleum empire, and he has a loving family. Between his good looks and his charm, he can have almost any woman he wants. The world is his oyster, and he really likes oysters. So why does it all feel so empty?

Nina Blunt is pretty sure she's cursed. She worked her way up through the ranks at Interpol, fighting for every step with hard work and discipline. Then she lost it all because she loved the wrong person. Rebuilding her career with McKay-Taggart, she can't help but feel lonely. It seems everyone around her is finding love and starting families. But she knows that isn't for her. She has vowed never to make the mistake of falling in love again.

JT comes to McKay-Taggart for assistance rooting out a corporate spy, and Nina signs on to the job. Their working relationship becomes tricky, however, as their personal chemistry flares like a wildfire. Completing the assignment without giving in to the attraction that threatens to overwhelm them seems like it might be the most difficult part of the job. When danger strikes, will they be able to count on each other when the bullets are flying? If not, JT's charmed life might just come to an end.

* * * *

Enchanted: A Masters and Mercenaries Novella by Lexi Blake

A snarky submissive princess

Sarah Steven's life is pretty sweet. By day, she's a dedicated trauma nurse and by night, a fun-loving club sub. She adores her job, has a group of friends who have her back, and is a member of the hottest club in Dallas. So why does it all feel hollow? Could it be because she fell for her dream man and can't forgive him for walking away from her? Nope. She's not going there again. No matter how much she wants to.

A prince of the silver screen

Jared Johns might be one of the most popular actors in Hollywood, but he lost more than a fan when he walked away from Sarah. He lost the only woman he's ever loved. He's been trying to get her back, but she won't return his calls. A trip to Dallas to visit his brother might be exactly what he needs to jump-start his quest to claim the woman who holds his heart.

A masquerade to remember

For Charlotte Taggart's birthday, Sanctum becomes a fantasyland of kinky fun and games. Every unattached sub gets a new Dom for the festivities. The twist? The Doms must conceal their identities until the stroke of midnight at the end of the party. It's exactly what Sarah needs to forget the fact that Jared is pursuing her. She can't give in to him, and the mysterious Master D is making her rethink her position when it comes to signing a contract. Jared knows he was born to play this role, dashing suitor by day and dirty Dom at night.

When the masks come off, will she be able to forgive the man who loves her, or will she leave him forever?

* * * *

Protected: **A Masters and Mercenaries Novella by Lexi Blake**

A second chance at first love

Years before, Wade Rycroft fell in love with Geneva Harris, the smartest girl in his class. The rodeo star and the shy academic made for an odd pair but their chemistry was undeniable. They made plans to get married after high school but when Genny left him standing in the rain, he joined the Army and vowed to leave that life behind. Genny married the town's golden boy, and Wade knew that he couldn't go home again.

Could become the promise of a lifetime

Fifteen years later, Wade returns to his Texas hometown for his brother's wedding and walks into a storm of scandal. Genny's marriage has dissolved and the town has turned against her. But when someone tries to kill his old love, Wade can't refuse to help her. In his years after the Army, he's found his place in the world. His job at McKay-Taggart keeps him happy and busy but something is missing. When he takes the job watching over Genny, he realizes what it is.

As danger presses in, Wade must decide if he can forgive past sins or let the woman of his dreams walk into a nightmare...

* * * *

Close Cover: **A Masters and Mercenaries Novel by Lexi Blake**

Remy Guidry doesn't do relationships. He tried the marriage thing once, back in Louisiana, and learned the hard way that all he really needs in life is a cold beer, some good friends, and the occasional hookup. His job as a bodyguard with McKay-Taggart gives him purpose and lovely perks, like access to Sanctum. The last thing he needs in his life is a woman with stars in her eyes and babies in her future.

Lisa Daley's life is going in the right direction. She has graduated from college after years of putting herself through school. She's got a new job at an accounting firm and she's finished her Sanctum training. Finally on her own and having fun, her life seems pretty perfect. Except she's lonely and the one man she wants won't give her a second look.

There is one other little glitch. Apparently, her new firm is really a front for the mob and now they want her dead. Assassins can really ruin a fun girls' night out. Suddenly strapped to the very same six-foot-five-inch hunk of a bodyguard who makes her heart pound, Lisa can't decide if this situation is a blessing or a curse.

As the mob closes in, Remy takes his tempting new charge back to the safest place he knows—his home in the bayou.

Surrounded by his past, he can't help wondering if Lisa is his future. To answer that question, he just has to keep her alive.

* * * *

Dungeon Games: A Masters and Mercenaries Novella by Lexi Blake

Obsessed

Derek Brighton has become one of Dallas's finest detectives through a combination of discipline and obsession. Once he has a target in his sights, nothing can stop him. When he isn't solving homicides, he applies the same intensity to his playtime at Sanctum, a secretive BDSM club. Unfortunately, no amount of beautiful submissives can fill the hole that one woman left in his heart.

Unhinged

Karina Mills has a reputation for being reckless, and her clients appreciate her results. As a private investigator, she pursues her cases with nothing holding her back. In her personal life, Karina yearns for something different. Playing at Sanctum has been a safe way to find peace, but the one Dom who could truly master her heart is out of reach.

Enflamed

On the hunt for a killer, Derek enters a shadowy underworld only to find the woman he aches for is working the same case. Karina is searching for a missing girl and won't stop until she finds her. To get close to their prime suspect, they need to pose as a couple. But as their operation goes under the covers, unlikely partners become passionate lovers while the killer prepares to strike.

* * * *

Adored: A Masters and Mercenaries Novella by **Lexi Blake**

A man who gave up on love

Mitch Bradford is an intimidating man. In his professional life, he has a reputation for demolishing his opponents in the courtroom. At the exclusive BDSM club Sanctum, he prefers disciplining pretty submissives with no strings attached. In his line of work, there's no time for a healthy relationship. After a few failed attempts, he knows he's not good for any woman—especially not his best friend's sister.

A woman who always gets what she wants

Laurel Daley knows what she wants, and her sights are set on Mitch. He's smart and sexy, and it doesn't matter that he's a few years older and has a couple of bitter ex-wives. Watching him in action at work and at play, she knows he just needs a little polish to make some woman the perfect lover. She intends to be that woman, but first she has to show him how good it could be.

A killer lurking in the shadows

When an unexpected turn of events throws the two together, Mitch and Laurel are confronted with the perfect opportunity to explore their mutual desire. Night after night of being close breaks down Mitch's defenses. The more he sees of Laurel, the more he knows he wants her. Unfortunately, someone else has their eyes on Laurel and they have murder in mind.

* * * *

Devoted: A Masters and Mercenaries Novella by **Lexi Blake**

A woman's work

Amy Slaten has devoted her life to Slaten Industries. After ousting her corrupt father and taking over the CEO role, she thought she could relax and enjoy taking her company to the next level. But an old business rivalry rears its ugly head. The only thing that can possibly take her mind off business is the training class at Sanctum…and her training partner, the gorgeous and funny Flynn Adler. If she can just manage to best her mysterious business rival, life might be perfect.

A man's commitment

Flynn Adler never thought he would fall for the enemy. Business is war, or so his father always claimed. He was raised to be ruthless when it came to the family company, and now he's raising his brother to one day work with him. The first order of business? The hostile takeover of Slaten Industries. It's a stressful job so when his brother offers him a spot in Sanctum's training program, Flynn jumps at the chance.

A lifetime of devotion….

When Flynn realizes the woman he's falling for is none other than the CEO of the firm he needs to take down, he has to make a choice. Does he take care of the woman he's falling in love with or the business he's worked a lifetime to build? And when Amy finally understands the man she's come to trust is none other than the enemy, will she walk away from him or fight for the love she's come to depend on?

Discover 1001 Dark Nights

Visit www.1001DarkNights.com for more information.

COLLECTION ONE
FOREVER WICKED by Shayla Black
CRIMSON TWILIGHT by Heather Graham
CAPTURED IN SURRENDER by Liliana Hart
SILENT BITE: A SCANGUARDS WEDDING by Tina Folsom
DUNGEON GAMES by Lexi Blake
AZAGOTH by Larissa Ione
NEED YOU NOW by Lisa Renee Jones
SHOW ME, BABY by Cherise Sinclair
ROPED IN by Lorelei James
TEMPTED BY MIDNIGHT by Lara Adrian
THE FLAME by Christopher Rice
CARESS OF DARKNESS by Julie Kenner

COLLECTION TWO
WICKED WOLF by Carrie Ann Ryan
WHEN IRISH EYES ARE HAUNTING by Heather Graham
EASY WITH YOU by Kristen Proby
MASTER OF FREEDOM by Cherise Sinclair
CARESS OF PLEASURE by Julie Kenner
ADORED by Lexi Blake
HADES by Larissa Ione
RAVAGED by Elisabeth Naughton
DREAM OF YOU by Jennifer L. Armentrout
STRIPPED DOWN by Lorelei James
RAGE/KILLIAN by Alexandra Ivy/Laura Wright
DRAGON KING by Donna Grant
PURE WICKED by Shayla Black
HARD AS STEEL by Laura Kaye
STROKE OF MIDNIGHT by Lara Adrian
ALL HALLOWS EVE by Heather Graham
KISS THE FLAME by Christopher Rice
DARING HER LOVE by Melissa Foster
TEASED by Rebecca Zanetti
THE PROMISE OF SURRENDER by Liliana Hart

COLLECTION THREE
HIDDEN INK by Carrie Ann Ryan
BLOOD ON THE BAYOU by Heather Graham
SEARCHING FOR MINE by Jennifer Probst
DANCE OF DESIRE by Christopher Rice
ROUGH RHYTHM by Tessa Bailey
DEVOTED by Lexi Blake
Z by Larissa Ione
FALLING UNDER YOU by Laurelin Paige
EASY FOR KEEPS by Kristen Proby
UNCHAINED by Elisabeth Naughton
HARD TO SERVE by Laura Kaye
DRAGON FEVER by Donna Grant
KAYDEN/SIMON by Alexandra Ivy/Laura Wright
STRUNG UP by Lorelei James
MIDNIGHT UNTAMED by Lara Adrian
TRICKED by Rebecca Zanetti
DIRTY WICKED by Shayla Black
THE ONLY ONE by Lauren Blakely
SWEET SURRENDER by Liliana Hart

COLLECTION FOUR
ROCK CHICK REAWAKENING by Kristen Ashley
ADORING INK by Carrie Ann Ryan
SWEET RIVALRY by K. Bromberg
SHADE'S LADY by Joanna Wylde
RAZR by Larissa Ione
ARRANGED by Lexi Blake
TANGLED by Rebecca Zanetti
HOLD ME by J. Kenner
SOMEHOW, SOME WAY by Jennifer Probst
TOO CLOSE TO CALL by Tessa Bailey
HUNTED by Elisabeth Naughton
EYES ON YOU by Laura Kaye
BLADE by Alexandra Ivy/Laura Wright
DRAGON BURN by Donna Grant
TRIPPED OUT by Lorelei James
STUD FINDER by Lauren Blakely

MIDNIGHT UNLEASHED by Lara Adrian
HALLOW BE THE HAUNT by Heather Graham
DIRTY FILTHY FIX by Laurelin Paige
THE BED MATE by Kendall Ryan
NIGHT GAMES by CD Reiss
NO RESERVATIONS by Kristen Proby
DAWN OF SURRENDER by Liliana Hart

COLLECTION FIVE
BLAZE ERUPTING by Rebecca Zanetti
ROUGH RIDE by Kristen Ashley
HAWKYN by Larissa Ione
RIDE DIRTY by Laura Kaye
ROME'S CHANCE by Joanna Wylde
THE MARRIAGE ARRANGEMENT by Jennifer Probst
SURRENDER by Elisabeth Naughton
INKED NIGHTS by Carrie Ann Ryan
ENVY by Rachel Van Dyken
PROTECTED by Lexi Blake
THE PRINCE by Jennifer L. Armentrout
PLEASE ME by J. Kenner
WOUND TIGHT by Lorelei James
STRONG by Kylie Scott
DRAGON NIGHT by Donna Grant
TEMPTING BROOKE by Kristen Proby
HAUNTED BE THE HOLIDAYS by Heather Graham
CONTROL by K. Bromberg
HUNKY HEARTBREAKER by Kendall Ryan
THE DARKEST CAPTIVE by Gena Showalter

COLLECTION SIX
DRAGON CLAIMED by Donna Grant
ASHES TO INK by Carrie Ann Ryan
ENSNARED by Elisabeth Naughton
EVERMORE by Corinne Michaels
VENGEANCE by Rebecca Zanetti
ELI'S TRIUMPH by Joanna Wylde
CIPHER by Larissa Ione

RESCUING MACIE by Susan Stoker
ENCHANTED by Lexi Blake
TAKE THE BRIDE by Carly Phillips
INDULGE ME by J. Kenner
THE KING by Jennifer L. Armentrout
QUIET MAN by Kristen Ashley
ABANDON by Rachel Van Dyken
THE OPEN DOOR by Laurelin Paige
CLOSER by Kylie Scott
SOMETHING JUST LIKE THIS by Jennifer Probst
BLOOD NIGHT by Heather Graham
TWIST OF FATE by Jill Shalvis
MORE THAN PLEASURE YOU by Shayla Black
WONDER WITH ME by Kristen Proby
THE DARKEST ASSASSIN by Gena Showalter

Discover Blue Box Press

TAME ME by J. Kenner
TEMPT ME by J. Kenner
DAMIEN by J. Kenner
TEASE ME by J. Kenner
REAPER by Larissa Ione
THE SURRENDER GATE by Christopher Rice
SERVICING THE TARGET by Cherise Sinclair
THE LAKE OF LEARNING by Steve Berry and MJ Rose
THE MUSEUM OF MYSTERIES by Steve Berry and MJ Rose

About Lexi Blake

Lexi Blake lives in North Texas with her husband, three kids, and the laziest rescue dog in the world. She began writing at a young age, concentrating on plays and journalism. It wasn't until she started writing romance that she found success. She likes to find humor in the strangest places. Lexi believes in happy endings no matter how odd the couple, threesome or foursome may seem. She also writes contemporary Western ménage as Sophie Oak.

Connect with Lexi online:

Facebook: Lexi Blake
Twitter: twitter.com/authorlexiblake
Website: www.LexiBlake.net

Love Another Day
Masters and Mercenaries 14
By Lexi Blake

A man born to protect

After a major loss, Brody Carter found a home with the London office of McKay-Taggart. A former soldier, he believes his job is to take the bullets and follow orders. He's happy to take on the job of protecting Dr. Stephanie Gibson while the team uses her clinic in Sierra Leone to bring down an international criminal. What he never expected was that the young doctor would prove to be the woman of his dreams. She's beautiful, smart, and reckless. Over and over he watches her risk her life to save others. One night of pure passion leads him to realize that he can't risk his heart again. When the mission ends, Brody walks away, unwilling to lose another person he loves.

A woman driven to heal

Stephanie's tragic past taught her to live for today. Everything she's done in the last fifteen years has been to make up for her mistakes. Offering medical care in war-torn regions gives her the purpose she needs to carry on. When she meets her gorgeous Aussie protector, she knows she's in too deep, but nothing can stop her from falling head over heels in love. But after one amazing night together, Brody walks away and never looks back. Stephanie is left behind...but not alone.

A secret that will change both their lives

A year later, Stephanie runs afoul of an evil mercenary who vows to kill her for failing to save his son. She runs to the only people she trusts, Liam and Avery O'Donnell. She hasn't come alone and her secret will bring her former lover across the world to protect her. From Liberia to Dallas to Australia's outback, Brody will do whatever it takes to protect Stephanie from the man who wants to kill her, but it might be her own personal demons that could destroy them both.

On behalf of 1001 Dark Nights,

Liz Berry and M.J. Rose would like to thank ~

Steve Berry
Doug Scofield
Kim Guidroz
Jillian Stein
InkSlinger PR
Dan Slater
Asha Hossain
Chris Graham
Pamela Jamison
Fedora Chen
Kasi Alexander
Jessica Johns
Dylan Stockton
Richard Blake
BookTrib After Dark
and Simon Lipskar

Made in the USA
Columbia, SC
08 June 2024

36862282R00133